...dently. Well, if she ...

...erself, she could.

More. More of him.

The kisses she'd had with Caelan had never caused this wanting within her. They had been tepid, unmoving kisses. Just between two friends, with no air of intimacy or longing.

Brodie's kiss had been possessive and enticing. He had tasted her and shown her how to taste him. He wanted her. She could hear it in his breathing and feel it in the way he held her and in the way his body...*changed* beneath her.

AUTHOR NOTE

Scotland's history is filled with stories about feuds between the clans. When I was researching a previous book I discovered a feud between the powerful Mackintosh clan and the smaller Cameron clan that went on to last more than three hundred and fifty years!

It began in the early 1300s, over claims to a piece of land, and expanded over generations and across the lands of both the Mackintoshes and the Camerons. It eventually even involved the King of Scotland. Since the Mackintosh clan led the larger 'Chattan Confederation'—a group of several clans and septs—it drew in large and small families over time.

After thousands of deaths, dozens of battles and attempts at truces and treaties, it ended in 1665, when the Camerons paid a fee to the Mackintoshes for the lands they claimed!

I have taken some liberties with the timing of some of the battles and the names or locations of some of the keeps, changing them to accommodate my story a bit, but the animosity between the clans is real. For when lands and titles and power and wealth are involved the truth can sometimes be stranger than any fictional story created to explain it all!

I hope you enjoy *Stolen by the Highlander*, the first book in my *A Highland Feuding* mini-series, and especially the sexy, brave Highlanders who seek to control their destinies and the strong women who tame them in the end!

STOLEN BY THE HIGHLANDER

Terri Brisbin

MILLS & BOON

Published in Great Britain 2015
by Mills & Boon, an imprint of Harlequin (UK) Limited,
Eton House, 18-24 Paradise Road, Richmond, Surrey, TW9 1SR

© 2015 Theresa S. Brisbin

ISBN: 978-0-263-24774-9

Harlequin (UK) Limited's policy is to use papers that are natural,
renewable and recyclable products and made from wood grown in
sustainable forests. The logging and manufacturing processes conform
to the environmental regulations of the country of origin.

Terri Brisbin is wife to one, mother of three, and dental hygienist to hundreds when not living the life of a glamorous romance author. She was born, raised, and is still living in the southern New Jersey suburbs. Terri's love of history led her to write time-travel romances and historical romances set in Scotland and England.

Books by Terri Brisbin

Mills & Boon® Historical Romance and Mills & Boon® Historical *Undone!* eBooks

A Highland Feuding

Stolen by the Highlander

The MacLerie Clan

Taming the Highlander
Surrender to the Highlander
Possessed by the Highlander
The Highlander's Stolen Touch
At the Highlander's Mercy
The Highlander's Dangerous Temptation
Yield to the Highlander
Taming the Highland Rogue

The Knights of Brittany

The Conqueror's Lady
The Mercenary's Bride
His Enemy's Daughter
A Night for Her Pleasure

Visit the author profile page at millsandboon.co.uk for more titles

I dedicate this book,
the first in my new series, to my editorial 'team'
at Mills & Boon® Historical Romances in the
Richmond UK office—especially Megan Haslam,
Kathryn Cheshire and Senior Editor Linda Fildew.
They constantly push me to make my work better and
stronger for my readers, and though we sometimes
disagree on how to accomplish that (LOL!),
they always do it in a kind and supportive way.
It's been great working with you over these
last several books—thanks for all you do for me!

Chapter One

Arabella Cameron understood how the layer of ice on a frozen lake felt. The smile she held on her face as another Mackintosh offered a poem about her beauty would crack soon, just as that brittle ice did when hit by a stone. She did not hold out much hope that she could keep smiling as the words reached a new level of ridiculous praise. The tip of her nose tingled and the worry over her face cracking disappeared when presented with the larger concern of laughing.

Drawing in a slow breath, she blinked several times, hoping the danger of being impertinent or disrespectful would pass soon. As she raised her eyes, Arabella was horrified to meet the dark and brooding gaze of Brodie Mackintosh. Seated at the end of the table to her right, the older of the two men who were possible heirs to The Mackintosh stared back at her, not flinching and not looking away. In the short time since they'd met, she did not ever remember him smiling.

Nothing in his mahogany-brown eyes gave her any indication of how he felt about these men regaling their clans with tales of her beauty and graciousness. Or how he felt about her. Or the possibility that they might, within a few months, be man and wife. Distracted by his intense stare, she had not noticed the poem had ended or that the room silenced in anticipation of her reaction.

Until he turned his glance away and angled his head towards... Towards the Mackintosh bard who had stopped speaking and now looked expectantly at her, awaiting her reaction to his words. Arabella nodded and clapped her hands.

'I am honoured by your kind words...' She could not remember his name.

'Dougal was not being kind, Lady Arabella,' Caelan Mackintosh interrupted. Seated to her left, he met her gaze and winked, knowing she'd forgotten the bard's name. 'He was speaking the truth as we all see it to be.' She turned back to the man who'd spoken and nodded.

'Still, I am honoured by your praise, Dougal. And I thank you for composing and sharing it with our clans.'

The bard bowed and returned to his seat amidst the cheering of those gathered for this feast. Caelan leaned in closer and whispered so that others did not hear.

'You have bewitched all of the Mackintoshes with your beauty and grace, Arabella. The Camerons could have won this feud long ago if they'd used you as their secret weapon.' He touched her hand, a slight caress, and then lifted his cup to his mouth, all the while his gaze never straying from hers. 'You have bewitched me.'

She'd heard these words before. She'd been praised for her beauty, a gift from the Almighty that had nothing to do with her own accomplishments, all of her life. But watching Caelan's piercing blue eyes deepen as he spoke now made her want to feel something for them. She wanted to believe them.

He offered her his cup, turning it so that her lips would touch the place where his had been. Arabella allowed this gesture, this small intimacy, from the man she might marry. The corners of his mouth curved into an enticing smile as she drank the wine. The heat that spread throughout her was not from the strong wine but from the way Caelan watched as she swallowed and licked her lip where a drop yet remained.

He leaned closer as though he would dare a kiss, here, now, and she held her breath, waiting.

The crashing sound of metal hitting the stone floor startled her and she turned towards the interruption. Brodie leaned over and picked up his heavy cup and placed it back on the table. Whether done a-purpose or by accident, it had ruined the moment between her and Caelan. And any hopes of rekindling it were dashed when her father spoke.

'Yer aunt awaits ye there, Arabella. Seek yer chambers.'

Although she might have challenged her father were they in their own keep and with only her clan present, she would never do so here and now. Not with so much depending on her being an obedient, dutiful daughter whose only task was to save their clan from continuing slaughter and destruction.

Forming that hated smile back on to her features, she rose and curtsied to her father and to The Mackintosh, before walking around the table and down the steps. Her aunt Devorgilla stood there, watching her every move. No doubt, there would be instructions this night about her behaviour and appearance. Arabella nodded and smiled at anyone who spoke or whispered her name as she passed and her graciousness, after so many hours of being forced to it, tired her.

With a servant leading the way with a torch, she followed through the corridor and up the stairs to the chamber assigned to her for her stay here. Once there, she waited for only a moment to pass after the door closed before collapsing on the bed, allowing her face to relax from the hours of tortuous smiling. Pressing her palms against her cheeks, she knew what would come next.

'You sat too close to the one and ignored the other, Arabella.' Even with her eyes closed, she could tell from the changing direction of the high-pitched voice that her aunt was pacing around the edge of the bed. 'You must not be seen to favour one over the other.'

'Aye, Aunt Devorgilla,' she said without opening her eyes.

'You were not paying attention during that last poem. You must not show disrespect to the Mackintosh's bard or his harpist or his—'

'I understand, Aunt Devorgilla,' she said before her aunt went on. 'And my mother would be terribly shamed by my lack of manners at the feast…and by not paying enough heed to your warnings…' Those words and more poured out of her and from the silence, Arabella knew she was not the only shocked person in the room.

'Child,' her aunt whispered. 'Your mother would be proud of you. Proud that you are carrying out the duty you were born to fulfil.' Her aunt's voice grew deep with emotion and Arabella raised her head to look at her mother's youngest sister. 'She would be proud that you are doing your duty when it would be easier not to. When it means you must live the rest of your life among our enemies.'

'Aunt Gillie,' she said. The tears would not be held back now. 'I am so sorry. I did not mean to act the wilful child to you. I value your advice, I truly do. I am exhausted and will be ready to face this on the morrow.'

'Here now, child,' her aunt said, stepping behind her. 'Let me help you ready for bed.'

'Nay. I can call for Ailean to help me.' Her younger cousin served as her companion and her maid when needed.

'Hush now,' her aunt said, unlacing her ties and loosening the gown and tunic she wore. Soon Arabella stood in only her shift. When her aunt began to unravel the long braid of her hair, she sighed. 'Sit,' her aunt directed.

First, her aunt slid her fingers into the woven

tresses and then she used a brush to ease out the snarls and knots. Each moment eased the tension within Arabella and allowed the exhaustion to creep closer to controlling her. Her eyes drooped closed and her body began to relax. All her worries drifted away with each long stroke of the brush through her hair.

'What are the plans on the morrow?' Forced to think of her future and the uncertainty of it, Arabella sighed again.

'A ride with Caelan in the morn and one with Brodie after the noon meal. Worry not, Aunt Gillie, Ailean will accompany me at all times when we leave the keep.'

'I do not worry over your safety, child. I worry over your heart.' The brush stopped and her aunt stepped away. Arabella turned to face her and found a sadness in her eyes she'd not seen before. 'Do not let your heart be engaged with either of these Mackintoshes until their elders decide on which will be tanist here. It will only lead to heartbreak and pain in the years to come.'

'Aunt Gillie, what—?' This was something unexpected. Something surprising and clearly with more of a story than she'd heard about.

'No matter, Arabella,' her aunt interrupted before she could complete her question. 'I think

I am more tired than I thought. I will seek my bed now.'

Without another word, her aunt placed the brush on the small table there, turned and left the chamber. Granted, the warning was one she'd heard before, but her aunt's words about heartbreak hinted at something more personal. She would pursue this on the morrow, but a soft knock foretold of Ailean's arrival. Arabella soon lay in the quiet darkness and pondered the differences between the two Mackintosh cousins and her future as the wife of one or the other.

Her aunt's counsel did not take into account how she truly felt about the one thing that would not change—no matter which she married, she was giving herself to her enemy. She would become part of the clan that had massacred her family over the past several generations and bear children to it. There were hopes that this feud would now end with her marriage to the next Mackintosh chief.

No matter, Arabella would be marrying her enemy very soon.

Brodie held out the cup to one of the women serving at table and watched as she filled it. Nodding his thanks, he continued to observe every

Cameron in their hall. They came under a flag of truce and accepted the hospitality offered, but Brodie did not trust a one of them.

As he glanced from Cameron warrior to Cameron warrior, he knew that some of them had killed Mackintoshes during their past skirmishes and battles. And some of the older ones did not want this truce or the coming treaty at all. Reasons not to trust them.

Not even the golden-tressed heiress of their clan did he trust. The chamber where the feast to welcome her had been held began to empty now that Lady Arabella Cameron had retired for the evening. Glancing around the hall, he met the gaze of each of the men he'd positioned wherever the Camerons sat.

Let their bard and hers pay homage to her beauty. Let his cousin fall all over himself flirting with the lass. Brodie saw to his duty of securing the safety of his clan while others played the courtier or ignored the dangers. When each of his men nodded their reply, he turned his attention to his uncle and cousin and their guests.

Content to observe and not get involved in the discussions, Brodie noticed the way The Cameron and his eldest son, Malcolm, sat and spoke and the way they watched him, too. It confirmed his belief that there was wariness on the part of both families. And possibly treachery, at which the Camerons excelled. His uncle stood and everyone at the table did, as well—a signal that the feast was over.

Brodie put his cup down and walked to his uncle's side as the Camerons followed their escort to the chambers assigned to them in the north tower. Keeping them together, in several chambers in the one tower, made it easier to keep a watch on them. And to keep them isolated in case of trouble. He smiled at that.

'You will escort the Cameron lass after the noon meal,' his uncle said, gaining his full attention now.

'Nay, Uncle. I have to see to—' Brodie began to explain.

'You will escort the lass, Brodie. That is your duty on the morrow.'

They'd already argued this point many times before the Camerons arrived on their lands for this visit. Brodie thought it premature for any of this, while the elders sided with his uncle. They thought it a way to assess the two cousins before making their choice.

After facing whatever tests the elders had planned, one cousin would be proclaimed tanist and heir to the chieftain of the Clan Mackintosh. With no other living male relative eligible, either he or Caelan would govern the Chattan Confederation after his uncle died. One of them would be selected by the elders to control the people and the lands and wealth of their clan.

He owed much to Lachlan for raising him after the death of his parents. The laird had taught him the skills he needed to live and to lead. So, even if he disagreed with his uncle, he would do as he asked, or ordered.

Now, his uncle had added courting the Cameron lass to the list of accomplishments required for the one deemed worthy to lead the clan. Glancing up, he saw his uncle's determined eyes and the look of merriment and victory in his cousin's.

Oh, aye, Caelan had a way with women, his soft words and caresses wooed many to him and his bed. Practised in collecting and discarding any willing woman, his cousin would use all his experience to soften the Cameron lass's heart. Brodie held no hopes that the woman who would, who could, be the means of ending the generations-long feud between their families would be anything but attracted to his cousin.

'Aye, Uncle.' Brodie would rather be attending to training the new guards or organising the defences of their borders than in this useless bit of courting. But, from the glare of his uncle's expression and the way he crossed his arms over his massive chest, Brodie knew he would be spending time with the lass, Arabella.

'Try not to put her to sleep,' Caelan taunted as he walked away.

As much as Brodie wanted to argue or come back at his cousin with some witty or even caustic reply, he could think of none. He was not known for his wit or sense of humour. He was also not known for his easy manner with women. Brodie let out his breath and strode through the hall into the corridor.

What he did do well was protect his clan and their holdings from the constant incursions by their enemies. He'd wanted an end to this feud for a very long time, even before his parents were murdered in an ambush in the hills around Loch Arkaig. With every new fight or battle that led to losing more of his family, his desire to find a way to peace between the Mackintoshes and Camerons had grown. And if it could be ended without destroying all of them, well, that was even better. He preferred peace through negotiation, but he would take it in any way they could obtain it.

Even if it meant he married the lass who wore a false smile like it was her second skin.

So, in spite of his suspicions and the cynicism he now carried with him as a constant companion, he would follow his uncle's orders and see to taking her on a tour of some kind. Then he would focus his attentions where they mattered—on being the one chosen to lead the clan next.

And, if that included marrying one of their enemies, so be it.

Chapter Two

It was going better than Arabella had expected when she left the keep in the company of Caelan Mackintosh. With Ailean and a Cameron and Mackintosh guard accompanying them, she rode at Caelan's side out through the gates and along the road through the village. Though she smiled, this morn it was because he made her smile. And laugh. And truly enjoy herself.

His compliments were not as overwhelming as she usually heard, but he placed them well and not too often. Caelan even brought a smile to Ailean's face and that was no easy task when dealing with her dour cousin. They rode along the road to the east and then followed the path of a large stream into the forest. For a time, they'd walked along the stream, leaving the others a short distance behind but always within sight.

* * *

When they returned for the noon meal, Arabella was amazed that the hours in his company had passed so quickly.

'I hope it has been a pleasant outing for you, Lady Arabella,' he said, lifting her hand to his mouth and touching his lips on her skin. 'Ailean, your company added much to the morn,' he added with a nod to the now blushing and stammering woman. Caelan had won over at least one Cameron lass and was well on the way to another.

'It has been, sir. And a welcome change to have a clear and sunny morn after the recent storms,' Arabella said.

'Almost as though the fates were smiling on us.'

Her aunt called out her name and she nodded at her. Time to move on to the next of her duties. At least the day had begun well.

'I will let you see to your duties,' she said, nodding at him.

His blue eyes sparkled and the appealing dimple in his chin when he smiled at her drew her attention. Attractive, hospitable and charming were not such bad traits for a potential husband, she decided as she walked up the steps to the doorway and entered behind her aunt. They did not speak until they reached her chambers and Devorgilla sent Ailean on some errand so they had a measure of privacy.

'From the colour in your cheeks and the light in your eyes, I would guess that this morning went well?' her aunt asked. A bowl of water awaited her and Arabella accepted the washing cloth.

'It did. He is…acceptable,' she said. Dipping the cloth in the water, she smiled as she cleaned her face and then hands.

'Acceptable? Only that, then?' her aunt prodded. 'Of the two, Caelan seems the more pleasant.'

'Aye, Aunt.' She handed the cloth back and removed the circlet that held her veil in place. 'You told me not to favour one over the other, so I am trying to follow your advice.'

At her aunt's direction, she sat so Aunt Gillie could gather her loosened hair back into a braid and to right her appearance before the noon meal. 'Though I suspect I am a bit optimistic over my chances for a happy marriage with one more than the other.' Her aunt shushed her as she tugged at the length of her hair.

'That is not why this match will be made, Arabella. Keep that firmly in mind as you spend time with these men. Their clan's elders will make their decision and you will marry their choice.'

Arabella felt the pleasure of the outing dissipate with each word of warning uttered by her aunt. She understood her duty and would do it, but that did not mean she could not enjoy these small moments when all the decisions seemed distant yet. A knock interrupted any reply she would have made. Ailean opened the door and entered.

'They are calling for the meal now,' her cousin said.

'Come, Aunt Gillie. We must not have them waiting on us.' She stood and shook out her gown.

Ailean led the way down to the hall, for her cousin was becoming familiar with the corridors and stairways of this large, stone keep. Arabella tried to clear her thoughts and not be worried about the next part of her day…with Brodie Mackintosh. He was the exact opposite of his cousin—dark and forbidding to Caelan's light and smiling countenance. When Caelan laughed and spoke easily with her, Brodie simply stared intensely and with an air of disapproval she could not explain. It was as though he looked at her and found her wanting.

So, it was a relief when his uncle announced that he would not join them at this repast. At least the meal would be pleasant.

And it was. Caelan sat a few seats away from her, next to her brother, and continued to pay attention to her. Her father smiled more and The Mackintosh did, as well. Each day they spent here seemed to ease a bit of the tension that had filled the air on their arrival four days before.

But soon, too soon, the informal repast ended and it was time for her to spend the afternoon with Brodie. She took a deep breath and nodded to her aunt and her cousin. The laird directed one of his servants to escort her to the yard and she noticed that Caelan began to offer, but was stopped by a shake of his uncle's head. So Arabella stood and followed the man out of the keep and into the yard. When she noticed Brodie standing next to their horses, she waved the man off and walked towards him.

Brodie leaned down and tightened the belt under the horse's belly, making certain it was secure. He stroked the animal, not one of theirs, but a beautiful beast, anyway. The Camerons could pick horseflesh and had some of the best in the Highlands. He whispered nonsense as he calmed the horse and finished his task. Or he would have if his friend Rob had not interrupted him.

'So, she is quite the beauty, is she not?' Rob said from the other side of the horse. Glancing down at the horse's rather obvious attributes, Brodie frowned at the man.

'Aye, *he* is,' he said, shaking his head as he checked the other belt and the reins.

'Are you daft or just trying to be difficult, Brodie?' Rob leaned in closer, his face just above the horse's back. 'The lass. The lass is a beauty.'

'Oh. The lass. Aye,' he mumbled out and saw to his task. He was beginning to think that asking Rob to accompany them on this ride had been a mistake. He should have asked one of the men on duty instead of his friend.

'Come now, you have to admit that it would not be difficult to marry her? To have her in your bed? To see that hair loose. Those eyes? That mouth?' Rob said in a low voice and then laughed at him. 'I would not mind ending up with her to wife when this bargain is struck.'

'A beauty? Aye, she is beautiful,' Brodie admitted aloud to his friend. Stepping back and giving the horse one more look, he shrugged. 'To be honest, Rob, I'd rather end up with another dozen head of cattle or horses like this one than her. Cattle and horses would be more useful to us, to me, than a woman who lives by her beauty.'

From the frozen expression on his friend's face and the sudden silence of those closest to them in the yard, Brodie knew she was there behind him. He closed his eyes for a moment and then let out his breath. His words had been harsh. Not meant for her to hear. She had heard and he needed to apologise. His uncle would have his ballocks if he did not make this right. Trying to think of the right thing to say, he turned slowly to face her.

If he had delayed only a moment more, he would have missed the fleeting dimming of her eyes and the slight downturn of the corner of her mouth. His stomach clenched at the sight. Then she smiled that empty smile of hers and walked up to him.

'It is kind of you to escort me around your lands,' she said, smiling at him. 'I know you have other duties to see to and appreciate your time.'

'Lady Arabella,' he began. Then...nothing.

Not the wrong words. Not the right ones. Simply no words.

'What do you think of him?' she asked, coming alongside of Brodie. 'Is he not magnificent?'

She was being gracious and giving him a way out of the insult he'd just paid her. He took it.

'Aye, he is. Strong and lively,' he said, slowly sliding his hand over the horse's withers and nodding. He glanced at the horse's legs. 'Stamina, too, I think.'

'Oh, he can ride for days,' she said, walking to the horse's head and rubbing it. 'He has taken me on many journeys.' She stepped back and met his gaze. He searched for some sign of hurt feelings or insult, but her blues eyes were empty of any emotion. 'Should we be on our way?' she asked, looking at the gathering clouds over them.

'Mount up,' he called out to the rest of their travelling group as he assisted her onto her horse.

Once she had settled, he handed her the reins and mounted his own horse. She sat as though born in the saddle, completely in control of the huge stallion. He could not help but stare at the way she looped the leather straps over and around her hands, keeping them at the right tension so that the horse had some freedom, but also could feel her commands. Brodie led them out of the yard, through the gates and in the opposite direction from where Caelan had taken her that morn.

Rob knew where they were going, so he rode ahead and the Cameron guard rode behind them.

The lass's cousin, a young woman named Ailean who wore the frown and had the bearing of an old spinster, positioned herself at Arabella's side, directly behind him. They'd crossed the stream a mile or so from the keep and continued towards the mountains that ran across their lands, from the loch to the sea. A few minutes after he heard whispering between the two women, Brodie found the lass riding alongside him.

'So, Brodie, where are we going?' she asked in a soft voice, her gaze not leaving the uneven road in front of them.

'You have seen our lands near the loch. We are going to a place up on the mountain for a different look.' It was his favourite place on all their lands, but he did not say that. 'A short distance ahead, we'll take the path up the mountainside.'

She did not drop back to ride with her cousin then. Nay, the lass continued to match his pace and remain there next to him. Which was probably what she had done with Caelan. Unease built in his gut—he'd rather fight a small army of Camerons than have to deal with this one. Worse, she did not even acknowledge the insult paid her—which made it the only thing he could think about as they travelled high up on the path.

After one curve in the road, they entered a

clearing, an outcropping that positioned them high above Mackintosh lands. The view was one he liked, one he visited often when he needed solitude. The clouds were low and heavy right now, but when the sun shone and the breezes blew, you could see for miles and miles, across the hills towards the sea and back to the loch.

'Beautiful.' Her breathless voice startled him, for he had forgotten for a moment that she was there.

'Aye.'

He dared a glance and found her usually empty gaze now filled with wonder at the sight before them. Brodie thought, for one daft second, that she might appreciate not only the view but the lands themselves. Lands much larger than those of the Camerons even if you considered the lands they stole all those generations ago. As quickly as it had appeared, her gaze changed at the sound of the others arriving. And the dreaded smile returned.

'I am confused as to our orientation,' she said. 'The loch is…where?'

Brodie turned in his saddle and pointed to the right. 'Loch Lochy is about five miles that way. Arkaig is north,' he said. 'And the sea is about thirty miles to the west.'

'And Mackintosh lands?' she asked, glancing from one horizon to the other.

'To the loch and as far as you can see to the west,' he said, not keeping the pride from his voice. 'And miles to the north and south, as well.' She stared out at the distances in the directions he'd indicated and nodded.

'You were correct then, sir,' she said softly, meeting his gaze then.

'Correct, Lady Arabella?' He tugged the reins slightly and turned his horse to face hers. A step or two closer and their legs nearly touched. 'Correct about what?'

Brodie could not remember a single thing he'd said to her other than the direction of their lands. And he knew he was correct about those. He knew their lands in the light of day or dark of night.

'That additional cattle or horses would be useful to you. Mayhap you should add that to the list of Mackintosh demands in the negotiations before it is too late?'

God save him, but her eyes blazed like icy fire for a moment and the smile left her face. Only when Rob snickered behind them did she regain control over her expression. It was the most he'd heard her say and the only time he thought he might be seeing the lass herself and it was gone. The ice maiden sat smiling at him for a moment more. Then, with a slight motion of her hand, she directed her mount around him and out of the clearing. The rest of them scrambled to follow her, leaving him alone to look out over their lands and ponder the mistakes he'd made so far.

First, he'd been so busy trying to ignore her and the possible match that he had not paid enough attention to her and had missed her true nature. For the man who oversaw the Mackintosh clan's spies, that was a huge failure.

Second, Brodie had failed at doing what he did best—notice things that affected the clan's security and preparedness for battle. He'd seen only what the lass wanted him—them—to see: a woman who had no mind of her own and did as she was told.

And last, and worst for his peace of mind, discovering that she was not a mindless, empty-headed beauty pleased him in some way he did not wish to think on or even acknowledge.

Riding out of the clearing and on to the road leading down the mountain, Brodie understood he would need to keep a closer watch on her. Why that brought a smile to his own face, he knew not. He caught up with them and placed himself at her side, edging her cousin ahead with Rob and the guards. He still needed to offer an apology for his coarse words of insult.

'Lady Arabella,' he said, slowing his horse's pace so that there was some distance between them. 'I would speak privately with you.'

When her maid glanced back across that growing space, the lady waved her off. The lass matched his horse's gait and they rode for a short time in silence as he tried to choose his words more carefully than he had earlier. Once again, she saved him.

'Sir...Brodie,' she began quietly without looking at him. 'I have been raised to carry out my duty for my family. Marrying whoever is named as the next chieftain of your family is that duty. And I will carry it out, no matter my personal feelings on the matter. I assume you will do the same?' Her blue eyes rose until they locked with his.

'I will carry out my duty,' he said, nodding. Brodie could not be certain what his personal feelings were on the matter when she stared at him so, but later he would sort through it all. For now...

'Lady Arabella, I...' He stumbled over the

words he now wanted to say. 'I should not have said such things about you.'

'Did you mean it? About needing cattle or horses more than me?' she asked. Neither her tone nor her expression gave away her feelings on his words.

'Do you wish to hear the truth?'

'I prefer the truth. I hear so little of it.'

'Aye, we need more cattle.'

Silence sat between them, but neither looked away.

'Then the good thing about getting a wife is that she'll be bringing the gold with which you can buy more cattle.'

The lass shifted in her saddle then, he could tell she was going to move away. Brodie reached out and touched her hand. She startled at the contact of their skin yet did not pull away.

'Aye. But I still should not have said that.'

'Aye,' she agreed as she lifted her hand from beneath his and gathered the reins. 'You should not have.'

Now, as she rode towards where the others were, he laughed aloud for the first time in a very long time. Arabella glanced back and nodded at him, wearing the first genuine smile he'd seen on her face.

There was more to this lass than he had thought. Mayhap marrying her, if he had to, would not be so bad at that?

Chapter Three

Malcolm approached the table, making his way through the crowd of Mackintoshes gathered for the meal. More than once, she noticed that he stopped to speak to one or another young woman. Her brother had that effect on women. Tall and handsome, he drew many an eye as he moved on towards the dais. He smiled at her as he took his place next to her.

'So, two more days and we will be gone from this place,' he whispered to her as his cup was filled by a very attentive and buxom serving woman.

'Two more days and, aye, we leave,' she said. 'I, however, will be brought back to remain here for ever in a few short months.' He stared at her, perusing her face and then her eyes.

'Are you unwilling to marry here? Have you

changed your mind?' He lifted her chin and narrowed his gaze. 'Tell me the truth.'

This was the only person with whom she could share her true feelings. They'd shared their mother's womb and spent much of their lives together since their birth.

'Willing or not, I will do what is expected of me. You know that,' she whispered. 'I just wish I knew more about the two of them. I wish I had more time. I wish…'

She stopped. Her wishes meant nothing in the negotiations or what would come after it. Her throat burned with unexpected tears and she lifted her cup and drank some of the ale to wash them down.

'What can I do to ease your burden and your worries, sister mine?' She knew he would help her, if he could.

'Marry the one selected as tanist?' she suggested. Malcolm laughed loudly at the inappropriate comment, loudly enough to draw attention. Her aunt frowned a warning, the one that meant her behaviour was unseemly.

'Think not that I shall escape a marriage bargain like yours,' Malcolm said. 'If there had been a daughter, have no doubt that I would have been offered like the sacrificial lamb that you are.' He leaned in and added, 'And think not that I can avoid being sold to the next highest bidder.'

Someone, one of his friends, called out his name and Malcolm emptied his cup before leaving her side. At the last moment, his expression grew serious.

'Truly, is there aught I can do to ease your mind on this marriage and the bargain made?'

'Find out what manner of men they are.'

That was her real question. She saw only what they showed her, just as they knew little or nothing about her. But as her husband, either man would have complete control over her—her body, her wealth, her future. They had nothing to fear going into a marriage for they lost nothing while she, as the wife, had many concerns. Concerns she could not voice or discuss, but ones that made her lose sleep.

'Find out…what?' he asked, nodding again to his friends.

'What kind of men they are. How they treat other women. How they are thought of by their clan. That sort of knowledge.'

'How big their co—!' She smashed her hand against his mouth before he could finish the word. The heat of a blush filled her cheeks. Only her irreverent brother would say such a thing to her. But, he revelled in shocking her.

'Malcolm!'

He lifted her hand from his face and kissed the top of it. Standing then, he bowed to their father and the Mackintosh chief and, with a wink, he was walking away. Soon, friends surrounded him and Arabella smiled. He meant what he'd said—he would seek what she needed to know. He would not fail her and would help her prepare for this new life she faced.

When Arabella turned her attention away from her brother, Brodie caught her eye. He never seemed at ease. Always watchful as he glanced around the chamber out of the corner of his eye, he kept everyone under his inspection. She thought she'd witnessed a few surreptitious nods and signals between him and several other men scattered around the gathering.

There! He'd done it again—exchanged some hidden message with a tall man standing in the back of the hall. She sipped from her cup and observed him over the rim. He repeated his actions—making contact, signalling in that same way, then moving on to the next one—over and over until his gaze moved back to the front of the hall…and to her.

Tempted to look away, instead she nodded to him and watched as he approached. Taller than his cousin, he wore his dark-brown hair long, tied back only at his temples. Though she rarely saw him smile, there were lines around his brown eyes and his mouth that spoke of the habit. His long legs covered the distance between them in a few paces and he stood before her, with his arms crossed over his chest, studying her much as she did him.

Their encounters since that day when they had ridden into the hills, when he had voiced his desire for more cattle rather than her, had been an interesting mix of politeness and challenge. Just last night, at their evening meal, he'd slipped in a question about crops and only the quiet 'harump' reply indicated his surprise that she could speak on such things. This morning, in the yard, he'd asked permission to ride her horse. He'd said the beastie needed a good run after being stabled through much of their business, but she recognised an appreciation for horseflesh that matched hers.

He stood there now, waiting for her permission to join her at table. She placed her cup on the table and nodded. Brodie sat in the chair vacated by her brother.

'My thanks for permitting me to take the horse out, Lady Arabella.' He smiled then and the combination of male beauty and the way his face lit with it made her breathless. How had she ever thought him intimidating and foreboding?

'What did you think of him?' she asked, waiting for his cup and hers to be filled. 'How far did you ride?'

'Several miles past the clearing,' he said. 'Into the hills and beyond. I gave him his head and he took it.' Brodie laughed then and she noticed as many in the hall turned at the sound. 'He tempted me to continue, but I did not want to overtire him with your journey home coming so soon.'

'I have yet to tire him out,' she admitted. 'Most times I am the one to surrender.' She laughed. 'Even my brother, Malcolm, cannot, so I know my skills are not so shoddy.'

He remained at her side, both of them watching as people gathered in small groups before them, clearing the space so that dancing could begin.

'Do you have any mares here he could be bred with?' she asked. The horse had wonderful traits that could be passed on to his get. Brodie choked then and coughed to clear his throat.

'Lady,' he whispered. ''Tis unseemly a topic...'

She turned to face him, shaking her head and putting her cup down.

'He is mine and will remain mine, sir,' she said. 'Even after my husband is given control over everything else I bring to this marriage, that horse is mine. Since you were interested in him, I thought offering him as stud would give you his offspring.'

Arabella knew her aunt and her father would be horrified, almost as much as Brodie was, to hear such words—or even the knowledge of such things—from her. She waited on his response.

He laughed.

Laughed. Raising his cup, he smiled and nodded to her.

'Then I accept your gracious offer, my lady,' he said. 'And I know just the mare to choose for him.'

Watching his eyes change from surprised to curious and then to appreciation made her wonder if marrying a man like him would not be the terrible thing she'd thought it would be. Shocked that she could contemplate such a thing without the fear she'd felt for so long, she listened as he spoke on the topics Caelan never did—lands, farming, animals and more.

Now at a greater ease with him, Arabella

wanted to ask him another question, one about the hand signals. Caelan's arrival and interruption prevented that.

'The music is starting, Arabella,' he said. 'I know my cousin cares not to dance, but that you favour it. So, may I?' He held out his hand and waited for her to take it.

She did not. For the first time during her visit, her curiosity won over her need to be gracious. Smiling as always, she shook her head and did not take his hand.

'My stomach is bit unsettled and I would like to wait before dancing,' she said. 'It must be the travelling and the excitement.' When both cousins wore a similar frown at her words, she added, 'Caelan, I am certain this will pass shortly and I will seek you out to accept your kind offer.'

'Should I call your cousin or aunt?' Brodie offered.

'Nay. I just need to sit for a short time.' She'd thought Caelan would be the one to offer such aid, so Brodie surprised her. Now, glancing at Caelan, she saw that he edged away from her and his usual pleasant expression had turned slightly grey.

'Very well,' he finally said. 'I will wait over

there.' He pointed to a seat at the other end of the table. And then he walked to it quickly.

Such behaviour came as another surprise. She did not know what to say about it, but Brodie explained.

'My cousin fears illness. He avoids being around those who are ailing or sick. He has since he was a child.' A hint of amusement filled his words. He turned to her then, examining her face with that intense stare she'd seen before. 'Truly, do you have need of assistance? One of your women? Our healer?'

Arabella could not resist a bit of mischief now, though he was being attentive and kind and, for once, not his irritating or insulting self. She looked up at him through lowered lashes and used her most feminine voice—the one that usually had any man she aimed it at doing her bidding.

'There is something you could do,' she whispered to him. Dropping her hand between them where no one else would see, she shaped her fingers into one of the gestures she'd witnessed. 'You could tell me what this means?'

His gaze followed hers down to her hand and then came back up to stare at her. Then down once more as though he did not believe what he saw there.

'I have my suspicions, but thought I would ask you since I saw you do it earlier.' His gaze narrowed for a moment and then something that resembled respect filled it.

'Do you think yourself clever, Lady Arabella?'

He reached down and eased her fingers out of the gesture. His hand was warm and strong and almost twice the size of hers, yet he did not use that size and strength against her. A shiver shook her at the thought of such a thing.

'You are ill,' he said, releasing her hand and turning to call someone. She grabbed his hand to stop him.

'I am not ill. I only wished to ask you about those gestures. What are you signalling to the others?' she asked.

'Others?' he asked in a rough tone. 'What others?'

He would not tell her. She had witnessed something he did not wish her to see. His reaction told her the truth—they were messages or words about her. Mayhap more insults about her between him and his friends? The thought of that burned her. Knowing only one way out of this situation, she lifted her face and smiled at him.

'Forgive me, sir, if I have overstepped the bounds of hospitality. I think my stomach has calmed now. I will seek out your...' She began to rise, but he took hold of her hand and held her there. 'Sir?'

'Brodie is my name,' he whispered harshly. 'And do not do that.' She did not force her way to her feet but remained seated there at his side. With her hand trapped within his.

'Do not do what, sir?' she demanded in a whisper that matched his. All the while, the smile remained in place. If anyone glanced at them, nothing would look amiss.

'Smile like that.'

'I do not understand. I am simply smiling,' she said through her teeth.

'Smiling like a simpleton, aye.' He yet held her hand in a firm grasp, one at odds with the anger she felt in him. She let her face relax and nodded her understanding. 'Better.

'I can only say this. Aye, you did see...what you saw. I am in charge of the guards. My uncle wanted them to keep watch discreetly. We use the signals rather than...' His grip eased but she did not pull away.

Not even when she felt his thumb begin to stroke her palm and wrist.

Not when heat crept through her veins and across her skin.

Not even when her words jumbled and she could not remember the question she wanted to ask him next.

'I doubt that anyone else, other than possibly your father, noticed them. Yet you did.' His eyes darkened then, changing from the deep brown they usually were to something closer to black. 'I would ask that you not share what you have seen.'

If she exposed his methods to the rest of her clan, it would render them useless. He was asking for her co-operation. It gave her some bargaining power and she almost laughed at that.

'I will not,' she said. Some tension lessened and he released her hand. 'If…'

'If?' The narrowing of his eyes and flaring of his nostrils warned her to proceed with caution, much as the same reactions in her horse did. It must be a male custom.

'If you tell me what this—' she made the gesture in the space between them again '—means?' He did not look down and he did not respond for a few seconds and she wondered if he would call her bluff. Or just refuse her outright?

'All is well.'

'Ah, so there is no danger tonight? No threats from the Camerons?'

'I would not say no danger,' he said, softly, his breath touching her ear, and she shivered once more.

'And if there was a problem?' The devil sat on her shoulder now, urging her on.

He let out an aggrieved breath and shrugged. He formed the sign with his hand to show her. 'Trouble is coming.' A different signal then. 'Trouble. Take cover.'

'I will not share that knowledge with anyone,' she said. Arabella stood then, as Brodie did at her side. 'I should go now. My aunt has noticed our conversation and I do not wish to be questioned on it.' She walked around the table and approached Caelan.

It took little cajoling or encouragement on her part to make Caelan smile and invite her to dance. As they walked, side by side, to the place cleared in the middle of the hall, she could not help herself. She glanced around the large chamber to see if those same men still stood guard. Then she looked to their leader to see if he signalled any of them. Brodie stared back at her, never looking to any of his men.

Worried that he was angry, she was glad to

see the slight smile curve his lips then. She
smiled back at him, over Caelan's arm, and felt
as though something had eased between them.

The rest of the evening passed quickly and
when her aunt mentioned that she seemed at ease
with both of the cousins, the truth struck her.
There was much more to Brodie Mackintosh than
she had first thought. And the thought of marrying him no longer threatened like a dreaded
outcome.

Nay, she thought as she reviewed the events
of the last several days, it would not be as difficult to find herself married to him as she'd first
thought. So, for the first time since her arrival
there, she looked forward to their next encounter.

Brodie sat in stunned silence for a few minutes after Arabella left the seat next to him. He
thought he was beginning to get a glimpse beneath the facade she wore, that damned smile
and the cursed frozen expression of graciousness. He'd told himself countless times that he
was only seeking out any possible dangers to his
clan, but the way his body responded to her fur-
tive whispers told him she was the danger.

No matter how many times he told himself not

to engage her in the silly bantering that Caelan did, and not to let himself get too close to her, and especially not to want her for himself, he failed. And from the insistent press of hardened flesh against his trews, he'd failed terribly.

Watching as she'd dropped her hand between them and then shaped her fingers into the sign he'd used to his men had caused two things to happen. The first was shock over his complete underestimation of the lass's intelligence and her skill in observation. Then a desire struck him as lightning in a storm, forcing aside his hard-fought indifference and leaving behind a clear, strong need to know her better. To know her at all, since he was now certain he knew little of the true Arabella Cameron.

Now the danger he felt growing was within himself. She put his sense of balance in jeopardy and the promise he'd sworn to support the next chieftain selected by the elders. Right now, as this unexpected need for her rose in his blood, Brodie was thankful that she would be gone in just two days and the elders would make their decision in a calm and reasoned manner.

And if they chose Caelan and she came to the Mackintoshes as his bride, Brodie would find a way to accept it. Now he realised, as he tried—

and failed—not to stare as she danced with his cousin, it would be difficult to do.

He strode from the hall and sought out a place far from her presence, knowing his men were still on watch. The next two days promised to be two of the longest in his life.

Chapter Four

The flames rose higher towards the night sky as the men circling it sat and drank. Against his judgement and as his uncle had ordered, Brodie posted no guards around the gathering or on the path to this clearing. Caelan and two of his friends sat across from him and Rob. Arabella's twin brother and two other Camerons made up the third side. In spite of the air of companionship and reverie, there was no lack of suspicion among the group.

'You are younger than your sister?' he asked of Malcolm Cameron. He wanted to know more about the lass, no matter how he fought the urge.

'Aye,' the younger Cameron replied. 'Only by a few minutes, but she is the elder.' Those minutes mattered not when there was a son to inherit the titles and most of the wealth.

'You fought well today,' Brodie said. 'Who taught you the sword?'

'My uncle Niall trains the young warriors. I know you held back in the yard,' he replied. 'Your control was well honed. Who taught you?'

Brodie got to his feet and walked over to sit nearer the young Cameron. Others talked amongst themselves and he did not wish everyone to hear his every question. 'My uncle Grigor,' he said, sitting down on the log there. 'I have heard the story of Niall and Grigor meeting in battle. Mayhap fifteen years ago?'

Malcolm shrugged and shook his head. 'Where was this?'

Malcolm held out a skin of ale and filled Brodie's leather cup and then his own. There had been skirmishes and battles between their families for generations and, unless this treaty was successful, there would be more.

'On the other side of the loch,' he said. ''Tis said the fight lasted a day and a night.'

'Yet both survived?' The brother's eyes glinted with suspicion.

''Twouldn't be a good story if they died,' he said, laughing. Raising his cup, he cheered, 'A Mackintosh!'

'A Cameron!' Malcolm added his own.

The others joined in the boisterous battle cries and then drank deeply. Caelan retrieved another skin and began to pass it around. This looked more and more like a drinking challenge each minute. Mayhap that was his uncle's intent? After things calmed, he turned his attention back to Arabella's brother.

'So who taught her to ride that beast?'

If he had not been watching the man's face, he would have missed the darkness that filled his eyes and the stark pain. But Brodie saw it and a tightness filled his gut for a reason he could not explain.

'She wasna supposed to ride it. The horse nearly died at birth, but she nursed it to health. Then, when it grew to the size it is now, my— our—father forbade her to ride it.' Malcolm drank deeply then, as though preparing for the telling of some terrible bit. 'He tried to train it and decided to break it when it would not come to heel. That horse threw every rider that tried, so my father ordered it destroyed.'

'What stopped him from doing so?' he asked, almost afraid now to hear the answer, for he knew the lass was in the middle of it.

'Bella did. She stood in front of the horse and refused to allow it. My father bellowed and shouted and threatened her and the horse, but she would not relent.'

'What did he do?' The Cameron was not known to be a soft man or one that would let a defiant daughter stand in his way. Or a defiant anyone.

'He told her the only way to save the horse was for her to mount it or he would break both of them.'

Even though Brodie knew the outcome, he found himself holding his breath. He knew Euan to be a harsh man, but this surprised even him. From the tremor in Malcolm's voice, he must have witnessed this.

'So, she whispered to the horse, climbed on his back and claimed him as hers.'

'I know him well enough to know that your father would not have let her disobedience go unpunished.' Why he said that, Brodie did not know. He just needed to know.

'He did not. She could not move or sit for more than a week.'

Brodie reached for the skin being passed around, filled his cup and emptied it. The wine did not ease his concern but it did send a burst of warmth through his body. Damn, the lass who seemed so compliant, so gracious and always smiling and obedient had a spine of steel.

He did not pursue anything more about her with her brother, for the wine affected him more than it did usually. The other questions he had dissolved in the face of its growing effects. The flames flared and the conversation grew louder and more boisterous. Brodie tried to rise, but his legs would not follow his will. Glancing around, he noticed that Rob's head bowed in sleep, like the Camerons sitting nearest to him and Malcolm.

He shook his head, trying to clear his thoughts, fighting the dizziness and the need to close his eyes. Struggling against the growing lethargy, he called out to Caelan but his vision grew dark and he felt himself falling...falling...falling.

His head pounded.

His mouth felt as though filled with sand.

His eyes would not open.

Brodie lifted his hand to his face, trying to wipe away whatever kept him from waking. But his hand was wet and it did no good. Dragging his arm, his sleeve, across his face, he could finally see...

Blood. It was everywhere. His sleeve and shirt were soaked with it.

Was it his?

Pushing up on to his knees and then to his feet, he looked in horror at the body lying there.

Malcolm Cameron was dead with Brodie's own dagger sticking out of his chest.

'Christ! Brodie.' Caelan's voice broke into the thick haze yet filling his mind. 'Why did you kill him?' His cousin grabbed him by the shoulders and shook him fiercely. 'What were you thinking?' More shouting and more voices clamoured around the clearing as Brodie tried to make sense of the scene before him.

And he failed.

He remembered nothing of the night after talking with Malcolm about Arabella and then a dark void. Looking around, he watched as the others got to their feet. Rob shrugged at him. Brodie did not remember ever getting this drunk before—and he'd had many, many nights of drinking to try.

A large group of men swarmed into the clearing, surrounding all of them with drawn swords. As he staggered forward, unable to regain his footing, his father and the Cameron chieftain dismounted and strode towards him.

'Why?' Euan Cameron demanded, grabbing his throat and pulling him forward. 'Why did you kill him?'

Brodie searched for words, searched for the truth of what had happened and could not find them. His uncle pulled him free and shoved the older man back.

'We do not know what happened, Euan. Hold until we do,' he ordered.

The Cameron dropped to his knees next to the bloodied body of his son, staring into unseeing eyes as they all watched. Brodie wiped his hands against his trews, trying to remove the blood there as he looked around at the others there. The only ones who appeared recovered were Caelan and his two friends.

'What happened?' he asked, his dry throat made his voice rough. 'How did this happen?' He gestured to Malcolm there. Caelan and one of his men walked closer.

'You do not remember?' his cousin asked. 'Truly?'

Brodie squeezed the bridge of his nose and pressed against the throbbing pain in his forehead and brow. The aching there and the queasiness in his stomach forced all rational thought aside.

'Nay, Caelan. I remember it not. Did Malcolm attack me?'

He had killed a fair number of men, in battle or other skirmishes, but he did not kill without thought. And he had no reason to this time.

'Attack you? Nay,' Caelan whispered so that only he could hear. 'You asked him about Arabella. Then you began to argue. Daggers were drawn and you struck first.'

'Take him,' the Cameron ordered his men. 'He owes his life for killing my son and heir.' The Cameron men tried to surround him.

'Nay!' his uncle Lachlan called out, stepping next to him. The other Mackintosh warriors formed line behind them. 'You are on my lands and have no power here, Euan.'

'So this is Mackintosh hospitality then,' Euan said through clenched jaws. 'We came under truce. We came in good faith. And yet my son lies dead at the hand of your nephew.'

His uncle crossed his arms over his massive chest and shook his head.

'We will sort this out back at the keep, Euan. Bring your son and meet us there.' Lachlan nodded at him. 'Bring Brodie.'

Two of his uncle's guards took hold of him, dragging and guiding him along the trail that led back to the keep. He turned back to look as the Cameron wrapped his son's body in a length of plaid.

'Caelan. Rob. I would have a word with you two.'

His uncle would want to know the truth before it was spoken in his hall, before their kith and kin.

Before he was branded a murderer.

The worst part was he could not even defend himself, for his dagger lay embedded in Malcolm's chest and the man's blood covered him.

Arabella heard the commotion below in the hall. The sun had not been up for long so it was not even time to break their fast yet. Her aunt came into the chamber with a haunted expression in her eyes.

'Dress. Now.'

'What has happened?' Arabella asked, as she pulled a shift over her head and a loud roar sounded below. 'Is it my father?'

With Ailean's help, she had her tunic and gown in place and her hair pulled into a hasty braid. It would do. Her stockings and shoes were next and then she turned to face her aunt. 'What is happening?' she asked once more.

'Lass,' her aunt began. Taking Arabella's hand in hers, she patted it gently. 'Nay, not your father. Your brother is dead.'

The room spun before her, with tiny sparkles of light dancing in her vision. If her aunt had not wrapped her arm around her shoulders, Arabella would have fallen.

'Malcolm is dead? How? When?'

It could not be true. Malcolm was her twin, flesh of her flesh, her first protector and friend. They'd just spoken last evening before he went off with the other young men. At her behest. She shuddered against this news, tears filling her eyes and spilling down her cheeks.

'I know not the details. We will learn it below,' her aunt said quietly. 'Are you ready now? You must be strong. You are the only daughter, only child, of Euan Cameron and must be strong.'

Arabella could only nod, for no words would come.

'Take a deep breath and we will go.'

She did as directed and soon found herself entering the hall, so lost in her thoughts and memories of Malcolm that she remembered nothing of their path there. Glancing across the large chamber, she noticed the divide immediately. Her kin stood to one side, the Mackintoshes the other. And in the middle, on a table, lay her brother.

Arabella pulled free of her aunt's hold and ran to him. Only his face could be seen from the shroud of plaid that cocooned him. She touched his cheek and whispered his name.

He could not be dead. He was not old enough to die. He could not. She stroked his face and said his name, willing him to open his eyes and bring this farce to an end. When he did not, she lost any shred of control she thought she had.

'Arabella,' her father whispered to her, softer than he had ever spoken to her. 'Child, come away,' he said, pulling her by her shoulders from her brother's side towards a chair in front of the dais. She did not want to leave his side, but her father's strength forced her away. He placed her in the chair and stood in front of her, blocking her from the sight.

'Father, how did he die?' she pleaded for an answer.

'Murder.'

Chaos ensued his claim, shouting and yelling, men surging and being held back, insults delivered across the ever-shrinking chasm dividing the two clans there.

'Who would murder Malcolm?' she asked

aloud, but no one was listening. The crowd shifted then and she noticed Brodie Mackintosh standing near the dais, covered in blood.

No. It could not be him.

Not him. He knew his duty. He was known for his honour.

She was beginning to like…

Arabella shook her head but when he met her gaze and regret filled his, she began to scream. Someone, someone strong, grabbed hold of her and held her in her seat until she stopped.

'Euan, come and let us speak of this privately,' The Mackintosh said.

She noticed her father did not refuse. The two chieftains strode into a small chamber off the corridor and the door slammed behind them. An uncomfortable silence descended over those left waiting, pierced only by the loud, arguing voices of the two men. With each curse that echoed out of the chamber, the tension grew.

She could not help but stare across at the man accused of killing her beloved brother. The realisation of his death struck her, making her sick to her stomach. Arabella began to retch. The hands on her shoulders released her and she fell to her knees, her empty stomach heaving again and again.

Her brother was dead. She'd sent him to his death.

She turned back to look on his body and then at the man who'd struck him down. Brodie's face might as well have been carved from stone, for there was no emotion there now. Whatever regret she thought she'd seen was gone, replaced by that empty expression. The only movement she could detect was that of his jaws as he clenched his teeth shut.

Her heart hardened against him in that moment. She would find a way to avenge her brother's death. Finally, her father and The Mackintosh returned. Now there would be justice for her brother's death.

'Did you kill the Cameron's son, Brodie?' the Mackintosh laird asked his nephew. Part of her wanted him to deny it. The part of her that was beginning to like this man wanted him to declare it a lie. She waited.

'I…' He shrugged and shook his head. 'I do not know. I do not remember.' Those gathered groaned and shouted at his words. How could he not remember taking her brother's life?

'There were witnesses?' her father asked. The Mackintoshes parted and Caelan and another man walked forward. 'What say you?'

'We were across the fire from them, my lord,' Caelan said. She could hear the resistance in Caelan's voice—he did not want to be the one who accused his cousin.

'What did you see?' her father demanded once more, walking closer to them both. 'I want the truth of this!' he shouted.

The Mackintosh stood at his side and nodded at the two. It was clear to her that Caelan was trying to protect Brodie in this. She clenched her hands into fists, awaiting the telling of her brother's last moments. The hall grew silent in anticipation, too.

'We were all drinking,' Caelan explained. 'All of us. Brodie drank more than was usual for him.'

'They seemed to be just talking, but then they began arguing,' the other man said. 'Over her, over Lady Arabella.'

She gasped as everyone turned to look at her and then Brodie. They had argued over her? Arabella met his gaze and could not hold it. Dear God, what had been said between them?

'Why did no one intervene?' The Mackintosh asked. 'You all know how important the truce is. How violating it would not be tolerated and could result in further bloodshed.' The other man looked at Caelan and back at his chieftain before saying anything.

'It happened so quickly. We were all…' He gestured as though trying to think of an explanation.

'Drunk?' her father offered. 'Too drunk to use reason? Too drunk to stop yourself from killing my son for defending my daughter's honour from insult?' Her father charged Brodie then, only being caught and held back at the last moment.

'Aye, too drunk to intervene, my lord,' Caelan replied. 'The daggers were drawn so quickly we did not see them at first, but then Malcolm fell.'

'He was dead before we could get to him,' the other whispered. The man looked as though he had more to say but her father interrupted before he could.

'I want him executed.'

Complete silence met those stark words. No one moved or spoke or even whispered.

'Euan, you agreed to settle this,' The Mackintosh said softly.

Her father let out a breath and returned to where the Mackintosh chieftain yet stood. Would he order the execution of his nephew?

'Aye, Lachlan, I did agree. Get to it then,' her

father said. What was this devil's bargain? What about the negotiations already completed?

'With witnesses that can speak of your guilt and with you not being able to refute their words, I find you are guilty of murder.'

A gasp went up, echoing through the hall. Whether the Mackintoshes believed him guilty or were shocked that his uncle declared him to be, she knew not. Next would come the…

'I sentence you to be outlawed from this clan and our allies. From this day forward, you are no longer kith or kin to the Mackintoshes or any of the Chattan Confederation.'

A few shouts erupted from the crowd—even Caelan called out against this punishment. The pronouncement shocked even her but she listened to the rest of it.

'You are no one. Your name is gone. Anyone who kills you does so with impunity and without fear of punishment or retribution. All ties of blood or marriage are torn asunder from this moment on.' His uncle's voice wavered then and Arabella found her throat and eyes burning with tears. For Brodie? For Malcolm? For them all? She knew not which.

She waited for him to argue, to plead for mercy or appeal in some way, but he did nothing. His face lost all its colour and other than a slight shake of his head, he remained wordless.

The Camerons there did not remain silent, the cheering began and spread through the warriors. They would have the chance to avenge their kinsman's death with no repercussions at all. She could see the lust for it in their eyes. It would not take them long to hunt him down and hang him like the mad dog they thought he was. She shuddered.

'You have two hours,' the chieftain continued. 'You leave with what you have on your back and nothing more.'

'Uncle...' Brodie finally spoke. When he would have said more, his uncle backhanded him across his face, sending him reeling back.

'You are not of my family, so do not call me that again. Go. Now. And never return here.'

She wanted to scream. She wanted...something. None of this felt real. Surely someone would wake her from this nightmare and tell her it was the stuff of dreams. Glancing over at her dead brother, she had to accept it as it was.

They released Brodie and he staggered through the hall and out into the yard. Though some looked as though they would speak to him, none did. Several minutes passed before her father and The Mackintosh spoke again.

'I declare Caelan Mackintosh to be tanist of the Clan Mackintosh and heir to me personally and to the chief's chair,' he called out.

'And I declare a betrothal agreement has been reached between us. My daughter, Arabella, will marry Caelan,' her father replied.

Her father motioned to her to rise and come to him. Marriage? They thought of marriage now while her brother lay unshriven and unburied there between them? She struggled to her feet, helped and escorted by her aunt. Her father took her hand and the Mackintosh took Caelan's and joined them. She could not breathe. She could not think. This was indecent and there was nothing she could do to stop it.

'The marriage date will be set and our clans will be joined. The feud will end,' her father said loudly. Releasing their hands, he walked away, calling out orders to ready for the journey home.

Lost, alone and in pain, Arabella did not know what to do.

'Come, Lady Arabella,' Caelan said softly, placing his arm around her shoulders and guiding her away. 'Let the servants see to the tasks at hand and I will see you to your chambers.'

'My thanks, Caelan,' she whispered. She appreciated his strength right now. She needed something, someone, to hold on to and he was there for her. At her side where Malcolm had always stood.

'This is not the way I wanted to win your hand in marriage, my lady. But we shall find a way through this. Together.'

Overwhelmed by the grief and shock, she allowed him to escort her to her chambers. In just a few hours, her entire world and family and dreams had been turned asunder. There would be a burial on their arrival back home. And a wedding to plan after that.

The only thing she could count on now was that she would be marrying Caelan Mackintosh. At least she'd learned the truth about the real nature of his cousin before she'd found herself married to such a despicable man.

Chapter Five

Four months later...

Arabella walked around the large chamber and came to stand next to the window in the north wall. Her father had slept in this room during their last visit here, but he slept below in a smaller one now. Ailean and Aunt Gillie occupied the chamber outside this one.

The storms battered the stone keep with relentless winds and rain. This one had begun as soon as they passed under the gates and entered the yard three days ago. It was as though the weather felt her sadness and responded in kind. She sighed then, peering through the rain down into the yard.

The last time she'd seen Malcolm alive was there, in the yard, fighting with his friends against some of the Mackintosh warriors in a training exercise. It was all in the spirit of the approaching treaty, when they would become allies instead of enemies. Wiping the tears from her cheek, she turned and glanced around the chamber.

It had been four months yet the pain and tightness in her chest crushed her now just as it had then.

Malcolm dead. His murderer exiled and still uncaptured. The Mackintosh chieftain dead. And, on the morrow, she would wed Caelan Mackintosh, the new chieftain, and seal their treaty. And any sense of excitement or anticipation had died along with her brother.

'Arabella?' She'd not heard Ailean open the door.

'Aye, I am ready,' she said. Accepting the gold circlet that Caelan had presented to her on her arrival, Arabella placed it on her head as Ailean adjusted her hair. She took a deep breath and tried to let the sadness leave her as her breath did. Attending a feast to celebrate your marriage was not the time to be crying and mournful.

Caelan stood waiting at the bottom of the stairs, smiling and nodding as he saw her. Ailean stepped aside and allowed Caelan to walk at Arabella's side. He took her hand in his and entwined their fingers in an intimate way. Lifting their joined hands to his mouth, he kissed hers and smiled again.

'All will be well, Arabella,' he whispered. 'I know that you are feeling the loss keenly right now, but I hope it will pass.' She felt a fool then, forgetting for that moment about *his* loss.

'My lord, your pardon please,' she whispered back. 'You have suffered your own loss and I have not offered my condolences.'

His eyes lost their merriment and he nodded. They entered the main hall and he escorted her to the table on the dais. Her father stood there waiting and nodded to both of them. Caelan introduced her to the chieftains of the other branches of their Chattan Clan, some young, some old, but none appeared happy. When they reached their places, he waited for her to sit and then raised his cup.

'To Arabella Cameron, soon my wife—' Boisterous and bawdy cheers interrupted his words and he laughed. Then growing serious, he added, 'And to the alliance our clans gain by this marriage.'

The hall erupted in cheering and clapping then, though some did not enter the frivolity.

Some of the Mackintosh elders did not seem pleased…by her *or* the alliance.

When he said those words, she realised that her attempts to remain gracious during that earlier visit were completely missing now. And it was critical to both families that this marriage happen and this alliance be confirmed. There had been more outbreaks and skirmishes since her brother's death and there would be more unless…

Unless she saw her duty through in good faith and humour.

Once the crowd calmed and Caelan sat beside her, she rose, cup in hand, and nodded at him.

'To my lord, Caelan, The Mackintosh, soon to be my husband,' she called out. She drank from the cup as they cheered and then raised it again. 'To our alliance!'

Caelan stood then, took her hand in his and raised them. After a few moments, he lowered them and leaned closer. His intention clear, he did not pause. He kissed her, on the mouth, and though the action surprised her, the kiss was as expected.

Nice. Calm. Friendly.

She watched his eyes and closed hers for a moment before he ended it. The first true kiss between them and not a hint of the things the married women whispered about in it. For part of her, that was fine and good. Since Malcolm's death, Arabella had been empty. She'd cried for days once they'd arrived home and through his burial for she felt as though part of her had died.

Then nothing. Empty.

Caelan waited for her to sit and then nodded at the servants to begin serving the meal. Since his uncle's unexpected death two months ago, he had assumed the chieftain's chair and inherited his titles and lands. Coming on the heels of… She could not keep her gaze from going to the other end of the table where Bro…*he* would have been seated.

The feelings she'd denied for months now began to bubble up within her then. Sorrow, loss, pain and hate pierced her heart and made her want to scream. Or run. Or both. Then Caelan reached over and covered her hand with his.

'Hush now, Arabella,' he whispered to only her. 'I know how difficult it is to sit at this table in this hall. I must force myself every day to sit in my uncle's chair and not to expect his entry into the hall. It will pass. For you and for me.'

Fighting back the tears, she nodded and he squeezed her hand once more before releasing it and turning back to speak with her father. Caelan was being kind in his understanding and she knew that she would do her duty and make this marriage work. She owed it to her father and to her brother who'd died because of her.

As they ate, she glanced around the hall. She noticed that not everyone was joining in the celebration. She searched for other Mackintoshes she might remember from the last time and could find none. What was his name? she thought as she looked for the man who'd ridden with them that one day to the clearing? Rob.

Arabella tried to be discreet while looking around. She realised that many people were not here. The hall, filled to the doorways and rear wall during previous feasts, stood half-empty this time. She knew that the number of Camerons was the same—well, but for one—so where were all the Mackintoshes?

'I thought you would appreciate it if we kept the ceremony small. Considering…' Caelan did not finish his words.

She sighed then. Their families had always had a history of pain and loss, caused by the other clan and visited on each other with severity and regularity. This was the way to end it. There would continue to be deaths and loss if she did not enter this marriage willingly. She'd been raised to this and not even grief would prevent her from bringing about peace between them.

'I thank you for thinking of such concerns, Caelan,' she said, nodding.

'Are you anxious?' he asked.

'Aye,' Arabella admitted to him. 'But my aunt Gillie told me that it is customary for the bride to be a bit nervous the day before her wedding.'

She did not want him to think she was not willing to fulfil her part of this treaty. She would do her duty even as he did his, in the midst of sorrow and loss, but with a hope for peace between their families. So, in the long view of this situation, she was glad it was him she would marry. He was kind and polite and even caring towards her and she would do whatever she needed to do to make this a good marriage.

'Ah, and so comes your aunt to claim you,' he said, standing at her aunt's approach to greet her. 'Is it time then?' he asked.

'Aye, my lord,' Aunt Gillie did her best curtsy before them. 'You will see her on the morrow.'

'Sleep well, Arabella. I will see you at the church.'

He leaned over and kissed her, on her mouth, much to the delight of those watching. They clamoured for more so he took her in his arms and kissed her again. Arabella tried to relax in his arms, knowing most of this was simply to demonstrate his willingness to accept her as his bride. He eased his embrace but held her close for a moment more before letting her go with her aunt.

'That bodes well,' Aunt Gillie whispered as they left the hall. 'I worried that this time apart would sour things between you.'

It took little time to ready herself for bed, but nothing she did seemed to bring on the sleep she needed that night. The morrow promised to be a long, emotional day and Arabella wished to greet it in good humour and without the dark smudges of sleeplessness that appeared under her eyes when she did not rest well.

As the sun's first light tried to chase away the fog, she yet stood by the window, staring across the yard and into the distance. Unable to sleep, she'd climbed from the bed some time ago and pulled on an old tunic and gown against the morning chill. This time of day was her favourite, just before dawn while quiet still ruled the land and the people. Stiff-limbed now from standing too long in one position, Arabella was about to turn away when one single ray of sunlight broke through the clouds and illuminated a spot on the hillside she could see.

The clearing.

The place Brodie had taken her to show her the extent of the lands that she would claim as wife to the next Mackintosh chieftain. She began to shudder before she knew it—her mind recognising the person who stood there now, outlined by the sun's light. Her breath froze and she squinted to be certain.

It could only be him. Standing there, so close to justice and yet no one knew. If she called a warning, he would flee before... Another shiver, this one bone-deep, shook her.

Even knowing he'd killed Malcolm, there was a part of her that did not want to see him dead. At least not until she learned his motives for taking her brother's life. At least until she knew the part she'd played by sending her brother to that gathering of men. She wanted to hear his explanation.

She moved around the chamber in silence, finished dressing and then crossed the outer chamber, passing the sleeping figures of her aunt and cousin. She was careful going down the stairs and through the keep and made her way to the stables. With a quiet word to a young boy there, she readied her horse as she usually did and climbed up on his back. Arabella was at the gate when it opened for the day and rode through it without a word, her cloak and hood pulled tightly around her.

Urging her horse faster, she leaned down low and pressed her knees to his sides. They covered the ground quickly as the horse's strides lengthened and his speed increased. With barely a tug on the reins, she guided him away from the keep and up the road that would curve around the mountainside to where he was.

She would finally get the answers that would allow her own guilt to ease. She would get the opportunity to confront the man who had killed her brother. She would…

Empty.

As she rode through the final line of trees into the clearing, she found no one there. Searching the area, she saw and heard nothing in the stillness of the early morning to indicate that anyone had been there.

Letting out the breath she'd been holding, she walked the horse around the level place, allowing him to cool down from their strenuous ride here. Keeping her gaze on the path, Arabella waited and listened.

The ride back was slower as she faced the

truth that it was not Brodie's guilt but her own that had sent her on this mad quest for the truth. Her heart hurt as she knew that she had sent her brother to his death. She had been the catalyst for the chain of events that caused him to die. If she had not asked him to find out more about Brodie and Caelan, to take their measure, there would have been no fight, no words, no altercation that ended with a dagger in his chest.

Somehow the horse found its own way back to the keep and she rode through the gates to the stable. And she had no idea when the two guards that rode at her side had appeared.

The only thing she could do now to honour her brother's death was to fulfil the purpose of their visit—to seal the bargain and end the feud. And she would.

No one could give her absolution for her part in sending him to his death.

'Get back!' Rob whispered harshly. His friend grabbed the back of his leather jack and pulled him deeper into the cover of the thick trees there. 'Are you daft?'

'They did not see me,' Brodie said, tugging free.

He could not believe the sight of Arabella,

riding at a full gallop on that beast of a horse up the road on the mountainside. She rode right into the clearing and he almost, almost, walked out to see her. A few minutes passed in the grey silence before she travelled back down towards the road to the keep. This time her mount walked and she stared off into the distance as they went by the copse of trees that hid him and Rob from view. He might have grabbed her then but for the two armed guards who rode up to meet her. And he knew that others would follow too closely now.

'Have you changed your mind then? You've given up your mad plan?'

'Not at all,' he said, pushing through the branches and walking away from the road. He made his way back to where three others waited for them. 'We stay true to the plan and do not let ourselves be distracted by surprises.'

'And the lady? Is she not simply a distraction in all this?' Rob asked from behind.

They'd argued this point many times over the past two weeks as the wedding date approached. Brodie would not be swayed from his intention— kidnapping Arabella to prevent the marriage. He turned so quickly that Rob nearly ran him down.

'Aye, she is *the* distraction. Caelan uses this wedding to disguise his true intentions. Everyone is so very busy looking at the beautiful bride that no one sees his true motives or actions.'

Rob ran his hands through his hair and shook his head, a familiar gesture his friend did without even noticing it. 'You are certain?'

He'd learned much during his past four months of exile and every bit of it pointed to his cousin's very comprehensive and long-planned plot not only to take over the chieftain's chair but to destroy the Camerons. Caelan's goal was not peace and compromise, but complete destruction of the other clan.

And though he loved power and control as much as most men, the other clan had much to offer both in terms of goods and trade and stability in the area. He saw no reason to destroy an entire clan when there was gain to be had in letting them live.

He smiled, grim and dark, at his friend. 'Aye. Completely certain.'

'And you must seize the lass? There is no other way?'

'The wedding and the treaty must be stopped, Rob. We have discussed this and you know what he's done. You, your sister, the others, would not be here, outcast and exiled, if you did not believe me. And believe we must take action.' They reached the others then and Brodie waited for them to gather closer.

'Go now and take your positions,' he said. 'The gates are open and many from the village will be entering now.' He drew in the dirt at his feet and continued, 'Hamish. Duncan. Ready the horses at the stables.' Nodding to Jamie, he said, 'Jamie, you trail us and warn us if need be.'

Brodie brushed the dirt from his hands and stood back.

'The kitchens will be the busiest place. Most of those attending the wedding will go on ahead and be waiting by the church.' The small stone building sat near the southernmost corner of the wall enclosing the keep, yards and other out-buildings. 'Her father and few others will remain in the keep to escort her there when ready.'

'But she'll not be ready,' Rob said.

They spent a short time going over the plan and then once more before they split up to enter the gates separately and disguised, so they would not be recognised. The sun was up in earnest when Brodie and Rob entered a little-used door and made their way up the stairway leading to Arabella's chambers.

Surprise was on their side as they opened the

door and met her aunt and maid. In the few seconds before they recognised them, Brodie and Rob were able to get control over them and keep them from screaming out an alarm—to either the guards below or the woman in the other chamber.

Once the two women were gagged and tied, Brodie lifted the latch and pushed the door to Arabella's chamber open. Moving quickly inside while Rob stayed in the outer room, he found her standing, back to the wall, with a very interesting dagger in her hand. Aimed at him.

Chapter Six

'It was you!' she said, turning her body to face him as he approached.

'Aye, my lady,' he said softly, easing his way across the distance between them. The one thing he needed to prevent her from doing was screaming and bringing the guards in on them. 'Did you see me then at the clearing?'

Keep her talking. Move ever closer. He thought those words over and over as he did both. Another step and pause.

'I saw you from the window,' she said, her gaze skittering over to it and back to him. 'But, the clearing was empty.'

'I am here now,' he said, holding out his hand to her. 'Give me the dagger, Arabella. I will not harm you.'

She stared at him then, with bleak and empty eyes that filled with tears. 'Is that how you killed

Malcolm then? Tricked him into giving up his dagger and used yours on him?'

Christ! He wanted to deny it, but could not. He still remembered nothing of her brother's death. Rob scuffed along the wooden floor and whispered a word to hurry him along.

'Give me the dagger, lass,' he ordered softly.

She raised her hand as though preparing to defend herself but it gave him the chance he needed. With a quick stride, he was in front of her, grasping the hand that held the weapon and twisting it down until she dropped it. Arabella gasped and opened her mouth to scream. It took but a second to cover it and nod to Rob.

Brodie wrapped the length of cord around her wrists after Rob gagged her with a piece of cloth. He wanted to laugh as his friend apologised, but this was too grave a time for any humour. Within minutes, she'd been secured— hands, mouth, legs.

'We are taking you from here, Arabella,' he said, as Rob threw a tapestry pilfered from another wall on the floor before them. 'Fight not and you will not be hurt.'

He might as well have thrown water on an angry cat, for she bucked and twisted, trying to free herself. With quick, efficient movements, he and Rob placed her on the tapestry and rolled her inside of it. They carefully lifted the tapestry and the lady and carried her from the chamber, closing the door tightly behind them. Her father would not seek her out until just before the ceremony.

Brodie and Rob walked quickly in the opposite direction and took the second stairway, the one used by servants now busy with wedding preparations, to the lowest floor of the keep. Once there, it took little time to find the secret doorway which opened into a long-forgotten tunnel. He'd played here as a boy and his uncle had planned to close it, but never had. Brodie doubted that anyone remembered this hidden path out of the keep that led to one of the storage sheds near the stables.

The plan in place worked exactly as he'd hoped—his men were in their positions and executed their parts precisely. Even better, those living or working within the walls or the keep were seeing to all of the arrangements for the day's celebration. With most of them so occupied, no one took note of two men carrying a rolled rug away. Soon, with the tapestry laid across his lap, Brodie rode the lass's horse out through the gates and into the hills. Rob followed him while the others parted ways and would meet them back at their camp in two days, each group taking a different route to avoid detection.

The horse had accepted the extra burden without effort and they rode for miles before Brodie realised that the lass had stopped moving beneath his hand that held her securely on his lap. He signalled to Rob and they slowed and then walked the horses a short distance before coming to a halt. Rob was at his side quickly and Brodie lifted Arabella down to him and dismounted. Rob tossed him the skin of water and saw to their horses while Brodie knelt down to release their prisoner. Easing her body and pulling the tapestry, he freed her and stepped back, waiting on her reaction.

There was none. Nothing moved. Her eyes remained shut. No struggle. Brodie leaned closer to check if she yet breathed and placed his hand on her chest to feel if her heart beat.

Alive, thank God, but unconscious. Pushing the hair out of her face, he slid his hand under her head. Lifting her, he loosened the gag over her mouth. He whispered her name.

'Arabella. Wake up, lass.' No response. He

tapped her cheek and spoke again. 'Arabella, wake up now.'

When nothing happened, he tugged the stopper from the skin and dripped a slight amount on her mouth and face. Her eyes fluttered then and she mouthed silent words before opening her eyes. It took a few seconds but Brodie could tell the moment she came back to herself. She pushed herself up to sit, or attempted to, before she realised her hands and feet were tied.

Brodie stood back, allowing her time and space to come fully awake. She struggled against the ropes and rolled over once, before calming a bit and meeting his gaze. The fleeting fear in her blue eyes quickly turned to anger and for some reason he was happier to deal with that. He held out the skin to her, allowing her the choice of it or not. She had not screamed and that was good, too. Arabella lifted her hands to reach for it and he crouched down closer and handed it to her. She took in two or three mouthfuls of water before stopping and holding it back to him.

An unexpected silence filled the space between them. He could not think of what to say to her and she simply stared at him, waiting. When he heard Rob returning with the horses, Brodie knew they must not stay there too long, for they had much more distance to cover before he would feel safe. He reached over and untied the rope around her ankles.

It was clear she fought letting him see a reaction, but she grimaced and clenched her jaws together as she tried to move her legs. A moan escaped as her legs began to spasm. Standing, he took her by the arms and lifted her to her feet.

'Come. Walk. They will feel better faster if you move them,' he said, holding her up and guiding her in a small circle. He felt her trembling begin to lessen and her legs started to carry more of her weight by the third time around the area. He walked them over to a fallen tree trunk and eased her down on it before offering her the skin of water once more. She rejected it silently.

She'd not spoken a word since he'd woken her. Only, accusations of all manner taunted him from the icy depths of her blue eyes. He wished he had Rob's easy way with women then, so he could say something to her.

'Are you hurt?' He forced the words out. From the way she gasped as she moved, he suspected she was.

'Bruised,' she said in a soft voice. Her hair fell about her shoulders, half still in an intricate braid and the rest loose and wild. His hands itched to touch it, but he drew back before he did. 'And battered,' she added, wincing as she pressed her tied hands against her ribs.

'Brodie.' He glanced at Rob, who signalled that they must be on their way soon.

'Does that mean that my father and Caelan are getting closer?' she asked. She pushed to her feet and began to look through the trees. Damn! She'd seen his hand movements again.

'It means we must be on our way,' he explained, sliding his hand around her arm and leading her to Rob and the horses. She pulled away when he reached to reposition the gag over her mouth. Sounds, especially screams, echoed through the woods and could be heard for miles away.

'I must…I must…' she whispered as he tugged the cloth up. 'I pray you…' The gag cut off the rest of her words, but she clutched at his arm and pulled on it.

'You must what, Lady Arabella?' he asked, anxious to put many more miles between himself and his cousin. He released his hold on the cloth.

'I must see to my needs.'

His male flesh reacted to a completely different need than the one she most likely referred to, but Brodie understood what she meant. They'd been riding for a few hours without stopping. He'd taken her after she'd broken her fast.

'This way,' he ordered, tugging her into a thicker copse of trees, one that would give her a measure of privacy to take care of her needs. 'Be quick now.' He released her and walked several paces out of the trees.

He'd no sooner walked away when something warned him that she would try to run. He whistled to Rob who would circle the other way and cut her off. Standing still, he listened until he heard the crackling of the leaves on the ground before pushing back into the trees to get to her. It was no surprise that she was not there. She had no more than a few paces' lead and no experience at trying to sneak away. The sounds of her escape echoed all around them and he had no difficulty following her. And when Rob cut her off and she changed directions, he was waiting for her.

She slammed into him, not seeing him before she hit him. They both went down, her from the force of the impact and him in trying to keep her from being crushed beneath his weight. His efforts failed for they landed in a heap, her bound hands trapped in the one spot where they could do the most damage. The only good thing was that he twisted at that last moment and Arabella came down on top of him.

It took barely a moment before he realised it was not truly a good thing at all. And when she shifted, trying to get back to her feet, it was more bad than good.

The fates or heavens smiled on him then, for Rob, on horseback, reached them, leaned over and lifted her off him. By the time Brodie jumped to his feet, Rob had replaced the gag and seated her before him. Brodie could do nothing but mount the black beast that Rob held there. With a grim nod to Rob and amazed at his own stupidity in handling, or mishandling, the lass, Brodie let his friend lead.

It was some time later, as they headed higher into the mountains and found the place where they would spend the night, that Brodie finally allowed himself to approach Arabella.

She ached. Every bone and place in her body hurt with every breath she took or move she made. If not from being wrapped in the tapestry and thrown over a horse, and if not from running into the wall of hard muscle of Brodie, then surely the past several hours spent in the saddle had been the final assault. If she had been allowed to ride how she was accustomed to riding—astride and not over the lap or in the lap of another—she might not be in as much pain as she was.

Or so she'd thought until they stopped their relentless climb high into the mountains. For now she added cold to the pain and the list of ever-growing complaints that she held against Brodie Mackintosh. And that was in addition to kidnapping her and preventing her wedding. And beyond his greatest sin. Her plan was to stay alive and somehow reclaim her horse to escape him and find her way back to Caelan.

If she could find her way out of these mountains.

She stood in silence, waiting for the waves of pain to lessen before taking a step or saying a word. The men left her standing there, as they took some supplies off the horses and led them away. The winds began to swirl and the coldness bit deeper into her as the last light of the sun dropped behind the mountains in the distance. Wearing only the clothes on her back and wrapped in a thin blanket that Rob had given her some time ago, it was not long before she began to shiver.

'Come.' So lost in her misery, she had not seen or heard Brodie approach. He pulled and tugged at the rope encircling her wrists until it fell free. Arabella shook her hands, trying to get the numbness out, and then winced as the sensations came rushing into them.

Brodie held out his arm to her, as though giving her a choice in this. All her intentions for his capture and punishment aside, she found herself clutching his arm more than she wanted to as they walked towards a small shelter built there. He helped her to sit and she watched him move around the covered space, gathering this or that and speaking a few words to his friend who did his bidding.

Neither had been cruel to her, even if binding her and rolling her in a tapestry was barbaric. So, they must plan to use her as a hostage or she would be dead by now, would she not? Rob sat near her, tore off a chunk of bread and handed it to her. Brodie took a place on the other side, blocking her in between them but also blocking the winds a bit. He held out a battered cup to her and, when she accepted it, he filled it from the skin.

Famished, she ate several bites of the bread,

first dipping it in the water to soften it, before asking the question that plagued her the most.

'Why?' she asked. Her voice surprised her as it echoed between them.

She said it once but wanted more answers than just to the obvious one. They glanced one at the other, some wordless message exchanged between these two men bonded by something she did not understand, and then Brodie met her gaze.

'To stop the wedding,' he answered with the most obvious answer. He held out a flask to her. 'Drink some of this,' he ordered. 'It will warm you.'

She tipped the flask back and drew on it. The fiery liquid burned a path down her throat until it hit her stomach. She'd drank this before, her brother...had shared it with her, out of their father's watchful eye. Now, it warmed her, spreading through her limbs and blood.

'Since you were not even certain you wanted me as a wife, why would you stop the wedding?' she pressed again. And she handed the flask back, knowing that imbibing too much of it would loosen her control over herself.

'It was necessary,' he replied, handing the flask to Rob.

'And now? What happens to me now?' His eyes flared then, some emotion flickering for a moment before it disappeared.

'You do as you are told and no harm will come to you,' he said. When she would have spoken, unable to resist the taunting nature of his words, he shook his head. 'There is much you do not know. There is much you cannot know.'

Living with her father, she'd learned at a very young age to choose rebellion carefully, for the cost was usually dear. Euan Cameron had discovered her weakness early and did not hesitate to use her brother as a substitute for her to punish her misdeeds. Her father expected absolute obedience from his children and she and Malcolm had learned early to give him that. Something told her that this was one of those situations, one that could turn against her on a moment's notice, so she paid heed to the feeling in her gut and allowed him to have the last word…for now.

The daylight disappeared quickly and the cloudy skies covered any light the moon gave off. Rob used his flint and some dry leaves to start a small fire. It would not give off much heat but at least it banished the darkness for now. Being midsummer, the night would not last too long here in the Highlands. Which meant they intended to sleep here.

A chance for her to escape? As if he'd heard her thoughts, he motioned for her hands. 'Give me your hands, Arabella.'

'There is nowhere for me to run, Brodie,' she said, glancing around at the darkness around them. 'I would be daft to try…'

'I saw it in your eyes,' he said, the smile that curved his mouth a grim one. One that spoke of his suspicions about her. Considering that the last time she'd been free for a moment, she'd run, she could not truly blame him for thinking such.

He wrapped the length around her wrist, only once this time, and then surprised her by wrapping the other end around his wrist. Brodie held it out to his friend who finished the task. They were tied together and she could not move without him feeling it.

'How will I…?' She could not voice the task she needed to see to right this moment, but from Rob's chuckle, he understood.

'Worry not,' he said as he tugged on the rope, leading her away from the light of the fire. 'It is too dark for me to see anything.'

Some mortifying minutes later, they walked back to the shelter where Rob had laid out some blankets and lengths of woollen plaid. Two places. Arabella looked from Rob to her keeper and shook her head. She would not sleep that close to him. She backed away until the rope stopped her.

'Your virtue is safe, lady,' he said. He guided her over to one of the blankets. 'As long as you remain quiet, I will leave the gag off.' She'd forgotten about that possibility.

Arabella decided that, if she wanted to escape, she needed rest and daylight. So, she would allow him to think her a compliant prisoner…until she was not. She must keep the element of surprise on her side since she was outnumbered. And a stranger in these lands. Her father and Caelan would be searching for her and she just needed to give them time to catch up with them.

It took one all-too-short minute for them to lie down. The pile beneath her was surprisingly comfortable, but her body went rigid when he lay behind her. Sliding as far away as possible, Arabella knew she would not sleep at all this night. Weariness and fear and anger proved her wrong, overwhelming her resistance as her body gave up then. As she drifted off, warmth surrounded her and she sank into it, dreaming of a huge fire burning in the hearth of her chambers.

* * *

Brodie could tell the moment she stopped fighting sleep, and him, because her body softened and leaned back against his. A soft sigh followed a shiver and nearly unmanned him. He tossed another blanket over her and slid his arm around her, pulling her closer.

To warm her.

So she would not sicken or grow weak.

She would be of no use to them if she sickened and died.

He was only taking care of her for the good of his clan and not because of any softer feelings he might hold for her.

He repeated those thoughts to himself throughout the rest of the night as she burrowed closer to him. He reminded himself also of his true intentions in this endeavour and that she was only a means to his end—to tear control of the Mackintosh Clan from Caelan's traitorous hands and save it from complete destruction.

When the meagre light of dawn pierced through the chilly fog, he was still telling himself those facts and trying to make himself believe them. Brodie knew that he had to endure this closeness to her for only two more days. Once they reached their encampment hidden high and well in the mountains, he would pass her off to be watched by someone else and not have to deal with her until he executed his plans.

Two more days.

Chapter Seven

Of hell. Of unadulterated misery.

Two days of it.

Mayhap if she'd cried or carried on, wailing and moaning, or whimpering, he could have withstood the pressure. If Rob had not laughed, silently or aloud, at his frustration in keeping a distance from her and not engaging her in discussions or arguments. Or if she'd not asked him questions so pointed he needed to check to see if he bled at her words and tone?

The worst of it was when he blindfolded her as they approached the final path to the hidden caves and clearings he and his lost souls called home. As he wrapped the cloth around her head, it tangled in her hair and she winced. Trying to free the mass of blonde curls, he could feel her breath against his skin. Worse, he wanted to wrap her hair around his hands, entwine it around his fingers and feel the silkiness of it. Brodie had to clench his jaw and complete his task, with Rob smirking from a few yards away. Now, as they crossed the stream and followed the well-disguised final approach, he wondered how he'd deluded himself for so long.

Her arrival at his family's home had raised the level of tension and expectation and he had planned to ignore her and focus on the important matter of protecting his clan. He had not set out to dislike her, but he had. With every false smile, Brodie had detested her. With each mewling attempt Caelan had made to woo her, he had disliked her even more.

So, it had been a surprise when he began liking her. And more surprising when he began to look forward to the time his uncle forced him to spend with her. He had seen through the facade to the woman beneath as she allowed him to see or hear bits and pieces of herself. What he had first thought was a shallow, vain, spoiled heiress was clearly not that at all. Arabella Cameron was much more than that.

And he wanted her for himself.

To have her, he needed to be chosen and named tanist, so he had inched his way towards that, both horrified that he wanted her so and fearing that he would never have her at the same time. It was during that time he had started to suspect that Caelan's plans and true aims when it came to the Clan Cameron might not be just the proposed treaty. He'd begun to ask questions when the terrible incident with Arabella's brother had happened.

Now, outcast and outlawed, proving his suspicions was nigh to impossible. All he had been able to collect were bits and pieces, reports from friends and those who supported him—so far nothing that would stand as evidence enough to remove Caelan from the chieftain's seat. And yet, if he was right, peace was not Caelan's goal at all.

For the past months, the part that had truly concerned him was what Caelan could have in mind for Arabella. Damn his weakness, but he had allowed his growing interest in a lass to distract him from his duties.

He heard the signal and replied to it as they turned at the bend in the road and walked their horses through a space in the trees that created a gate-like opening. Brodie nodded to the men they passed who would see the trees and branches put back in place. He raised his hand with another gesture, another safeguard to those whose lives were in his hands now. Two men crept out from behind more brush and greeted him.

'Take her to Margaret,' he said, as he lifted her down to the ground. 'She is a prisoner, not a guest.' He tried, with no measure of success, to ignore the shudder that shook her whole body at his words. 'She stays as she is until I get there.'

'Aye, Brodie,' Rob answered, taking her arm and leading her away.

He had things to see to and could not waste time thinking about her now. Turning to one of the guards, he asked, 'Duncan? Hamish? Jamie?'

'They all returned yesterday. Said no signs of being followed.'

'And Caelan? The Cameron?' he asked. He held the reins of the black tightly as the beast fought this new unfamiliar place. Tugging the horse forward, he led him to the small enclosure where they held the horses. Ranald followed along, keeping his distance from the horse even while giving his report.

'Search parties have been sent out several times a day. Sometimes Caelan leads them, sometimes others,' Ranald said. 'All to the west.' So, their plan of leaving signs of the lady along the roads leading west had succeeded.

'Anything else?' Brodie stopped, nodding to several men as they passed.

'Nay, Brodie. All is well.'

'Watch the lower roads. I do not underestimate Caelan's response to this insult. And tell the others to have a care. There will be more men watching and searching in the woods.'

Ranald nodded and went off to spread the warning, leaving Brodie to figure out what to do with Arabella's horse. His presence with the other horses would cause problems. Just as his owner's would. He handed the stallion off to one of the lads with instructions on his care and walked off to see to tasks undone because of his absence these last days.

Mayhap that would help relieve the restless tension within him before he had to deal with his prisoner?

Caelan waited in his chambers for his man to return from the latest search. He paced from door to window though it did no good in hastening his wishes and orders. Finally, the heavy tread down the hallway outside his room foretold of results. A sharp knock heralded Gavin's arrival. He offered no hospitality before speaking.

'Have they been found?' he demanded.

'Nay, my lord,' Gavin began, but Caelan had no patience for prevarication right now. Days had passed with no sign of either his outlaw cousin or his missing betrothed.

'Has Euan returned yet?' The Cameron laird had been relentless in searching for his daughter. A great help, since it kept him busy and out of the way.

'He has been sighted on the road, my lord. He should arrive momentarily.' He'd hoped the old man would stay on the road, following the signs of his daughter's abductors and keeping out of his way.

'Do any of my cousin's friends yet remain here or in the village?' he asked. In a manner of thinking, his cousin had made things easier for him by staying alive. Until this escapade at least.

Over the past months, while Brodie had been on the run, Caelan had weeded out those who had supported him in the past, by either pressuring them to leave or evicting them. And all of it done discreetly so blame did not come to him. His uncle's *unfortunate* but timely passing had given him the position and power to accomplish that and more. Now, though, Brodie's return and his taking of the Cameron heiress threatened his goal.

'I canna think of any, my lord,' Gavin replied.

'Go and seek out any of those who were known to be his friends. Or their families, Gavin,' he said. Grabbing the man and dragging him closer, Caelan finished his warning. 'You do not want me to suspect your loyalty in this. Find someone and find my cousin!' He flung the lackey back towards the door and turned away, waiting for him to leave.

In slow and measured steps, Caelan had put his plan into play and stood to gain all he desired. The Camerons cowed and conquered, their heiress his, their gold his, their lives his. Chieftain of the Mackintosh Clan and head of the Chattan Confederation. Complete control over a large part of the Highlands and the esteem and power that came from that.

As he'd watched the Camerons arrive for the wedding, he'd reminded himself that he could keep up the charade before them until the dowry was transferred into his control. He could play the pleasant, interested, magnanimous laird and make people believe it. He had been doing that and doing it well most of his life. With his objective so very close, he could continue.

Even if his cousin now interfered.

When there had been no outcry at Brodie's

exile and Euan Cameron had been convinced to keep to their bargain with his uncle's sweetening of the pot with concessions, Caelan had been pleased and had inched forward. When his uncle's death had brought no suspicion on him, another step forward. Now, all he needed was Arabella Cameron in his grasp to finish.

And he would.

Not even Brodie Mackintosh—damn him!—would stop him.

The sounds out in the yard spoke of Euan's return, so Caelan curbed his temper and prepared to greet the man. By the time he reached the yard, the older man had dismounted and walked towards him.

'No sign of them past the river,' he said, pointing off in the distance. 'Your man Magnus thinks we are being led far afield from their real direction.'

'Magnus? He said that?'

Magnus had trained under Brodie though he held no liking for his cousin. Some woman or another had got in between them, breaking whatever friendship or bond they'd had. But he knew Brodie's ways.

'Gavin, summon Magnus to the hall,' he called out. 'Come, Euan. I found the other maps that may help us.'

He hated the man next to him and it took all his will to keep from plunging his blade into the man's chest. For in his uncle's attempts to mediate their feud, Lachlan had never known that Euan was the one who had tortured and killed Caelan's parents after losing a battle. His mother had been first, her throat cut, in front of her husband…

And her son.

Euan had forced him to watch then and did not even remember it now. Today, he acted the wise leader, seeking peace.

Though so many, too many, thought to forget the past and forgive the trespasses of those on both sides in an effort to gain peace for the future, Caelan would never forget. And he would never forgive. He would seek revenge for those who had died at the hands of the thieving Cameron bastards. He would make them pay so dearly that no one would ever claim the name of Clan Cameron again.

First, he needed to retrieve his betrothed and kill his cousin. Then he would see to the rest.

Arabella did not fight Rob as he led her over the rough terrain. Indeed, she leaned on his strong arm as the uncertain path ahead continued. With her eyes covered as Brodie had ordered, she followed Rob's instructions. But being blind like this did not mean she did not hear things.

Whispering voices as she passed. The laughter of children in the distance. Her name spoken, both in surprise and derision. Several people called out to Rob, though he never slowed or stopped along the way to their destination.

Margaret. She was being taken to Margaret, whoever she was, and to be treated as a prisoner, he'd ordered. She shivered then, for his tone had been ominous...and angry. The anger frightened her. Remembering the beatings and punishments of her childhood, they had always come after something had drawn her father's close attention and ire. Another shiver and Rob stopped then, cursing under his breath again.

She wanted to smile at that realisation for he did utter a surprising number of profanities and impolite words. Usually in response to something Brodie had said or ordered and usually they stood unanswered by that man. He was the opposite of his friend who rarely spoke and seemed to parse out each single word. But that wordless man might yet take her life as he had her brother's, so she needed to keep her wits about her now. They began walking again but this time only for a few minutes before he drew her to a stop.

'Margaret?' Rob called out. A few moments and then again, 'Are you in there, Margaret?' He released her for a moment and then took her arm in his hand and guided her forward. She heard no reply but he must have seen something in answer to his call.

'Here now, my lady,' he said. She felt his hand on her head. 'The opening is a bit shorter than you are, so you must bend slightly to enter.'

She allowed him to guide her head lower and she followed him inside...some dwelling. It was warmer now, the smell of a fire and something cooking made her stomach grumble unexpectedly. A few more steps and they stopped, then Rob took her by the arms and placed her on a stool or chair. Someone, Margaret most likely, scuffled and moved around from behind them.

'Brodie said she is a prisoner, Margaret, not a guest,' he repeated the words to this woman.

'Did he now?' the woman asked. 'And is she to be trussed up like that the whole time she is his *prisoner*, as well?'

'Until he says otherwise,' Rob answered from

further away now. 'And you'd best heed his orders.'

Arabella thought she heard humour in his voice, but surely that was not possible? Then he was gone and she could only hear Margaret moving around near her. A few minutes passed in silence, the gag preventing her from saying anything to the woman who seemed her gaoler. As she sat in the warmth, her body protested the long hours on the road and her bindings. She felt herself begin to sway and feared falling over. The touch on her face surprised her.

'Here now, my lady,' Margaret said as she tugged the gag free of her mouth and removed it from around her face. 'Let me take these off.'

'Nay,' she warned. 'He said…' She did not want someone else to be the target of Brodie's anger.

'Ah, pish,' Margaret whispered as she untied the cloth covering her eyes. 'The man says many things, but I still do as I please.'

Arabella opened her eyes then and looked around. They sat inside a tent that had a small brazier at one end, creating the warmth. A pallet lay in one corner, a small trunk in another. Then she looked at the woman Brodie had sent her to.

It took no time at all to see the resemblance between Margaret and Rob. Siblings most likely.

'First, drink this.' Margaret held out a steaming cup of something and she reached to accept
it. 'That man!' she huffed out in an aggravated
whisper.

Then, after she put the cup down as she
tugged and loosened the rope around Arabella's
wrists, Margaret continued her hushed diatribe
against Brodie. Brother and sister, for certain,
she thought. Once freed, Arabella took the cup
and sipped from it. Some kind of brewed tea or
concoction. She did not recognise the flavour
but the warmth of it eased some of her shiver-
ing. When her belly grumbled once more, Margaret shook her head and began another string
of curses under her breath. Soon, a hearty soup
filled the same cup and Arabella spooned it into
her mouth so quickly, she barely tasted it.

Once her belly was full and her body warm,
the exhaustion gained control and she drifted to
sleep where she sat.

She only discovered when she was awakened
by the loud whispers close by that Margaret had
guided her to the pallet and covered her with a
thick blanket.

'I gave orders, Margaret.' Brodie's voice was harsh and demanding. 'She was to remained blindfolded and bound.'

'Oh, aye, you did,' Margaret replied. Arabella dearly wanted to open her eyes and watch this exchange but pretended sleep so that she did not interrupt them. She would learn more this way.

'And you dragged that puir lass for days and miles, without proper food or care. I thought you knew better than that, Brodie?'

'She is a prisoner, Margaret. Something you need to remember,' he said, letting out a loud breath. 'The blindfold was for your protection and for the others. If she did not see you, she could not report back to Caelan who was here. Now she can identify you.'

'Then leave her to me since she has seen my face,' Margaret replied in a calm voice. 'No need for the others to be endangered.'

'Do not answer her questions. She will poke and prod and pry, but say nothing about any of this,' he warned.

'Should I wake her now?' Margaret asked.

'Nay.' He paused and she knew he was dragging his hands through his hair as he did when frustrated. 'Nay. Let her sleep. Send someone for me when she wakes.' She heard his movements as he stepped out of the tent. 'And send to me if you have need of anything.'

'I will, Brodie,' Margaret said.

When they finished speaking, Arabella intended to say something but the cocoon of warmth and the first real rest in days tugged her back to sleep.

How much time had passed she knew not, for she woke to the quiet of night outside the tent. Pushing the layers of wool off her, she sat up and stretched her arms and back. With a care to be quiet, Arabella found the end of the useless tangle of her hair and freed it. With her fingers, she combed through the length of it and wrestled it back into something that resembled a braid.

The indrawn breath echoed across the air as she raised her arms and tossed it. Gazing into the dark and shadowed corner of the small dwelling where the sound originated, she watched as a large form moved closer.

'Did I wake you?' he asked. Brodie.

'Nay,' she said with a shake of her head. 'How long have you been sitting there?'

He shrugged his massive shoulders. 'Since I finished seeing to matters I needed to handle.

And after I'd eaten,' he said, pointing to a bundle next to the pallet. 'Some for you.'

Refusal was on her lips until her stomach answered for her. A few chunks of bread, some pieces of cheese and meat and water had not been enough for her over the days of their journey. She'd noticed that both Brodie and Rob had given her the larger portions so it had not been their aim to starve her. She reached for the bundle and unwrapped it, finding some type of roasted fowl, more cheese and bread within. It took little time to finish the food and drink some of the ale he then offered her.

'I have questions,' she said. When he grunted but did not refuse, she continued. 'I want to know what you expect to accomplish by kidnapping me? Was it to stop the wedding?' That made her think of another question. 'Why would you want to stop the wedding?'

He reached out his hand and placed his fingers against her mouth then, shocking her with the intimate touch. Arabella drew back but remained silent then.

'The less you know, the safer you may be, lady.'

'Why?' she asked, before he pressed his finger again to her lips.

'If you know not, Caelan cannot force it from you,' he said, his deep voice tinged with sadness or something like it. She moved out of his reach and shook her head.

'Caelan would never...'

'Hurt you?' he interrupted. 'Harm the ones you love? I fear you have not seen the true man that Caelan is. He would do both of those things without hesitation or remorse, lady.' He pushed to his feet, towering above her.

'But Caelan was not the man who harmed one I loved, was he?'

Though she needed to say it, his eyes darkened to the colour of night in an instant and she knew the moment the words of accusation left her mouth that it was the wrong thing to say. His hands clenched into fists and his jaw tightened as she watched.

'Nay, he was not,' he forced out.

He walked out without another word, leaving her in the darkened tent alone. She scrambled to her feet and trailed him out of the tent. This might be her chance to escape and she did not want to miss it.

So, why did she want to run to him and take back her accusation? She stopped just outside and watched as he walked away without even looking back. Instead of running in the other direction, she grabbed up her gown and followed him. With each moment and each step, she waited for someone to stop her or catch her again. Arabella ducked behind some trees when he slowed and then skirted several tents and huts to stay just a few paces away.

Then he stopped and she realised he'd reached the edge of a cliff. For several minutes Brodie stood staring off into the darkness without moving. The winds shifted and spiralled around her, reminding her that she'd left without any cloak or blanket to protect her from the biting cold of the night and high mountain air.

'Go back to Margaret's tent, Arabella,' he ordered without looking back.

She left him there and did as he said. Arabella did not doubt that he would force her back. Her folly was, as she turned and discovered, in believing that she could have escaped. Not only was Rob watching her, but several other armed men, as well. Without a word, she retraced her path back to the tent where she'd been held. Rob held back the canvas flag so she could enter.

Arabella still wanted answers, more so now that his reaction puzzled her. Witnesses had called him guilty. He could not dispute their claims. Yet, he did not accept the blame or responsibility for her brother's death. It was there, in the tone of voice when he responded to her question. He admitted the deed, but did not accept it.

Since it was clear he meant to hold her until some purpose of his was achieved, she would have time to discover the truth. And she would.

Chapter Eight

For the first time in his life, Brodie felt helpless.

Even on the day he faced the accusation that would change his life for ever, he had not felt this helpless. When the words of exile were spoken, he knew he could survive on his own. He knew their lands better than any of them. He knew his own abilities and weaknesses. He would survive.

Then, as the first few trickled or were sent out of the keep and village and found their way to him, he remained confident in his plan to survive without kith or kin. The growing number of exiled Mackintoshes who joined him and brought him information about Caelan's plans and activities added to his burden, but helped him in so many ways. When the winter came, they would survive because of their numbers, not in spite of them.

Work continued on the caves and they would

be their shelter when the snows came. He regretted that they'd turned to reiving for some of their supplies and needs, but they did as they had to until they could reclaim their clan.

And they would. Brodie had been gathering information and proof to use against Caelan and it was only a matter of time before he was ready to implement his plan. Arabella's kidnapping gave him the time he needed.

He stood before Margaret's tent again, once more not even knowing how he'd got there and cursing himself for taking so much notice of the lass. With all other tasks, when he handed off the chore or assignment, he did not concern himself with it unless there was trouble or a problem. He allowed those with him to carry out their duties without interference.

Yet, when it came to her, he lost all semblance of self-control. And all the words he had been able to speak before meeting her. Two nights ago, he had wanted to scream out that he had not killed her brother. But those words would not leave his mouth.

No matter how much he tried to remember that night, no matter how much he wanted to remember, it remained cloaked in a thick fog. After Malcolm had spoken about Arabella's horse…nothing. Rob's memories of that night were similar. Knowing now what he did, Brodie had no doubt that Caelan had manipulated them. But without proof, he could not deny killing her brother.

Her voice inside the tent captured his attention then. She laughed softly at something Margaret said but that stopped as he ducked and entered the tent.

'Margaret,' he said with a nod at Rob's older sister. A widow, she had been one of the first to follow them into the wilderness when Caelan had forced her out of the cottage she had lived in since her marriage some years ago. Caelan had excuses, but none that were the real reason—she was Rob's sister and Rob was Brodie's friend. 'Lady Arabella.'

Glancing around, he noticed a lamp lit and several candles. She held out something to Margaret and stood before him, shaking out the length of her gown and smoothing it with her hands. Then she entwined her fingers, even clenched them tightly, as she watched him in silence. Then she blurted out the first question.

'Is there news? From Caelan? From my father?'

'There will be no news from them, lady,' he

replied. Margaret whispered something under her breath that sounded much like one of Rob's favourite oaths. 'You are here until this is done.' Damn! He realised what he'd done as soon as the word slipped out.

'When what is done?'

She loved nothing more than to pick at him with dozens of questions. All at once. Sometimes without drawing a breath. Some silly, ridiculous ones, but always a sly, intelligent one hidden amongst those to lure him into revealing something he did not wish to say. Rob said she did the same to him when he took her from the tent to stretch her legs.

'If you want to walk outside, come with me,' he offered, ignoring the query and knowing that being kept inside the small tent was not a pleasant way to spend the whole day.

Her blue eyes narrowed and she seemed to be considering it a choice. As though she weighed the chance of getting answers against the desire to be out in the crisp night air. He'd given her her parole, she would not be tied nor gagged as long as she remained with Margaret. So far, she'd not tried to escape or raise an alarm.

Brodie knew that, too, was only a matter of time.

She nodded and waited for him to lead. Stepping through the flap, he held it out of the way for her. It must be his imagination but she smelled of flowers. He shook his head at that daft thought as he took a few paces away from Margaret's tent.

'Come this way.'

They walked around several tents, huts and other makeshift shelters. He made certain to take her along the darker of the two paths, the most deserted one, so that they avoided those who lived in the camp. He did worry about her counting their numbers or memorising their faces or hearing their names. The camp had nearly been discovered only a month ago and he could not risk it again.

The rain that had plagued most of the day had moved on along the valley below and now the stars twinkled in a storm-washed sky. At this height, the clear sky also meant the cold would set in quickly after the sun set. The cloak he'd found for her lay tossed over his shoulder, forgotten until he watched her shiver.

Yet she did not complain. Not about the cold, nor the lack of accommodations suitable for a lady of her stature. Arabella Cameron was unlike any woman he'd ever met. If only things had been different for them.

'Lady,' he began, stopping near the path leading to his own shelter. 'This is for you.'

He held out the cloak, a plain brown one with a hood. She surprised him again, turning her back to him so he could drape it around her. Arabella lifted her hair to better allow him to place it. The urge to take the braid in his hand and wrap it around his palm until he could pull her to him took his breath away.

'My thanks,' she whispered as she took a step away. He closed his hands to stop from taking hold of her.

'You can walk down to that outcropping if you would like time by yourself.' Mayhap the distance would also give him a chance to clear his head, as well?

'Why?' she asked. She tugged the ends of the cloak around her and stared at him. 'Is this a trap of some kind?'

'A trap?'

'I go down there without you and something will happen to me and you can claim no knowledge of it. Was this your plan, then? To kidnap me and kill me?' Her voice had dropped lower and sounded too calm. The stark terror shining back at him belied that.

'I told you that you will not be harmed. I give you my word, Arabella.'

And in that moment, as she met his gaze, he realised that she did not trust him and would never trust him as long as her brother's blood was on his hands.

She ran then, ran back the way they'd come, running too fast in the growing shadows of night, in a cloak too long for her. He knew these paths in the darkness, but she did not. And now, she took the wrong turn and ran in the direction of the cliff.

Brodie ran faster, catching up with her just before she took the last step off and wrapping her in his arms. Fearing his momentum would carry them over, he was relieved when he felt others grabbing at them and pulling them back on to firmer ground.

'What the bloody hell are you doing, Brodie?' Rob asked as he climbed to his feet and dusted his hands off before reaching for Brodie.

'Chasing her down,' Brodie answered. He got to his feet without letting go of her. She pulled away then, glancing between him and Rob and waiting for something to happen. 'We are high in the mountains, lady. There are more of these—'

he pointed at the cliff they'd barely avoided '—that will take your life faster than I could.'

She gasped, her mouth opening and her head shaking. Rob said something under his breath... again. Brodie closed his eyes for a moment, praying for forbearance and wisdom and not receiving it.

'Come. Give me your hand,' he said, holding out his to her. It would have been easier on his peace of mind to let Rob escort her right now, but he did not want to relinquish her to him.

She hesitated. Then her hand slipped out of the cloak's folds to him. Rob cleared his throat and walked away then, taking the two other men who'd followed them with him. Brodie took her hand and tugged her closer, laying her hand on his arm. The trembling lessened as they walked wordlessly back along the path.

He had things to say to her and this would be the best time to say them. No details or specific information about his plan, but she did deserve to know some of the truths he'd discovered...because there was every chance that he would fail and she would return to Caelan.

'I brought you here to stop the wedding and the treaty, Arabella. I am keeping you here until I can make certain that Caelan is stopped.' He waited for the barrage of questions or the accusations he knew she would make.

Silence.

He accused Caelan once again and Arabella did not argue this time. This fear that sprang free and controlled her was her enemy as much as the man standing before her. And if she did escape, and she planned to try, anything she could tell Caelan would make it possible for him to destroy his outlawed cousin and bring this, this, well, whatever Brodie planned to an end. It would be wise to learn as much as she could and not antagonise him.

'If you will not reveal your plans, will you tell me what you think Caelan is planning?' she asked. Better to focus on something he would speak of. 'The treaty will bring peace between the Camerons and Mackintoshes and an end to bloodshed. Is that not something to be desired?'

'A true and honourable truce is to be desired and pursued, as my uncle did with your father. But Caelan twists that now.' He turned his gaze to her and she lost the ability to breathe. 'The duty to which you and I were raised is not what you should expect from Caelan if he succeeds, Arabella.'

He spoke of duty. Of a shared duty. Months ago, that might have worked to gain her support. It had surely helped to break down her resistance or reluctance to accept him as husband. There was comfort of a sort in knowing that they would put their duty to their families above their personal desires or wants.

But that was before he killed her brother. And was outlawed from his own clan. Before he kidnapped her.

'What should I expect? Caelan accepted the high chair and swore to protect your...' She began to say *his* clan but it was not his. Not since his exile. 'Caelan took his oath of loyalty and promised to see this treaty to the end.'

He let out an exasperated sigh then and she half-expected to hear him curse under his breath as his friend did. Instead, he shrugged and shook his head.

'Caelan has made many promises. Fooled many people. He fooled me for too long, Arabella. I thought you of all people would have seen through him by now.'

'Me of all people? I know not what you mean by that, Brodie?'

'You wear your beauty like a mask, hiding

the woman you are beneath it. I would think you could recognise when others did the same.'

She wanted to deny it, to say he was wrong, but he had seen through her. And if Caelan was hiding something from her, she had never thought to pay heed to any clues. But what should she say to him now? Should she admit it?

'You owe me no explanation, lady,' he said, nodding to the path ahead of them. 'I just want you to know that there is more to my cousin than he shows until he no longer needs you. When you become expendable, you will learn his truth.'

She shivered against the words and against the fear that he now spoke the truth. Could Caelan be hiding something from her? Arabella needed to think about this, but Brodie's presence, staring at her as though willing her to believe him, made it impossible.

'May I return to Margaret's now?' she asked.

She needed to get away from him. Too many words threatened to spill and too many accusations burned her tongue. Worse, too many questions bubbled within her. Letting them out would not find the truth for her or get Brodie to reveal anything more. Since her questions angered him and his reaction was to ignore her and them, it did her no good to pursue them now.

'This way,' he said, pointing to the left.

He did not offer his arm, but instead, motioned for her to precede him. This part of the path was familiar to her. Soon they reached the tent where Margaret stood waiting. Without a word she walked inside, seeking a place of refuge from the creeping tendrils of doubt that taunted her now.

'Margaret,' she heard him say. 'Do not let down your guard with her.'

She should have been insulted by his words. Instead, she felt as though he saw that there was more to her. That he'd acknowledged it and saw her differently than anyone save her brother had done before.

And the warning was well warranted, for she had begun making plans for an escape. The darning and sewing she'd offered to help Margaret with gave her the opportunity to work on garments from others in this encampment. She started collecting clothing that would disguise her appearance. Once she had enough, she would find her horse and get away.

Even if she did not know the location, she knew she must go down, down from this place high in the mountains, down and towards a loch. Once on the main roads, she would find her way or find someone who knew how to reach her father's lands.

It might take only another day or two, for she'd hidden away a pair of breeches under the pallet where she slept. The cloak she wore now would work nicely to cover her face. She yet needed a shirt or tunic and she would try. Margaret always left her at dusk to get their meal and it would be just dark enough to obscure her from anyone guarding the area.

One more day, two at the most, and Arabella would, at last, being taking some action and not sitting around waiting for rescue or release. And when she returned to Caelan, she would find out if Brodie spoke the truth.

From the tiny twinges of suspicion that plagued her now, she worried that he might have.

Obtaining the needed garments proved easier than she thought it would be. Though she could not guess how many lived here, clearly there were not enough women with sewing skills to mend and fix torn clothing. Or mayhap it was Margaret's way of keeping her occupied during her imprisonment. For whichever reason, she'd welcomed it, for she liked nothing less than laziness. And it provided her with time to give thought to her plan.

Now, she watched the growing shadows outside the tent each time the flap moved in the wind and knew she would need to act quickly once Margaret left. Arabella had taken note of the twists and turns in the pathways as she was permitted to walk last evening with one of Rob's men. Finally, Margaret put away the garments and pieces of fabric and sewing needles and shears and went off to get their evening meal.

Her stomach clenched with nervousness and she thought she might vomit from the tension in her. She stood and tugged and shimmied until she got her gown off over her head. Grimacing from the smell of too many days in the same gown, she shoved it in the space between the pallet and the side of the tent. With a speed her maid would laugh over, Arabella pulled the breeches and stockings into place. The fabric outlined her legs in a way she'd never seen before.

With a length of linen, she bound her breasts and put on the tunic. Gathering up her braided hair, she shoved it down the back of the shirt and hoped the cloak would hide all manner of mistakes. With the hood in place, she lifted the flap of canvas and looked around the immediate area before stepping out.

With a deep breath to calm herself, Arabella walked away from the tent. Remembering the cocky strides of her brother and other young men, she lengthened her steps as she tried to imitate it and mask her feminine sway. She quickened her pace and tried to follow the path she'd laid out in her mind.

Left. Left. Right. Straight on to the area where they kept the horses. Although the night was clear, there was no moon and she would have little time to get down the mountain or away if she did not hurry.

She looked neither left nor right and never raised her head to meet the gazes of others. Soon, she heard the sound of horses and saw her black there in the pen. Climbing over the hastily made fencing was much easier in the garb she wore and soon she stood before her horse as he nuzzled her face and neck. Then he sought out the treats she usually brought him.

'Next time, laddie,' she whispered as she found a bridle hanging on the fence and quickly fixed it in position. Leading him out through a gate, she tried to avoid scaring the other horses there. She did not, could not, be discovered yet.

With no time for a saddle, she used the fence once more as a step and swung herself over the horse's back. This would not be the first time she rode without one, nor the last. With fast, familiar motions, she wrapped the reins around her hands and grabbed on to his mane. Then, with a touch of her heels to his sides, she guided the black out of the camp.

Or she would have if not for the obstruction in their path.

Brodie stood in their way, hands on hips and a dark expression in his eyes. She was still far enough from him that she could get the black into a running start that would force Brodie to move or be trampled. Before she could, he strode quickly at her, his long legs eating up the space between them.

The horse reared up and whinnied loudly, blowing and huffing his displeasure at being threatened so. And it was a threat. Arabella thought Brodie would keep running at them and grab for the reins, but he stopped a few yards away and waited for her to control the horse. She did, with some whispered words and caresses.

'Are you willing to take the risk, lady?' he asked in a quiet voice and not in the loud, angry shout she expected.

'Risk? He is mine. He knows me. He can take me out of here,' she said.

'The dark of the moon is upon us. The fog rises quickly in the mountains. And you would take that horse on to a hillside path that you do not know and have never seen? If you have not a care for your own life, I thought he was more valued to you than that, Arabella.' He crossed his arms over his massive chest and glared at her.

Accusation mixed with disappointment. That was what she heard in his voice. And, worse, it bothered her though she did not wish to admit that. She wanted to run. She wanted to knock him out of their way and escape. But, damn the man, he was right.

He walked the final few paces and reached up to take the reins from her. The horse shuffled his hooves in the dirt and nuzzled him just as he had her. The traitor!

'Give me the reins,' he ordered.

'I want to go home, Brodie. Just let me pass.' She hated that her voice trembled and sounded, even to her, as though she begged this of him.

'Give me the reins, Bella,' he said.

So shocked to hear that name, she let the reins slip from her hands. No one called her that except…except…Malcolm. And this was the man who had taken his life. The same one who now held her life in his hands. She stared at his hands, remembering the sight of them and him covered in her brother's blood that terrible morning.

Arabella did not realise she'd launched herself at him until they tumbled to the ground.

Chapter Nine

The only warning he got that she would attack was the briefest flash of complete and utter devastation in her blue eyes. Then, her eyes darkened and she leapt from the back of the horse at him, throwing her full weight onto him. Her knee landed a blow in his gut and he could not breathe from the power of it. Then, she screamed unintelligible words as she clawed at him with her nails.

The black reacted, too, dancing and shuffling next to them—too damn close to them—as Brodie tried to get control over the she-demon who raked his face with her nails. If he did not get them out of the way, they would both be trampled to death by the huge stallion. And there was no way that the horse would not be injured in such a situation. A shrill whistle pierced the air, alerting him to help.

Brodie managed to get both of her hands in

his and rolled over, straddling her in the muddy path. Rob ran to them, first throwing his hands up to try to scare the horse away and then, when it had backed up, grabbing the reins and bringing it down on all four hooves and trying to calm it.

As he did with the wild woman beneath him.

They were both covered in mud from the wet ditch next to the path that collected the rain. Her cloak had loosened and she lay there, struggling against his hold as she called him a murderer over and over.

'Arabella,' he ground out through clenched teeth. 'Stop. Now.' He leaned more heavily on her softness, trying to make her cease her fight and her accusations.

He wanted to stop her words. Others were gathering, drawn by the sounds of their struggle and her screams, and he did not want them to hear. They might all think the same thing. They might not believe him guilty, but hearing the claim spewed aloud before all of those who threw their lives and futures in with his was not something he wanted right now. Not here.

'Stop,' he whispered. 'I beg you. Just stop.'

His quiet plea broke through her hysteria and she stilled. He knew when she had gained control over herself, for her eyes finally centred on his face. Everything in her gave up in the same moment. Her body softened beneath him, all trace of resistance dissolved away so quickly he thought she'd fainted. Her breathing came heavily then, moving her breasts against him and reminding him of his promise not to harm her.

Brodie eased up, releasing her hands slowly, ready to capture them again if he needed to. His face stung and his stomach hurt. Pushing to his feet and wiping the blood and mud off his face, he reached out to help her up. Her empty gaze filled with confusion and shame as she lay there unmoving.

Rob had taken the beast away and his men cleared out of the area, so Brodie leaned down and scooped her into his arms. She did not fight him—indeed, she did nothing but slump against his chest. Only then did he realise she wore another man's garments and not her own gown. And he felt the outline of shapely, feminine legs on his arm and knew that he would feel much more if he moved his hands.

Walking towards the small cave he claimed as his, he nodded to one of his guards to follow. Once he carried her inside and let her stand, he returned with orders for buckets of hot water and cold and for Margaret to attend her.

* * *

The night was full dark by the time she had cleaned the mud and muck from herself and he'd used the nearby stream. The frigid cold water had shocked him back to his senses. He thought it might dampen the growing desire he felt for her, but that came roaring back as soon as he entered his shelter and found her there, sitting on his pallet, wrapped in a blanket and staring at the far wall.

He approached quietly but without trying to be silent. An air of fragile emptiness filled her—something he'd never seen before. This was not the beautiful Lady Arabella, nor the falsely smiling one. And not the intelligent, resourceful, frustrating one, either. Something had broken inside of her. He searched his memory for the moment that she'd lost control and attacked him.

Bella.

He'd called her the name her brother had used for her.

Then Brodie searched his memory for the time when Malcolm had said it to him and remembered their conversation *that* night. But he could not remember much more after that.

When it had slipped out in that moment and had caused this strong woman to fall apart, he also knew he had yet another sin laid at his feet that he would answer for. He let out a sigh and sought the jug he kept in his trunk. Taking a mouthful and swallowing the burning liquid, he observed her.

The edge of a gown peeked out from beneath the blanket, but it was not the one she'd worn since he'd kidnapped her. He'd given no thought at all to her care and comfort while making his plans to bring her here. Her hair was loose now, hanging damp down her back. Margaret had helped with that, too.

Carrying the jug, he walked over and poured some in a cup for her. When she did not take it, he placed it on the floor before her. Brodie used the wall to slide down and sit across from her. He stretched out his legs and then drank from the jug once more.

'Where did you get the garments? Do I need to see if one of my men lies unconscious somewhere in the dark?' he asked, never expecting her to answer. She was deep in shock, an emotional one, brought on by many things, including his kidnapping and imprisonment of her. He should've expected it sooner, but that was a testament to the lass's strength.

A spine of steel.

Familiar words, but again, no clear memory of when he'd heard them or said them.

'Nay.' The soft whisper shattered the silence and drew his gaze to her. 'No one is hurt.'

'Well, that is good,' he said, nodding. He did not think she would harm someone, not truly. 'And the garments?'

Without looking up or moving at all, she continued. 'I have been helping Margaret repair clothing.'

'Ah. So you fixed them and hid them away until you needed them for your plan, then?' Smart lass.

She did not answer him, but she did lean forward and take the cup in hand. After sipping from it once, she placed it back on the floor and slid away to lean against the wall as he was.

'Too strong for you, is it?'

She nodded and touched the back of her hand to her lips. He walked over and got the jug of water, adding some to the golden liquid in her cup. Then he returned to his place on the other side. They sat quietly for a few minutes and then he asked the question he'd not been able to ask anyone else.

'Were you there when my uncle died?'

The look of betrayal in his uncle's eyes as

he spoke the words exiling Brodie would haunt him until he died. Worse, he could not deny the charges and clear his name.

'Nay. We had returned home. We only heard the news afterwards.'

He'd never had a chance to reconcile with Lachlan, a man who'd raised him and taught him and challenged him into manhood. And he'd died believing that Brodie had betrayed him and their work to ensure a peaceful future for their clan.

'My father said he did not seem to suffer. That he began to have trouble keeping food down and two days later, he…he…'

Brodie nodded for he'd heard the way of it. 'Aye.'

He sank into sadness, thinking about all the people he'd lost due to his cousin's plans. Brodie had avoided this, avoided allowing his feelings to seep through but now he could not. If only. If only. His own plan could not bring back the lost, but it would prevent further destruction of his own clan and that of the Camerons. So distracted was he by the memories he never heard her approach. Her hand on his cheek startled him into awareness.

Arabella knelt next to him, touching his face. 'You are bleeding,' she said quietly, almost a whisper. He had washed the deep scratches but had not worried over their condition. Reaching up to staunch the bleeding with his hand, he found them pushed away by the lass. 'I will see to them.'

Her ministrations, gentle and sure, wrecked any sense of self-control he thought was his. With her this close, he felt her breath against his skin as she traced the path of each slash and pressed on it with a cloth. And he would have been fine, he would have been able to resist her nearness if she had not slid her fingers in his hair to move it away from his face.

Brodie turned his head, bringing his face level and close, very close to hers. Her sharp gasp and shallow breathing told him she was affected, too. A quick glance at her eyes revealed no fear there. They darkened to a deep blue and her mouth opened ever so slightly. And then he lost his battle.

Her fingers stilled in his hair as he leaned over and touched his mouth to hers. Brodie pressed against her, teasing and touching her lips with his and with his tongue. He slanted his face, moving closer to capture her. At first she stared into his eyes, but when hers drifted shut, he slipped his hand into her hair and pulled her to him.

Her body leaned against his, her breasts against his chest, and he felt the rise and fall of every breath she took. Her mouth and body softened and he slid his tongue along the seam of her lips until she opened to him. Dipping deep inside, he tasted her.

Sweet. A hint of *uisge beatha*. Arabella. And so much more.

He smiled against her mouth when she allowed him in. Sweeping again, he found her tongue and suckled on it, gently then stronger. She intoxicated him. Attracted him. Lured him to her. Brodie eased his arm around her shoulders and guided her down until she rested over his lap. Waiting for some sign of hesitation or rejection, instead she touched the tip of her tongue to his.

He waited then, allowing the curiosity that was as much a part of her as her beauty to push her on. And he was not disappointed for she began to stroke his mouth with her tongue, then, taste him and suck on his. It stirred his desire and his body hardened.

What he really wanted to do was to lay her down there, strip her naked and taste every inch of her. Now, after hearing her soft gasps, he wanted to hear more of the sounds she would make in passion. What noises would she make when he kissed her breasts or touched that place between her legs or when he entered her? He drew back to see her face and exulted in the passion-glazed expression her blue eyes held.

Then, something just outside the cave's entrance crackled loudly, startling them both back to their senses. Arabella pulled back, pushing herself out of his intimate embrace until they did not touch at all. Kneeling there, with her mouth swollen from his attentions and with his flesh swollen from kissing her, he only knew he wanted more…of her…with her.

Footsteps outside the cave drew his attention, so he moved away from her and her disconcerting nearness and stood. He had duties to see to. He had people he was responsible for. He had things to do. Worse, he knew she would never be his. Time ran against him, as did his resources, and the commitment of the people here.

Brodie wanted to explain everything to her, but he knew Caelan's methods. If he failed, he did not want her to answer for his sins. The less she knew, the better. Though if he failed, there was every possibility that she and her family would suffer, too.

'Take your rest there this night,' he said, pointing to his pallet.

She raised her chin as though she would argue. Their gazes met and she looked away, with a slight nod of her head in acquiescence. Almost out of the cave, her soft question called him back.

'Why did you call me that?' He did not pretend to misunderstand. He shrugged.

'I heard you called that once.'

'When? By whom?' she asked. She stood now, twisting her hands together. 'No one is permitted to use that. My father would not like it.'

The fragility was back. Her spirit seeped out of her body as he watched, some memory forcing her into surrender. With what he'd heard and what she just revealed, Brodie knew there must have been some punishment wrought in the past by her father. Just as with the black.

He hesitated in giving her the answer. Would it hurt her more to hear the truth? Would it send her careening out of control once more? Something told him she would value the truth, even though he could not give her all of it. Nay, for now he would not risk it.

'I am sorry, Arabella. I do not remember,' he said, turning away.

'It was Malcolm, was it not?' she asked. He could hear her walking up behind him. The touch of her hand on his arm was no surprise then.

'What else did he say?' A mournful, pleading tone in her words nearly took him to his knees.

'Aye, it was your brother. I just do not remember when he said it.' He did not look at her then, knowing he could not hide the lie from her gaze.

She released him without another word and he stalked out of the cave, leaving her there. Rob waited for him, waving him on, but he dared a glance back at her.

Arabella stood without moving for several moments before lifting her hand to touch her mouth. She slid her fingers over her kiss-swollen lips and then turned away. Rob called his name and he nodded. After posting two guards at the only entrance to his dwelling, he went off to see what had chased the usual mirth from his friend's face.

It could not be good.

The way her body throbbed could not be a good thing.

Her lips were swollen. Her skin tingled. A place deep within her ached for something she could not identify. Well, if she was honest with herself, she could.

More. More of him.

The kisses she'd had with Caelan had never caused this wanting within her. They had been tepid, unmoving kisses. Just between two friends with no air of intimacy or longing.

Brodie's had been possessive and enticing. He had tasted her and showed her how to taste him. He wanted her, she could hear it in his breathing and feel it in the way he held her and in the way his body…changed beneath her.

She'd asked her question because she'd needed to force herself out of this seductive haze and back into remembering who he was and, more importantly, who she was.

Months ago, her growing curiosity about him had been appropriate for they might have married. Now, now he was her captor, the man who'd kidnapped her and killed her brother. And his wanting her could lead to nothing but more heartbreak and dishonour. And he could not be the man she thought him to be those months ago if he did these things.

Instead of doing his duty to his clan, he'd torn it apart. Instead of honouring his uncle's and his elders' wishes, he had destroyed everything they'd worked for. And instead of being a man she could have loved, he was a man she loathed.

Worse, he made her hate herself for the part she had played in this tragedy. If only she had not asked Malcolm to go with them that night, he might yet be alive and none of this would have happened.

And Brodie made her detest the weakness within her that allowed her to enjoy his kisses. Knowing what she knew of him, her reaction— permitting him such intimacies—was deplorable and pointed out how correct her father was in his assessment of her. Whenever she tried to go against his will or use her own methods, disaster struck.

As it had been with Malcolm, both when they were children living with an angry father after the death of their mother, and then in causing his death.

She should learn…she would learn…before her poor judgement cost more lives.

Chapter Ten

'Caelan has Magnus,' Rob said as they walked from the cave towards the small gathering of men waiting for them. These were his most loyal friends, men and a few women who had left or been exiled from Drumlui Keep. With their help, he'd been able to find the caves and keep their existence from Caelan.

Magnus...well, their friendship had been broken over the love of a woman, but Magnus remained loyal to his cause. Though Brodie had not been able to offer Isabel marriage because his own future had not been decided yet, he did love her in his fashion. Magnus had offered what he could not. Isabel had chosen neither, leaving Drumlui and moving to live with her sister in another village. Magnus had blamed Brodie for losing his chance with her.

But the man knew the locations he used

to hide and from which he or others spied on Caelan. And Magnus knew the identities of everyone involved. And, he did not wish any man to be left to Caelan's mercy, for he had none.

'When? For how long?' he asked.

'Two days. We just got word of it,' Rob said.

'In the keep?' It would be difficult if not impossible to get him out of the keep, so he hoped Magnus was being held some other place. Rob's grim expression gave him the answer without a word. 'Who do we have there?'

'Grigor is about the only one who could do anything. The others...' Rob paused and looked at Hamish and Duncan for confirmation. The nods and shrugs said it all.

Grigor was an elder and knew of Brodie's plans. He'd supported him in his efforts to be named tanist. But this, helping with this went well beyond any expectation Brodie held for his co-operation or assistance.

'How long do you think he has?'

He met the gaze of each one and they understood his question. How long could Magnus hold out before betraying their location? Not truly a betrayal, for few if any men could withstand the measures and methods Caelan would use against his resolve. But the others did not know that Magnus was working for him. Jamie was the first to speak.

'I doubt much longer. We should move further north now,' he offered.

'Too dangerous,' Duncan replied before Brodie could. 'Too many people to move without a place to go. And with winter coming...' Everyone nodded in agreement—they'd discussed this before to the same conclusion. Many times. 'It might be easier to get someone close enough to kill him.'

Though the suggestion should have shocked them, it did not. A quick death would be preferred over Caelan's torturous path. But Magnus was too important to leave there.

'Send more men to keep watch on the approaches,' Brodie said. Jamie nodded. 'Send word to Grigor to help if he can. If he can find a way to get Magnus out of the keep, I want men ready to get him away.' Rob and Duncan nodded then. 'And have a care for I know this is a trap of some kind.'

'Bring him here?' Rob asked. 'Is that wise?'

That was the true question here, for could they trust a man who'd broken under torture? Brodie let out a breath. What choice did they have? Even knowing it was most likely a trap, they had to try to free him. He nodded.

'Aye. Bring him here. You ken how to do it.'

'And if he's in a bad way?' Rob seemed to be asking all the difficult questions this night.

'Do what you can. Do what you must.'

The silence allowed them to realise once again that this was a war and not the usual way of things. Brodie wanted it to be different. And he wanted it soon.

'Rob, tell Grigor I am out of time.' At Rob's questioning gaze, he nodded. 'He will understand.'

The others took their leave and Brodie was left alone with Rob. It took no time at all for his questions to begin. He thought mayhap it had been a mistake to allow him to spend time with Arabella, a woman who was made of questions.

'What do you need from Grigor, Brodie?' he asked. 'You have not told me.'

'The fewer people who know, the better for all.' Rob pushed his chest, forcing him a pace back.

'You can say that to me? I have risked much for you. I deserve to know.'

Brodie had kept crucial information and documents to himself, for fear of betrayal or the need to rush this and strike too soon without adequate preparation. He'd let no one too close to all of the proof he'd collected to stop Caelan's path of destruction.

And if anything happened to him, all hope would be lost for those who lived here. With the evidence, they could forge their own path and gain protection from one of the clans allied with the Mackintoshes. For Caelan's plans were as huge as his ego and did not stop with dominating just the Camerons; they extended to their allies in the Chattan Confederation. Allies who would not be happy and step aside for the young, untried, headstrong, power-hungry chieftain.

Brodie nodded his assent and returned to the cave to retrieve the strongbox holding their evidence. Arabella startled as he entered but did not speak. She yet stood in the place where he'd left her, looking lost. He moved his trunk and lifted the cover from the hole he'd dug. The strongbox was locked and chained so that only he could open it. Carrying it under his arm, he stopped before her.

'Is aught wrong?' he asked. He studied her face for a moment, waiting for her to speak. A slight shake of her head was all the answer she gave him. 'I will return later. Speak to one of the guards if you have need of anything.'

They walked to Margaret's tent where they would have some measure of privacy and he explained everything to his friend. Some information he'd held back from the others, he now shared with Rob. And Rob's reaction to the scope of his cousin's perfidy was the same as his had been when he'd realised the patterns and methods—first complete shock and then anger. Then utter determination to stop him from destroying their clan with his plans.

They had talked late into the night and then he had secured the strongbox in another place. With Rob at his side, they walked the perimeter, checking the guards and looking for signs of trouble. Then, as dawn's light crept over the horizon, Rob left with Duncan and a few warriors to help as they could to retrieve Magnus from Drumlui Keep. For the first time since discovering the first of Caelan's secrets and in spite of the odds they yet faced, Brodie felt a burden lifted just knowing his friend would be there for him.

He strode towards the cave, wondering how he should deal with his lady prisoner. The cave was more easily watched and harder to escape from. Though, knowing Arabella, he had no doubt she would try again. Crouching down, he slipped into the cave in silence, hoping to avoid waking her and to get an hour or two of sleep before the camp roused.

Arabella lay on her side, facing the wall. He knew not if she was awake or asleep, so he tossed a blanket on the floor where he'd sat earlier, hours ago, and leaned against the cool stone surface. He dozed but never found the sleep he wanted, not with her being so close and the memories of the touch and taste of her fresh.

His name being called roused Brodie quickly and he left the cave, an order to the guard to see to her being the only time he would be able to think of her for the rest of the day. Some sort of warning deep in his blood told him the situation with Magnus was a trap. Though Rob had about an hour's start over him, he knew he could catch up with them...and would. Something was wrong. Some danger lay waiting for them. The last time he'd had this kind of warrior's warning, it had been a near thing for Caelan's minions had almost caught one of the small groups of men he'd sent to watch over Drumlui.

This time? He knew not what lay ahead, only that it did. He saddled the black, gathered another few men and was on his way before the full light of morning was on them.

Margaret visited her at what seemed to be mid-day, bringing food. And, bless her, she brought something for her to do. Sitting or pacing here in his place gave her time to think about things— too much time to think as it proved. The sack of clothing would give her a task to keep her hands busy.

'Will you be planning another escape with these?' Margaret asked her, without a note of censure in her voice.

'I had thought to attempt it in a different way next time,' she replied as she fell back into the companionable way of things between the two of them.

'Wise.' Margaret nodded. Handing her the shears and needles and thread, Rob's sister laughed. 'He'll be counting the pairs of breeches and shirts from now on.'

'I do ask your pardon if I caused you harm,' she offered. Others would pay for her mistakes, they always did, but she had not meant for this woman who'd shown her kindness in her captivity to bear it.

'Harm, my lady? What do you mean?'

'Brodie. Did he punish you for allowing me to escape?' she asked, hoping the consequences had not been too grave. Her father would not brook such disobedience. Her father had not...

Margaret put her mending down on her lap and stared at Arabella for a long minute before speaking.

'Have you seen or heard him punish any man, woman or child since you arrived here, lady? My tent is in the middle of everything—did you hear him yelling or beating anyone? Did he raise his hand to you?'

She'd overheard her father and Caelan discussing Brodie's brutal attacks on the outlying village. And about his ruthless control over the band of brigands he used to defy and harass the Mackintoshes. Yet, here, being held as his prisoner, she'd seen none of that.

He could have used brutality against her, to pay her back for whatever blame he held against her father and Caelan. And he did not. He made certain she was fed and warm and gave her charge to a woman he had to know would defy his orders and keep her well. Other than those kisses and the desire she saw burning in his eyes, he'd not abused her and had surely not forced himself on her.

'Nay,' she said, glancing away. Sometimes it was hard to accept the truth and easier to believe the lies.

'Just so.'

She tugged and pulled at some loose threads and avoided meeting Margaret's gaze for a while then. They traded some of the pieces back and forth, for her skills lay in the intricate, fine stitches while Margaret's were in adjustments and cutting to size. It was Margaret who spoke first.

'My lady, a question, if you do not object?' She shook her head and Margaret swallowed several times and cleared her throat before continuing. 'The scratches on Brodie's face…did he…?'

Arabella felt the heat of mortification fill her cheeks. She understood what the woman meant. It must look as though she had fought off his advances rather than that she had attacked him.

'He did not,' she said. If her tone was too vehement, she could blame it on her embarrassment and the guilt that yet pierced her over allowing him to kiss her. 'If the truth be told, I did it when he stopped my escape.'

* * *

They worked for some time, the rest of the afternoon, and ate together when one of the men brought food. Then, when Margaret prepared to take her leave, she explained that Brodie would be gone for some time.

'Did he return to Drumlui, Margaret? Will he seek to ransom me back? Certainly gold or supplies would go far in seeing to your survival here?'

'Oh, my lady, this is about far more than gold or supplies,' Margaret said. Surely this woman was not involved in whatever Brodie planned? Or was she?

'What do you know of his plans?' she asked, walking to Margaret's side and lowering her voice so that the guards just outside would not hear her words. 'Why will I not be ransomed?' Margaret pulled away, but Arabella grabbed her and held her fast. 'Why will he not bargain to return me?'

'Because returning you to Caelan would mean your death, just as it would for anyone here who returned to Drumlui.'

Arabella stumbled away from the woman and her words. It could not be true. Caelan wanted to marry her. Caelan wanted peace. 'It cannot be true,' she insisted. Even if it were, why would he care if it meant her death for she was nothing to him?

'Lady,' Margaret whispered to her, 'we women are kept out of such matters for ours is not the choice, until it is too late. My husband died and I was forced from my house by the new chieftain before I accepted the truth of it.'

'Your husband?'

'Aye. Killed in front of me for questioning Caelan's right to our home. Worse, Rob had tried to convince Conall to leave before that and he would not listen. He believed Caelan was a fair man and an honourable laird.'

Her mind filled with questions and possibilities and doubt as Margaret whispered her tale of sorrow. Arabella prided herself on being intelligent and curious and yet she had missed this entire side of Caelan. Raised to be beautiful and trained to be gracious, the perfect wife to a nobleman who would need her wealth, her honour and the children he would breed on her, Arabella was never supposed to look too closely at her prospective husband. Chosen by her father and his elders, the flaws mattered not, only her obedience did.

'I...'

Words would not come from the chaos that swirled in her thoughts. Could this woman and the others be telling the truth? Had she, and her father, been played as fools this whole time?

'Margaret!' A man called her from outside. 'You are needed.'

She left without another word, but a string of murmured oaths told Arabella how upset Margaret was. Brodie had told her quite openly not to answer Arabella's questions and now, in one outburst, she'd said more than Arabella knew from all those months before and after her brother's death.

Standing alone once more, Arabella wrapped her arms around herself and listened. Though the sun had set, the camp was still awake and busy. Because Brodie and others were gone? She suspected so from Margaret's words. She picked up a woollen blanket and wrapped it around her shoulders before sitting just next to the cave's entrance. She could not be seen from outside but she could hear people and snatches of their conversations as they passed by.

She needed to learn more. Once Brodie returned she would speak to him and ask for the true reasons for his actions. Mayhap if she knew more, she could sort this out and come up with a way to mediate between Brodie and his cousin. And get word to her father to be on his guard.

As Arabella sat there over the next hours, bits of memories and conversations returned to her. Soon she realised she had indeed been oblivious to many facets of her betrothed's true personality and methods of ruling. Oblivious to what was truly happening around her.

The night had flowed into the next day and even into another before Brodie returned to the camp. And with him, he brought proof that she would not be able to ignore or explain away.

Chapter Eleven

A bloodbath. It had turned into a damned bloodbath.

Once ready, they had sent word to Grigor that they waited. Then, using the secret tunnel, Brodie had met with a few men still loyal to him and got Magnus out of the lowest level of the keep. Brodie's men had expected a trap so they were prepared to face opposition and thought themselves ready. Upon exiting the tunnel in the same place he had when he'd kidnapped Arabella, the trap was sprung and then were exposed in the yard.

Luckily, his men had their horses there and they rode to safety just as the alarm was called. Everything was going as he'd planned.

He had thought.

Even with the precautions they'd taken approaching Drumlui, the attack had come when they had not expected it and in a way they could not have imagined: from the village as they passed through it. Once surprised by the people with their pitchforks and other homemade weapons, it had not been long before Caelan's warriors had caught up with them from behind and attacked.

Worse, the Mackintoshes who fought for Caelan had dragged the villagers into the middle of the chaos.

Brodie wiped the blood from his face as they reached the final pathway to their camp and looked over the group who'd survived. In saving Magnus, they'd lost two other men and several more were seriously wounded. If he added in the number of villagers—innocents caught in the battle—it rose to seven dead. At least four of Caelan's warriors lay dead behind them.

Mackintoshes all.

And that was the thing that tormented him the most. All those injured or dead were his clan. This escalation in hostility had cost a terrible price. Brodie stopped and waited for the others to pass him on the path, meeting each gaze as they did.

'Rob, get Magnus to Margaret first. Then the others can be seen to,' he ordered softly.

He'd sent a man ahead to warn of their arrival and to put additional guards in place along the lower approaches to the camp. By the time he rode in, the wounded were being carried to Margaret's tent and Magnus was already within. Brodie was going to wash off the blood that streamed from his head and his side when Margaret called to him.

'Bring the lady, Brodie. I need her help here.' She ducked back inside before he could refuse.

Would Arabella help their wounded? She was a prisoner here and a Cameron, so she had no reason to do so. The few women in the camp were already at work, so the more hands, the better. If she would consider helping them?

'Now!' Margaret's voice carried over the chaos.

He ran to his cave and entered. She backed away from the entrance and stood there, her arms tucked tightly at her waist and her eyes wide with fear.

'Is there an attack?' she asked. 'I heard many voices and yelling about horses approaching.' Then she looked at him, her gaze moving from the blood on his head, face and neck down to his tunic that was soaked through with it. 'You are wounded.'

'Aye, I am. But…' He was going to ask her and realised that their last leave-taking had been less than affable. If the request came from him, she might refuse. 'Margaret has asked if you would help her.'

First her gaze glanced at the entrance, then at him. Would she refuse?

''Tis daylight out,' she said, pointing to the sunlight's play on the ground near the opening in the rocks.

In the confusion, he did not understand her meaning at first. Then he did—she had only been outside during the night or the dark, at his orders, so she could not identify the people here or their location. Now, that mattered not.

'Will you help?' he asked again.

'Aye. Of course I will,' she said. She looked around the cave as though searching for something. Arabella went to the pallet and picked up a pile of clothing there. 'We…she might have need of these.'

He took her arm and led her out of the cave. She threw her hand up to block the sun from her eyes as they walked quickly away from the cave and towards the turmoil in the centre of the camp. He nodded and answered questions as they walked, never stopping in their progress towards Margaret's tent. The woman herself opened the flap and stuck her head outside as they arrived there.

'I was about to send someone for you, lady.' She nodded at Arabella. 'Your skill with stitching would be most helpful inside. Now.'

He released Arabella and she followed Margaret back inside. Brodie could hear only some whispered words. Leaving the lady to Margaret, he went about his own duties and the next hours passed quickly as he organised the others in the camp for a quick escape if one was needed. He saw to gathering what supplies the women would need to treat the injured. He summoned his friends and set up plans for more defence around the camp and in case they needed to move.

Night had begun to fall as he finished his work and stood outside Margaret's tent, awaiting word of Magnus's survival or passing. Rob walked to his side and handed him a cup of ale and an oatcake. He answered Rob's raised brow with a shrug. No word had been given or asked about the man's condition.

In a way, Brodie did not want to ask, for in the absence of an answer, he could continue to believe his friend was alive. The birds of night, the ones who roosted on the mountainside, sang their songs. The winds, dry all day, now carried a hint of moisture, of storms coming on the morrow.

'I think the burden of trying to appear friendly towards the Camerons is wearing on my cousin,' he said. 'He expected his plans to be further along by now and is running out of patience.'

'Patience?' Rob asked. 'I have never known Caelan to be a patient one. Even as a child, he wanted what he wanted at the moment he wanted it. Not later, certainly.' Rob had actually grown up as Caelan's friend until the three had trained as warriors and fought in their first battles, skirmishes truly, against the Camerons. Something Rob saw had made him turn away from Caelan and never be his friend again.

'Oh, he can be when it works in his interest. But now, the delays I caused by bringing the lass—the lady—here have worn it thin. This—' he waved his hand at the ongoing activities around them '—this is a sign of his desperation.'

'What will he do next, Brodie? Do you think he will come here?'

'I think the Camerons might be asked to leave so he can focus his attention on wiping us out.'

'But what about Lady Arabella? Her father would not simply leave without her, would he?'

Brodie considered the question. Caelan was playing both of his enemies against each other in this—blaming Brodie for Malcolm's death and Arabella's kidnapping while using the troubles with Brodie to manipulate Euan Cameron. Knowing his cousin, Caelan had most likely promised to accept another Cameron lass if Arabella was not returned alive and...marriageable.

And if, as he suspected, Euan did want a lasting peace between their clans, he would agree. If Lachlan and Caelan had increased the concessions after Malcolm's death, it would be done again, until the bargain could not be refused. But then Caelan knew the eventual outcome—it would all be his—when Euan did not.

'Would he, Brodie? Would my father abandon me here?'

He turned to discover Arabella standing outside the tent, staring at him. Her face had lost all its colour, whether due to what she'd heard or what she'd seen this day, he knew not. She stepped closer and he read the exhaustion on her features. And the blood splashed on the gown she wore and along the edge of her jaw where she must have missed wiping it.

'Arabella…' he began. He glanced at Rob, who deserted him and walked into his sister's tent. 'Not here. Not now. I need to check on Magnus first.'

'He lives,' she said. 'Thanks to Margaret's skills and the man's determination not to die.'

He nodded and went inside as Margaret left to go out. Magnus's battered and bruised face and body had been patched up with stitches and bandages, but he was alert and ready to talk. They questioned him quickly, getting the most important details from him before allowing him to rest. Before leaving, he gave Rob new orders to protect the man.

Stepping outside, he found the area empty. Margaret and Arabella were gone. Trotting towards the cave, he found Margaret returning alone.

'Margaret?' he said, stopping in front of her. 'The lady?'

'Waiting for you, Brodie,' she said. She laughed softly and shook her head. 'And she has many questions for you.'

'Margaret, I told you…'

'Oh, aye, you told me this and that, but the lady deserves the truth now, Brodie. She did well today. Her stitches saved Magnus from bleeding to death. And she never shied away from doing anything I asked of her. She's a right one, she is, and not the woman most think her to be.'

'Is that right?' He already knew there was a depth to Arabella that she did not let many see. But at this moment, he did not want to be reminded that he, like the others, had underestimated her.

'Ask her to see to your wounds.' She pointed to his shirt which showed signs of fresh bleeding. 'I will send some ointment to you.'

'What did you tell her, Margaret?'

'I did not share your secrets, Brodie. I but told my tale, for it was mine to tell.'

He exhaled loudly and wanted to pick up their custom of cursing under his breath just then. 'I asked you not to.'

'She wasna ready before, but she is now. Arabella Cameron would be a good ally when the time comes.' She began to walk away but faced him once more. 'And it is coming, is it not? Everyone will have to choose their side. Give her reasons to choose yours.'

Having made her point, she walked away then. Margaret had suffered the most grievous loss because of her brother's friendship and backing and so he took her counsel seriously. With her skills as a healer, she had saved dozens of lives many times over. And her abilities to organise and oversee supplies and souls made her as indispensable as any or all of his warriors.

Most times in the past, she'd left the leading to him, but clearly she had wanted her say on the matter of Lady Arabella Cameron.

The only problem, the insurmountable one, was that the lady would never marry the man who had killed her brother. She had agreed to marry into the clan responsible for it, but would never allow herself to be joined in marriage to him. And he knew how strong her resistance could be.

A spine of steel.

Those words again! He rubbed the back of his hand across his brow, pressing against the pain that throbbed there now. Would he ever remember? Why could he not remember, for other memories of that night trickled in through dreams or random thoughts? Yet when he tried to make them come, they fled.

Like the name *Bella*. It poured forth from him and he knew her brother had used it in his company. But her reaction told him it was something dear to her, something only shared by brother and sister who'd been born from the same womb. And in spite of their father's forbidding it.

The weight of these past days, with hours on horseback, a battle and a harrowing escape, suddenly crashed down on him. Exhaustion stole his resolve and his ability to focus his thoughts. Even though he knew he must be on his guard with her. She was in danger and was a danger to him. Every time he saw her, the wanting within his body and soul grew stronger.

And knowing he could never give her the explanation she craved simply made it worse.

He washed at the stream to get most of the dried blood off his skin. The fabric of the shirt was stuck in the deep gash of his side, so he took some time and eased it loose. The bleeding began once more as he walked back to his dwelling. Mayhap if she was still awake, he would ask her to stanch the bleeding and bandage it for him.

It would matter not how close she stood to him or how her gentle caresses stirred him, for he vowed that he would not repeat the liberties he'd taken the last time.

He might be exhausted from lack of sleep and the tumultuous journey and battle, light-headed from the loss of blood and lack of food and even resistant to the fact that she could never be his—

but—his honour demanded that he not press his affections on her.

So, Brodie entered the cave filled with complete and utter determination that he would not kiss her.

Although she'd helped the healer at Achnacarry Castle since her mother had passed, nothing in her life had prepared her for this day's work. Mixing a concoction, mayhap. Applying a bandage for certain. But, sewing muscle and skin back together? Never.

And yet, Arabella had.

As she stood in the cave now, she glanced down at her hands. Traces of blood remained under her nails and the length of the gown she wore was stained in it.

Margaret had praised her work, said that Magnus lived because of her abilities and skill with a needle. For the first time in as long as she could remember, she was appreciated for something other than her God-given beauty. A laugh bubbled out of her then, inappropriate considering how many had died or had suffered grievously but she let it out.

If her father saw her now he would be horrified by her appearance and condition! Covered in blood and sweat and who knew what else, her hair a tangled mess down her back and a borrowed gown that did not fit. The Cameron heiress looked more like a serving woman than a noble bride.

He'd been very precise about how she should behave and appear in public since she was his heiress. Though her brother would eventually sit in the chief's seat, she would inherit a good part of her father's, and mother's, wealth and so be a bargaining tool for his use. Once her mother had died, he'd lost the benefit of her tempering and his will had become iron. His goal was to make the Cameron Clan the strongest and always to come from a position of strength. To do that, infractions were punished, rules were enforced and his children learned his ways.

So, the graciousness and false smile became her best defence and were always in place. She and Malcolm had been careful not to let their small rebellions be seen. Only Aunt Gillie ever saw her as she was.

Today felt like the biggest rebellion of all.

And it felt wonderful.

She had saved a life today. She had helped others. Her actions were meaningful and not gracious or frivolous. It had taken being kidnapped and held against her will to feel this freedom.

Now, she waited for Brodie to return. Many questions plagued her about what she'd overheard between the two men and from the pain-filled murmurings of the man they'd treated. Even worse, she'd heard men talking as they walked by Margaret's tent, about the fighting that had happened. More tales that revealed Caelan's two faces—the one he had shown to her and the one seen by those who lived here or questioned him.

Margaret's own words had been the worst to hear and the hardest to accept, but the woman had no reason to lie to her. Indeed, she owed the woman much for being the one who understood Arabella's place and still spoke to her about the truth.

Margaret had urged caution on their walk back here. Emotions flared all day, from anguish and pain, to anger and hot-headedness. The worst time to deal with her father was when his anger was high.

Though she did not know all of the details about what had happened at Drumlui, what she did know was upsetting, even to her. Men Brodie knew and counted as friends had died. From some of the talk, she'd learned that innocent villagers had been caught in the middle and had perished, too.

Letting out a breath and feeling the bone-deep exhaustion seeping in, Arabella decided to wait before asking him everything she wanted to know. She would still be here on the morrow and there would be time. Searching the chamber, she did not see water for washing. And she had no brush or comb to use on her tangled hair. She took the empty jug to the entry and asked one of the guards there if he could fill it for her.

Arabella sat on a stool and lifted the length of her hair over her shoulder, using her fingers to ease out the knots. She needed to wash it. She needed a bath. She needed a good night's rest. She needed to sort through this situation and figure out how this was going to end. Only when a soft indrawn breath drew her attention did she look up to see Brodie there.

Watching her wordlessly. Intensely. Her mouth went dry from the way he gazed at her.

He wore no shirt, instead he held it in his hand and pressed it to his side. His long hair, made darker by the wetness of it, dripped rivulets of water down over his shoulders and chest. It was not the bare-chested part that shocked her, for she'd watched him fight like this all those months ago. It was the nearness of him and the size of him and the intimacy of being able to hear his breathing and see his muscles move.

She might have been able to look away but he stared at her mouth as if he remembered the kisses they'd shared. Her tongue slipped out to moisten her very dry lips and he groaned and closed his eyes. His hand dropped from his side, exposing the deep slash there that bled freely now.

'Your wound. No one saw to it?' she asked, moving towards him. He took a half step away before stopping.

'Nay. I washed it, then.' He turned and walked to the large chest where he kept garments.

'It will keep bleeding. Here—' she pointed to the stool that she'd used '—sit. Let me see if I can stop the bleeding.'

He followed her instructions without arguing which told her that the wound did pain him. She needed better light to see the gash more clearly, so she sought out a few candles and a lamp and set them around him. It took only a few minutes to gather what she needed and then she was ready.

Nay, not ready. All she did was look at him there and her hands began to shake. Her legs trembled as she walked closer to him. As much as she tried to convince herself it was just the exhaustion taking over, Arabella knew the true reason for the way she felt—the man before her. The thought of touching his skin, feeling the heat she knew his strong body produced...

'Come now, lady,' he said, his voice deep and dangerous, as he lifted his head and met her gaze. 'Margaret told me of your daring deeds this day. Surely, this—' he glanced down at his injury and then back at her '—is nothing to worry over.'

All the confidence she had in herself fled as he opened his long legs to allow her closer. The gash went from under his arm towards his chest and she would need to see it better. Sitting on the stool would not work. Standing here would not work, either. She moved to his side and knelt next to him. Bringing candles closer, she reached out to test the length and depth of the wound.

He hissed at the first contact, his back stiffened and she drew back, glancing up at his face. His lips, the ones so recently kissed, thinned in what she knew was pain. Remembering where he kept his jug, Arabella found it and held it out to him. She was nervous enough, the thought of touching him and the thought of piercing his skin with needle and thread made her own stomach clench. As if reading her thoughts, he lifted it up to her mouth.

'I think you need this more than I do, lass.'

His voice was as deep and smooth as the *uisge beatha* in that jug he offered. She tilted her head a bit and let some slide into her mouth. Its heat trickled down her throat and into her belly, spreading through her. Licking the last drop from her lips, she glanced at him.

A mistake, that was. A huge error in judgement.

His mouth was on hers before she could take a breath, his tongue dipping inside, chasing the heady liquid towards her throat. Any sense of calm the brew had given her exploded as his hot mouth slanted across hers to taste her.

Brodie slid his hand into her hair and held her to him. When she would have eased back away, for fear of hurting his wound, she told herself, he would have none of that. His other arm came around her shoulders, holding her there.

Now the heat piercing her had nothing to do with the potent whisky but everything to do with the man. Her blood did not rush, but it thickened and heated with every caress of his tongue in her mouth. She opened wider and took it in more deeply, suckling his in response. Her breasts grew heavy against his naked chest and she fought the ridiculous urge to peel off her gown and feel the heat of his skin against hers.

Only when the feel of his hair tickled the sensitive skin in between her fingers did she realise she'd reached up to touch him. Without moving her mouth from his, while he plunged in and possessed her, she wrapped her hands around his neck and pulled him closer. She wanted... she wanted...she wanted...

Him.

The shock of that thought made her pull back and stare at him. His breathing came shallow and fast, matching hers. His eyes bore the glittery glaze of passion and stared at her mouth as though hungry for it, for her. Her body shuddered, recognising the extent of his desire and answering it with a throbbing tightening within her. His expression turned fierce, possessive, primal as he slanted his face and pulled her in to him once more.

'Brodie.'

He stopped at the sound, his mouth scant inches from hers, open and ready to take hers. She blinked, trying to dispel the powerful attraction to him.

'Brodie,' the man said, louder this time.

He released his hold on her and she on him. Sitting back on her heels, Arabella tried to slow her ragged breathing. Her body did not wish to and she felt aching waves that pulsed through her. Then he stood and stepped around her, walking to the opening of the chamber to speak to one of his men.

When he turned back towards her, she tried to keep her gaze on the small crock in his hand. But her efforts failed for she could not help but notice how aroused he still was as he crossed the space between them.

How could she be so drawn to the one man she could never love? Where was her honour when all she wanted to do was fall into his embrace?

Taking a deep breath, Arabella prepared to do battle—with herself.

Chapter Twelve

'You just thought of him, did you not?' he asked quietly. His gaze searched her face and for a moment she did not realise to whom he referred. Then she did and the pain struck her. 'And again just then, too.'

'Aye,' she said, turning her face so he could not stare at her in that manner.

'And you feel disloyal to his memory because we…kissed?'

She nodded as tears gathered in her eyes, stinging her throat. If only…

'Arabella, look at me.'

It took a few moments to gather her strength and meet his gaze.

'I would deny it if I could.'

She waited, her heart pounding as she knew she wanted him to refute his part in Malcolm's death. She'd waited to hear his explanation, his attempt to mitigate his part in it, but now she knew it would not come. It could not come because he was guilty. No matter if she wished it. Exhaustion and sadness overcame her then and her shoulders sagged.

'Take your rest, lady,' he whispered, kneeling next to her. 'You have done more than I expected of you and you have earned your rest.'

'Nay,' she said, reaching for the needle and thread. 'I'll see to your wound, as Margaret asked me to do.' She retreated safely behind the woman's request.

He nodded and sat on the stool, spreading his legs once more around her and leaning back to give her access to the gash on his side. In silence, she repaired the wound, using small, close stitches, mopping the blood as it welled and spilled down his side. Then he held out the small crock and she scooped out some of the ointment with her fingers and dabbed it over the area. Other than stiffening once or twice, he did not move or speak.

Or reach for her. Or stare at her mouth. Well, if he had, she'd not seen it for she kept her eyes on her task and tried to ignore the man beneath her touch.

When she wrapped several lengths of cloth

around his chest and tied it off, her task was done and she gathered up her supplies. As she stood, her legs trembled and she would have fallen if he had not caught her. Resting her hand on his shoulder, she regained her balance and stepped back. And saw the other gash on his head.

'You did not tell me your head was injured,' she said as she took the needle and thread in her hand. 'Hold that candle higher so I can see this.'

''Tis nothing, Arabella.'

'It must have pained you when I...tugged on your hair?' This tear followed the line of his hair from above his right eye down to the side of his cheek.

'Nay.' He hissed this time when the needle pierced his skin, the area being more tender than his side.

'I will finish quickly.' She bent to her task, not wasting time on words. It took only a few minutes to repair that cut and put the ointment on it. No bandage would be placed over it.

'My thanks, lady,' he said as he rose.

Brodie walked to the trunk and pulled a shirt from it. She saw the wince as he lifted his arms and tugged it over his head but did not comment. Men generally did not want to be reminded of weaknesses or injuries—she'd learned that early in her years of caring for her family after her mother's death.

'Seek your rest now. And you have my thanks for your help this day. Especially since...'

'Since?'

'Since you are here against your will. And...'

'And a Cameron?' she asked.

'Aye. A Cameron.' She sensed that those words were to remind her of the line drawn between them. A safe distance from which they could observe and interact but not engage.

'Even Camerons are capable of mercy, sir,' she retorted.

'It would appear that some are, Lady Arabella.'

And he was gone. No warnings to stay within. No admonitions of any kind.

Tomorrow would see new battles between them, but for now she walked to the pallet there and collapsed into a fitful sleep.

Brodie wanted nothing more than to sleep, but he could not allow it to take control that night. He paced his way around the camp, from end to end, checking on his men, the guards, the horses and the supplies. And then he found himself standing before the cave he'd claimed as his some months ago. Jamie moved away as he approached. He crouched down to look within and saw her on his pallet.

Damn, but he felt himself surge and harden at the sight of her lying there!

She'd been extraordinary all day. Margaret yet sang her praises, as did every one of his people who'd come into contact with her. Magnus's life was owed to her actions—actions taken without hesitation. A prisoner. A Cameron.

What was he going to do with her?

His body responded with its own suggestions, the same ones that had been trying to take control for months now. The same body that she'd repaired with her gentle touch and sure movements. Did she know he had inhaled her scent as she knelt between his legs? Had she been able to see his erection that had lasted through the whole time they were together? Had she any idea of what could happen if she but gave a word or sign to him?

She was an innocent, he had no doubt of that. But that simply made it worse. He could read the signs of her own arousal, he'd noticed the tightening buds of her nipples and the way she breathed there next to him. Her eyes had darkened and her mouth had opened just a bit to allow her to pant in shallow, quick breaths.

Never to be his.

He let out a sigh as he noticed her condition. It looked as though she'd crumpled to the pallet with no attention paid to her comfort. She lay as she'd fallen. Brodie crept silently into the chamber and stood over her as she slept the sleep of the exhausted. If she remained as she was, she would pay the price come morning when her neck would hurt and her hands would be numb.

Brodie leaned over and untwisted her arms and gently lifted her head on to the folded blanket that served as a pillow. She mumbled as he straightened her legs and untangled her gown. Then, after removing her shoes, he covered her with several thick blankets against the chill. Satisfied that she would be more comfortable now, he stood and watched the soft rise and fall of her chest with each breath.

And he wanted nothing more in that moment than to lift those blankets and crawl in next to her. To wrap his body around hers, to sleep with her in his arms. He'd not realised he'd groaned until she began to rouse.

He stepped back into the shadows so she would not see him and wake fully. She rolled on to her side and whispered into the dark corner. Her brother's name floated in the air between them.

Just where it would always be.

Brodie stood and walked out, nodding to Jamie as he left. Seeking a place in Rob's tent, he would get a few hours' sleep before dawn came.

And on the morrow, he would hear counsel from his closest friends and supporters over their path forward. The events and bloodshed of this day had shaken his resolve—not in his determination to bring down his treacherous cousin, but in how he would go about it.

Something must change.

The sun shone bright and clear, its light piercing the darkness of night and of the cave and waking her. Arabella discovered that unaccustomed hard work demanded its price and, for her, that cost was that every one of her muscles ached. As she rose from the pallet, tossing aside blankets she did not remember placing there, her arms and back screamed in protest. She forced herself to move, stretching her arms over her head and bending to ease the tightness in her back and hips.

She was no stranger to work, but attending to

the needs of so many was new. Her father's healers dealt with the worst of the wounded after an attack or skirmish. Aided by servants, Arabella's responsibilities had been but to monitor their efforts and offer comfort to the wounded.

Here, she'd lost count of how many wounds and cuts she'd cleaned, stitched and bandaged. How many doses of Margaret's potions and pain medicaments she'd administered. How many pieces of cloth she'd torn into bandages. She'd given no thought to the cause of this until she'd overheard some of the men talking outside Margaret's tent.

An ambush. A rescue gone bad. Caelan's attack using villagers as shields. If not for Brodie, more would have died.

A terrible feeling in the pit of the stomach told her she, and many others, might have been fooled by Caelan Mackintosh.

'Lady?' Arabella went to the opening where Rob stood waiting.

'Aye?'

'Good morrow, my lady,' he said as he entered. She expected he would carry the customary morning bowl of porridge but he was empty-handed instead. In the light of day, she noticed the bruises on his jaw and under his eye. He'd fought, as well.

'And to you,' she replied. Before she could ask his purpose, if not to bring her food to break her fast, he spoke.

'Brodie said that if you give your word not to try to escape, you can have the freedom of the camp, lady.'

Startled, she met his gaze and found all seriousness there. This was an unexpected offer… and chain of a sort.

'He would accept my word?'

'Aye. He said so himself when he sent me here.'

After spending so many days within dreary tents and this cave, and on an especially sunny day, it would be a welcomed change to be outside. But she would have to give up any attempts at escape.

'Can I trust him when he says he intends to release me?' she asked, watching Brodie's closest friend carefully. Without a moment's hesitation, he nodded. Could she trust him?

She would learn nothing sitting inside every day until she was released or rescued. Her father must be searching for her. He would not allow this action, this insult, to go unanswered, for it was not his way. She must be ready for whatever happened and being kept here would not work.

'Aye. He has my word.'

Rob nodded and escorted her outside. An unusually warm day greeted her, the sun shone from a cloudless, brilliant sky, promising to dry up the mud and remove the chill from the air. They walked along the path and were met by nods from those they passed.

'Margaret asked that you see her, if you would?' Rob said, as he pointed in the direction across the camp. 'You can break your fast there, as well.'

Arabella nodded and began to walk away when he stopped her.

'Lady, there are some here who do not welcome a Cameron within our midst, even one brought against her will.' Rob glanced around and then back at her, his brown eyes intense. 'So have a care as you go.'

'Old ways die hard,' she whispered.

Decades and generations of feuding did not fall away easily. Old attitudes took years to form and even longer to dissipate. Even marrying a Mackintosh would not smooth over all the hurt and deaths of their feud.

'Just so.' He nodded then and waited as she walked away.

Arabella stood there, alone for at least the moment, breathing in deeply of the cool air. Glancing across the area, she noted the cluster of tents and shelters erected towards the cliffside and more back along the path to the cave. Several fires burned in pits and women stood cooking around them. Children, a surprising number of children, played nearby.

The encampment stood surrounded by a thick growth of trees, hidden from view of those below. Above them was only the highest of the mountains in the area. From what she could tell, they faced north, but whether Drumlui Keep was to the north or south of them, she could not tell. A woman waved her towards one of the fires and held out a bowl to her as she approached. The woman looked familiar, but she could not remember her name.

'Good morrow, my lady,' she said, offering a cup to her, too. 'I am Bradana. Ye treated my husband, Duncan.'

'How does he fare?' she asked, smiling as two little boys played around their mother's skirts, peeking at her and hiding when she glanced back. She scooped the hot porridge up and ate several mouthfuls of it as they scampered about.

'He is complaining this morn, so he must be improving,' Bradana said. ''Tis the way of men, is it not?'

'Aye, it is.' She smiled at the wee ones as they played their game. She finished the last of the thick porridge and handed the bowl back.

'Have ye need of a cloak, my lady? This bit of warmth will disappear by day's end and ye will catch a chill.'

'Brodie gave me a cloak, Bradana. I left it behind but I will fetch it later. My thanks for your concern,' she said, drinking the water and giving the cup back to her, too.

She walked on and found her way to Margaret's. She called out softly before lifting the flap of the tent and entering. Magnus lay sleeping and Margaret tended to him. Soon, she followed Margaret throughout the camp, seeing to those injured yesterday. If it was strange to see Arabella Cameron there, or having her help these rebel Mackintoshes, no one said anything. Though she feared some retaliation or insult, none came.

The morning passed quickly and all the injuries had been checked and new ointments and bandages applied. The only one she had not seen yet was Brodie. Had he ridden out again? Arabella kept watching to see a glimpse of him as they moved all around the area, but he was not there. When Margaret said she did not need her any longer, Arabella went looking for her horse.

Remembering the path she'd taken the night she tried to escape, she circled the tents and walked towards the makeshift yard where the horses were kept together. Had Brodie ridden the black back to Drumlui? She walked to the fence and spotted her horse there. Recognising her, the black came at her call and nuzzled her hand.

'Poor lad! Did you think I'd forgotten you?' she joked, stroking his nose. Reaching inside the pocket of her gown, she drew out a piece of carrot she'd got from one of the women and held it up on her palm to him. He gobbled it down and pushed her hand, demanding more. 'Next time, lad. Next time.'

'I think you could forgive me for taking you, but not the horse.' She turned and discovered Brodie standing with his back against a tree there, watching her.

'You may be correct in that,' she admitted. 'Are you giving him a chance to run? He gets restless if he does not.'

The horse under discussion nudged against her shoulder just then, sending her stumbling a few steps. Laughing, she regained her balance and walked back to the fence. She heard Brodie walk to her side and glanced out of the edge of her eyes when he stood next to her.

'I have been tending to him, lady. And he proved the difference between life and death over these last few days.'

'You did ride him back to Drumlui, then?' she asked, facing him. She sensed a readiness in him to reveal some of his story.

'Aye. He is stronger than any horse I've ridden. And has the heart to give his all.' Arabella watched as Brodie reached out his large, strong hand and stroked the horse's side. 'He saved Magnus and me.'

She turned back towards the yard and kept her eyes focused on the horse as she took in a slow breath and let it out. 'How did he do that?'

'He was strong enough to carry both of us. Magnus could not ride on his own when we got him out. Then when we were trapped between the villagers and Caelan's men, he got us through. Carried us all the way here.'

'So the villagers are against you now?' she

asked. Glancing at him, she saw his jaw clench and grind as he heard her words.

'Nay, not all of them, lady. Most of them have avoided taking sides in this.' He paused then and she thought him done. But he was not.

'Some were ordered to stop us as we escaped through the village. So they took up what weapons they had—pitchforks and shovels and the like—and got between us and the road out. We could not fight them, would not fight them, but it slowed us up enough for Caelan's men to catch us there. Then, they attacked all of us, my men, the villagers, anyone in their path, without regard for their part in any of this.'

She must have gasped for he turned to her and she saw the bleakness in his gaze and feared the rest of it.

'Some were trampled. Some were struck down because they were in the way. Four, possibly five, died there.'

He stared at her, as though willing her to make the connection he wanted her to see. If she believed his words, Caelan had caused these deaths and more. Where was her father during this?

'Did my father take part in this? Did he send Camerons, too?' she asked. She needed to understand.

'Your father? I did not see him. Magnus said he might have left for Achnacarry Castle some days ago.'

'Left? He left me here?' she asked. Her heart pounded in her chest as the pain of being abandoned struck her.

'More likely, Caelan convinced him to leave so he could see to this family matter. I am certain Caelan does not want your father asking too many questions or seeing too much of his plan.'

'You keep saying that. You say Caelan has this plan. That he is the one tearing your clan apart. That he is forcing people off their lands. Killing them.' She heard her voice rising but could not stop it. 'So tell me then, what is this plan? Why am I a pawn in his game?'

'A pawn, lady?' he asked, his voice growing hard-edged and angry. 'Nay, you are the queen he will eventually sacrifice to protect himself in this game.'

Anger filled her then, for she was tired of talk of games and tired of being held here. And tired of not knowing the truth of the matter into which she'd been drawn.

'And your part in this game? Do you stand out here in safety while he plays?'

He took a step towards her and she backed a

step away. His hands fisted and his face grew fierce and dark. But she never feared for herself. Strange, that.

'I am the one trying to put an end to his game. I am the one trying to save *his* queen from destruction. I am trying to save my clan, lady.'

'And this is how you protect your clan? By hiding in the mountains, collecting the exiled and lost and trying to avoid capture? What kind of life is this for them?'

He stepped away from the fence, the black and the other horses were sensitive to the rising anger between them. As she turned to face him and hear his answer, she looked past him.

Chapter Thirteen

Brodie noticed her face lose all its colour and go pale and looked over his shoulder to see what she saw.

Some of those exiled and lost people stood behind them, obviously hearing her accusations and words and being none too happy about them. Rob had warned him that having a Cameron in their midst during such a dangerous time could lead to disaster, but he had disregarded it. She was his prisoner after all was said.

'Brodie protects us,' called out one man as he spit in the dirt at Arabella's feet.

'He is the rightful Mackintosh,' a woman said, nodding her head at him. ''Tis he who should be sitting on Lachlan's seat, not Caelan.'

The grumbling began within the crowd and Brodie knew it was time to step in. None of this was Arabella's fault and she should not bear the brunt of it.

'The lady is under my protection here, just as each of you is,' he said, crossing his arms over his chest and stepping partly in front of her. The movement was deliberate.

'But she's a Cameron,' someone in the back argued.

'Aye, she's a Cameron,' he said, nodding in agreement. 'But she came to Drumlui to do her duty and end our feud with them.'

'She is to marry that bastard!'

'She carries out her duty to her father and her clan. That was the agreement Lachlan negotiated. The one I supported and pledged to uphold. 'Tis not her fault that Caelan took matters into his own hands and hatched his plot.'

Now whispers echoed through the group as they took in his words. Some of the old ones would not, could not, ever release their anger at the clan responsible for so many deaths and so much destruction. And that, in spite of the shared part the Mackintoshes played. Then Bradana stepped forward, mirroring Brodie's own stance, and nodded at Arabella.

'She may be a Cameron and unwelcome as that by many, but that did not stop her when we needed her help. She worked at Margaret's side and on her own to help our men. And, according to Margaret's own words, 'twas her that saved Magnus.' She nodded, glancing around the crowd and meeting the gaze of most of the women there. Women who were as much pawns of their fathers or husbands as the lady was.

'So, if you have a problem with the lady being here, just stay away from her,' he said, meeting each gaze. 'A problem with her is a problem with me.'

The ones who'd voiced objections nodded, accepting his words, and walked off. Bradana looked as though she wanted to approach Arabella but glanced at him first. Brodie turned and saw what Bradana saw—a very fragile, pale Arabella, standing there trembling. With only the merest shake of his head, he warned Bradana off. The crowd dissolved, all going back to their tasks and duties, understanding that this moment had passed.

Except for the lass.

He would have approached her if he could have thought of words to say that would comfort her. Since none came, he waited on her. After a few silent moments, she lifted her head and turned back to the yard. The black walked slowly across the yard and whinnied at her, waiting for a sign of affection.

'I am sure you have duties to see to, Brodie. You do not have to stand here by me.' Her voice, recently strong and strident, now trembled and shook.

He fought the urge to take her in his arms and soothe away the insults. He fought the need to apologise to her for dragging her into this fight. And, worse, he fought the doubts within his own heart and mind that he was on the right and true course. In the end, he allowed her the privacy she desired and walked away, his boots crunching in the dirt the only sound between them.

Several paces down the path, the guard remained as he'd been ordered, watching the lady from a distance. Brodie nodded to him and stopped to look back.

The black now nuzzled her shoulder as she buried her face in the horse's neck. Though he could not see her face, the way her body shook told him she cried. The sight of it tore at him.

This was not her fight. She would honour her family and her brother by marrying as she was ordered to and give herself, body and soul, over to her enemy. She would live among her enemies and never truly be part of them, known as a Cameron even when her children would be called Mackintosh.

All to gain a lasting peace.

Brodie turned and walked away, knowing that his actions in kidnapping her had caused Caelan to accelerate his plan. And, it had caused the violent repercussions that had resulted in the deaths of his own people. His other choice was to allow the marriage to go forward and intervene later.

But the thought of placing Arabella under his cousin's control and, worse, in his bed, had forced his hand. He had no doubt that once she was Caelan's wife and once he'd gained her dowry, the real destruction would begin. As The Cameron's heiress, she would bring wealth to him immediately. And if Caelan got her with child, that child would be heir to both clans' titles and power.

He had no doubt that Arabella would bear the terrible cost, for Caelan would never countenance a strong wife. He would beat down her intelligence and never accept her for all she could offer him. Now that she'd heard the stories and questioned his falseness, he might not even allow her to live...

She would never be his, but Brodie had sworn

he would see her safely through this. It was the reason he'd taken her on her wedding day. It was the reason he protected her even now. She had accepted her duty even when it was not what she wanted. He would honour that commitment. Arabella would probably still find herself married to a Mackintosh when this ended and the elders chose a new chieftain, but he would make certain that it would not be Caelan.

Brodie went to Margaret's tent to speak with Magnus. He was the one man who could help him assess how close Caelan was to success and how much time they had to stop him. They'd gathered almost enough proof to show that Caelan was paying off men to do his bidding. That he was amassing his own army, a collection of mercenary warriors from all over the Highlands, to destroy any who stood in his way.

Brodie and his men would be first. Then the Camerons.

Sending word for Rob and the others to meet him, he went about his business and tried not to think about the desolation etched into the lovely face of Arabella Cameron.

Over the next hours, he thought about her more than he did his own problems. And as he headed back to his cave to try to get some rest, he knew how he could bring a smile back to her face.

Each day here seemed to bring its own disaster. And each disaster unmade her in some way.

Sometimes it was his words that did it— challenging her beliefs. At other times, it was his actions—standing between her and his people and protecting her. And then there were his more intimate approaches—touches, caresses and kisses that made her want to forget her name, her family and her honour.

The only thing she knew for certain was that she was not the same young woman who'd arrived in Drumlui those months ago, with a clear purpose and the intention of carrying out her duty. That smiling, beautiful, false woman was gone, left behind after tragedy and upheaval. The problem was she was quickly losing more of herself and her beliefs every day here.

For so long, for all her life, she had believed what her father told her. She believed that she owed her mother and all those who'd died the duty of unquestioning obedience. That the only way to honour the dead was to give herself to their enemy and use her body to make peace for a new generation. But what she'd seen and heard and done over these past few weeks underscored what a stupid, naive young woman she'd been.

She'd seen, for they'd only shown her, one facet of this conflict between the clans. Now, these people who hated her for nothing more than the name she carried, had shown her more honesty than anyone in her family, save Malcolm. They'd not shown her the genteel, pretty parts, but the gritty, honest, life-and-death parts.

So what was she supposed to do now?

She desperately wanted to speak to her father, to argue and to warn him of the possible treachery afoot that was aimed for them. Arabella wanted to determine whether Caelan could be as duplicitous as everyone here claimed him to be. If she believed them, not a word he'd spoken to her was true.

As the sun began to dip towards evening, she found herself following the guard across the encampment, for he brought word that she would spend the night elsewhere. Too distraught to question it and not really wanting to see Brodie right now, she did not argue. Soon, they arrived at another cave and he bade her to enter. A girl stood there but that was not what caught her attention.

In the middle of the chamber which also held

all manner of supplies stood a large wooden tub. It was the kind used for laundry, but now it was filled with steaming water.

'My mam said I am to help ye with yer bath, my lady.'

'And what is your name?' she asked, already crossing to the tub. Nothing would feel so good as a soak in a hot bath.

'I am called Fia, my lady,' the girl said.

'How many years have you, Fia?' Arabella gazed at the girl and saw the resemblance immediately. Bradana's daughter.

'Almost ten, lady.' Fia came to her side.

'A perfect age,' Arabella said, as she began to untie the belt around her waist. 'My hair is not easily managed in a bath and I would appreciate your help.'

Within a short time, she was undressed and sinking into water so hot, it made her skin tingle as she sat down. The tub was not large enough for her to stretch out, so she dipped her shoulders down first and then drew her knees up. Knowing what a luxury this was, she would find a way to make it work. Fia might be only ten, but she was more than an able helper. Before the water could cool, her hair was washed and rinsed and her skin scrubbed clean of the dirt of the camp.

A clean shift, gown and stockings awaited her there once she'd forced herself out of the water. It took some time, but Fia helped her dry and comb her hair and then took her to a different place in the camp. Bradana waited there, smiling at both of them.

'Better, my lady?' she asked, taking Fia under her arm and squeezing the girl. 'Did ye help the lady as ye were told to, Fia?'

'Aye, she was the best helper I have had,' Arabella said, wanting to reach out and hug the girl. But these people were strangers and she was… she was…not one of them.

'Mama, her hair is long enough to touch the ground!' Fia exclaimed.

'But ye kept it off the ground?'

'Oh, aye,' the girl said brightly. 'I could not let it get dirty all over again.'

Out of habit, Arabella reached for the small purse she always wore on her belt, to give the girl a small coin in thanks for her help. She ran her hands down her gown, realising nothing here was hers.

'I would give her something for her help, Bradana, but I fear I have nothing,' she admitted.

'Yer words of praise and thanks are enough for her, lady. She will be the centre of all the chatter for days to come.' The girl scampered off to some friends who waited nearby.

'And my thanks to you, as well,' Arabella added. 'For all your help, earlier and with the bath. I know it could not have been easy to stand against your people for me.'

'Old hatreds run deep, my lady. Ye ken? But there comes a time when it just does not matter.' She pointed to a stool there, outside the tent. 'Here. Sit and I will braid yer hair. To keep it clean and from yer eyes.'

Arabella could not resist such an offer. Nothing soothed her more than having her hair brushed and braided. Such a small comfort but it meant so much. Though her own mother had died when she was but a wee lass, Arabella imagined that this was what it felt like to have her tend to her comforts.

'Lady?'

A touch on her shoulder and a slight shaking brought her awake. She did not remember falling asleep. Sitting up, she found Bradana tying off the braid.

'I did not mean to…'

'Anyone with eyes can see ye are exhausted,' Bradana replied, shaking her head. 'Worry not over it.' The woman stood and moved towards the small fire there. 'Have ye eaten yet? Are ye hungry?'

More tired than hungry, she thought until her stomach grumbled loudly. Bradana chuckled and handed her a bowl of stew and a chunk of bread. 'Rest a while and eat, then,' she said.

'And Fia?' Arabella asked before taking the first spoonful.

'The lass will come when she is hungry. Or she will eat with Glenna and her da.'

'So this is like your village, then? You have a care for the others?'

Arabella glanced around. The fires cast shadows across the tents and shelters. Men and women finished up their tasks and would be seeking sleep soon. Certainly not cottages and crofts and not the orderly layout of the village next to Drumlui Keep, and yet here in the midst of it all, it did have the atmosphere of a village.

'For now, lady. Once Brodie…weel, once this is all settled, we have a hope we can return home.'

'And if things do not settle? If he remains an outlaw? Where will you go? What will you do?'

'I have faith in him, lady. It will all work out.'

Bradana nodded and smiled. 'He's a good man. A good leader. He'll see this to rights.'

Before she could ask another question, Bradana stood and patted her on the shoulder. 'And he will see to yer safety as weel, my lady. Fear not.'

'My thanks for this food. And for the bath,' she said, standing and facing the woman. 'I am not certain where I am supposed to go now.'

'Why, right inside, my lady!' Bradana said. 'I have a pallet prepared for ye. Take yer rest and worry not over what ye cannot change.'

Arabella wanted to hug the woman who offered her such comfort and did not realise it. For so long, all she'd known were the duties she must perform and the people she must see to. No one saw to the small needs as this woman had. The simple offer of braiding her hair. The words spoken in her defence. And now this offer of a protected place to rest.

As if she'd made her request aloud, Bradana opened her arms and welcomed Arabella into them. She stepped close and allowed the embrace and all the comfort it offered. It should not matter as much as it did. But this kindness of strangers during a time of need eased so much of her pain. After a few moments, Bradana released her and held open the flap of the tent.

Whatever else came her way, she would remember this moment of peace among the chaos, the moment of kindness. She stepped inside, feeling lighter than she had in a long time. Mayhap Bradana was right? Mayhap Brodie would see things settled and this would work out for the best?

Unfortunately, her optimism lasted but one day and then the real mayhem began.

Chapter Fourteen

Arabella walked along the path that led from Brodie's cave to several of the others that lay hidden among the trees. A connected cluster of deeply cut chambers invisible until you were at the entrance to them. From below or above, no sign of them existed. An ingenious place to hide.

Having little to do that morning because Margaret saw to the remaining injuries, she had inspected the caves and found a large amount of supplies hidden away in them. If undetected, these people could live here for months.

Deciding to see if her horse was here or if Brodie had left the camp, she turned down one of the paths into a more wooded area and walked only a short distance when she was taken from behind.

An arm wrapped around her shoulders and covered her mouth. Another arm tucked around her waist and then she was dragged deeper into the shadows. Struggling against her attacker, she found herself held against a tree, gagged by a hand.

'Hush now, Arabella!'

The voice was familiar. It could not be. She met the man's gaze and discovered it was indeed her cousin Alan.

'Alan!' she whispered furiously. 'How did you find me?' He let go of her and she grabbed him in a tight embrace.

'I have been tracking you for weeks.' Her father called him his best. Though he was too young at ten-and-two to hunt and fight with the men, he would prove valuable when he reached manhood. 'Then I saw them escaping with the wounded one. I followed them here.'

'Where are the others?' she asked, peering over his shoulder.

'I came alone. Your father had to leave Mackintosh lands and took the others with him.' Alan stepped back and held out his hand. 'I have been waiting and watching for the chance to get you out of here. Come. Now.'

If he'd been able to sneak in, he might be able to lead her out. She reached out to take his hand when the oath she'd given echoed in her thoughts.

'You have to get out of here, Alan!' She pushed

him away and pointed back at the path. 'If you hurry, they'll not see you.'

'I am not going without you,' he said, taking her hand and tugging.

She held her breath when the sound of metal scraping metal surrounded them, knowing that swords had been drawn. Brodie stepped forward from the shadows first.

'Neither of you is going anywhere.'

Alan reached to draw his sword in answer, a gesture she knew would be his last, regardless of his age or inexperience with that weapon. So Arabella threw herself between her cousin and the men now threatening him.

'Nay! He is just a boy!' she cried out.

'Take him,' Brodie ordered as he took her by the arm. His hand was like an iron band, pulling her from Alan and holding her still as his men took her cousin prisoner. Then just before Rob left with him, Brodie stopped them.

'Wait. Let me look at him.'

Brodie's tone was a strange one, almost choking on the words, as he walked up to Alan and stared at him. Then he examined his face feature by feature and shook his head. 'Take him. I will be there in a moment.'

They followed his orders and she watched

in silent helplessness as Alan was dragged off. Then, when they were gone, he turned to her.

'Who is he, Arabella?'

She saw no reason to lie. 'He is my cousin Alan.' When he frowned, she added, 'You met him during our visit. He was forever trailing after...' She could not finish it, but he nodded his understanding.

'How did he get here?' Glancing around the area and listening for a moment, he tightened his grip. 'And where are the others?'

'He tracks. He has since he was a wee one. Animals. People. 'Tis a game for him.'

'And the others?'

'He said he came alone. That my father left Mackintosh lands days ago, just as Magnus told you.' He released her and she stumbled a few steps away.

'Go, then,' he said, nodding in the direction of the camp. 'Be about your day.' Without another word, he turned from her and began following those who'd taken Alan.

'Wait!' she called out, running to catch him. 'What will you do to him?' Arabella couldn't help but remember the horrible things she'd heard from Caelan and her father about how he treated those Camerons he captured.

'I will deal with him, lady. 'Tis none of your concern now.'

What could she do to keep him from torturing the boy and killing him? That would be his fate now that he'd found this place and could tell others. She had nothing to bargain with for his parole or treatment. Then she met Brodie's gaze and remembered the way he'd looked at her and how he'd kissed her.

'I pray you to treat him with mercy,' she said softly. 'If you agree not to mistreat him—' she looked away for a moment and then met his eyes once more '—I will give you whatever you wish.'

She knew the moment her offer was understood for those brown eyes turned darker and his body shifted. It lasted only seconds before anger filled that heated gaze. She found herself pulled up against his hard body before she knew what happened. His mouth descended on hers and took it in a wicked, hot, possessive kiss. Then he let her go and stepped away. Her body shivered in anticipation and not fear.

'That you question my honour now and in this is disappointing, Arabella,' he said, his voice as harsh as his gaze now. 'I do not kill children.' He leaned in towards her and she thought he was going to kiss her again. His voice dropped low then. 'And no matter how much I might want you, and I do want you, Arabella, I will not take what is not mine to have.'

Her body would not draw a breath after hearing the fierce and erotic words spoken. He was gone, yards and yards away from her before the spell was broken. Her legs gave out and she knelt on the ground, forcing air into her lungs.

She had, once more, misjudged him badly and not trusted him. She had allowed more falsehoods to guide her opinion and not relied on her own judgement of him. Nothing in the way he'd treated her matched the stories she'd heard. Nothing in the way he dealt with his people gave any indication that he was less than honourable. Nothing.

Again, the world in which she lived became a quagmire, swirling with untruths and rumours, and undermining her sense of everything and everyone. The sound of leaves crunching underfoot brought her back to her senses.

'My lady? Are ye unwell?'

She turned and found one of Brodie's men there. She did not know his name, but he held his hand out to her and she took it, gaining her feet.

'I am well,' she said, brushing leaves from the

length of her gown. Glancing at him, she saw only concern in his eyes.

Had he witnessed her encounter with Brodie? That kiss? A hint of embarrassment entered his green eyes and he glanced away. He had.

'My thanks...' She looked at him and knew him in that moment. 'Dougal.' The bard. Now, though, what purpose did he serve? 'Are you following me?' She knew the answer before he spoke.

'Aye, lady. I am to see that nothing happens to you while you are here.' Said like that, it sounded much better than prison guard or gaoler.

'So you saw my cousin, then?' He shook his head. 'And you summoned help?' Another nod.

In the tumult of those minutes, she had not heard any voices or cries of alarm. And then she remembered Brodie's system of communicating with his men in the keep. He must have something similar here so that they could wordlessly signal danger or attack. A begrudging respect for his methods grew within her.

'He is no danger to anyone here,' she said. He nodded, but doubted the man agreed. 'Where will they take him?'

Dougal shrugged. Whether ignorant or wilful,

he would not tell her. But now, she accepted that Alan would not be harmed.

'Am I free to go?' she asked. Had the man's instructions changed since this incursion into their camp?

'You should stay nearer the tents, my lady.' Just so.

Arabella walked back towards the centre of the encampment, keeping a watch for any sign of Brodie or Rob and seeing none. She decided to keep busy until she could seek Brodie out, to explain and to apologise. For she owed him that much.

Brodie stood in the shadows as Rob began questioning the boy. Struck by how familiar the boy looked, he first thought he had to be a Mackintosh. Then Arabella named him her cousin and Brodie realised his mistake. Now, though, every time the boy stared over at him, something tugged at his memories.

To the boy's credit, he'd said nothing of value when Rob asked. Instead, he glared and shook his head in refusal. But Brodie could read the fear in the boy's expression—he knew worse was coming and feared it.

Still, the fact that he had tracked them down

and got close to Arabella spoke of his abilities. His dangerous abilities at that. The only thing that had worked in their favour was that he was a Cameron and would report back, or take Arabella back, to The Cameron at Achnacarry Castle rather than to Caelan.

'How many follow you, boy?' Rob asked in his most menacing voice. Grabbing the boy's shirt, he pulled him up close and repeated his threat. 'Do not make me hurt you.'

Rob would not do any such thing without Brodie's consent, but using fear to loosen the boy's tongue was the first step. If he believed the same stories that Arabella believed, it should take no time at all to break him. He watched the boy—Alan, she'd called him—tremble, but the lad never answered.

For a moment then, he saw the lad's face outlined by the light of a fire. Not here. In the woods. The flames flickered higher and Brodie almost called to him. Then he was gone. Brodie blinked at the apparition before realising Rob called to him.

'Brodie? Are you well?' At Rob's call, he shook off the vision or hallucination and looked at the lad as he sat here, his hands tied behind his back.

'Nothing?'

'Nay. He will not tell us anything.'

Brodie walked forward then, close enough to force the lad to lift his head and look up at him. 'Are you certain you have nothing to tell us?'

Alan shivered even more but his lower lip slid out in a stubborn, belligerent gesture that gave his answer. Brodie shrugged and walked out of the cave, leaving the rest of it in Rob's capable hands.

One way or another, the lad would share his secrets.

After he'd eaten and given Rob about two hours or so to get the information from their captive, Brodie made his way back to the cave. Unfortunately, the lady stood there on the path, arms crossed and ready for battle. He did not know whether to gird his loins or call for help from her fierce expression.

'I know you have Alan within,' she said. 'I want... May I see him?' Her tone surprised him. He expected fire and brimstone to rain down on his head, so the polite request was a shock.

'Nay. We are not done questioning him yet,' he answered.

'You have had him for hours. How much can he bear?'

Tears glistened in her blues eyes and somehow Brodie managed to stand firm, in spite of the need to wipe them away. Damn, but she found his every weakness! If she offered herself to him again, he doubted he could refuse.

'Rob,' he called out. His friend came out of the cave and nodded. 'Done, then?'

'Aye. He told us what we needed to know,' Rob said before he noticed Arabella. Then he saw her and nodded. 'Lady.'

Brodie could see her struggling with her need to castigate him and to ask questions. Knowing the stories passed around about him, he understood her fears. He did not like that she believed them, but he understood.

'Go on, then,' he said to her.

Arabella bolted into the cave and they followed. Alan slept in the corner. She knelt next to him and touched his face. Brodie fought off the jealousy of such a tender gesture and watched as she whispered the lad's name several times. Rob nudged him with his elbow and leaned in to tell him what they'd learned.

'He truly did come alone. The lad is quite talented. His uncle may or may not know of this, but he has returned home at Caelan's request.'

Just then the lad opened his eyes and greeted his cousin in a drunken, slurred voice.

'Arrrrabelllllla,' he whispered, tilting his head this way and that and squinting his eyes to try to see the lady.

Young lads could rarely hold their own against *uisge beatha* and Rob had used it to loosen young Alan's tightly sealed lips.

'Are you drunk, Alan?' she asked, leaning in and sniffing the scent of her cousin's breath. 'Whisky? You have been drinking whisky?'

She sat back on her heels and turned her attentions to him now. He waited for the eruption of anger and accusations from the lady. In preparation, Rob, the coward that he could sometimes be when it involved women, backed away, heading for the entrance to the cave. Her gaze narrowed and she nodded at Brodie.

'That was well done of you, sir,' she said. 'Well done.'

Something that looked like respect filled her eyes and she nodded at him, the slightest curve of a smile appearing on her mouth. Before he could say something foolish, the lad interrupted.

'It would have worked, you know.'

Then he shrugged and tilted his head again in the other direction as though unable to find his cousin to speak to her. She turned to say something and he shook his head so hard and fast he fell over laughing. The lady helped him right himself as she clearly fought the urge to smile.

'She would not come, you know. It took much time and you found us. If she'd only come when I told her, we would be free now.'

They would not have escaped, but it somehow made him glad to know she'd kept her word to him. Especially in a situation where he'd have difficulty honouring a promise not to try to escape.

With that admission, Alan gave up fighting against the effects of the powerful liquor and fell back to sleep. Arabella eased the boy down to the blanket on which he lay and then stood. When she was right in front of him, she looked up at him.

'You thought I would brutalise him to get what I needed.' The words hung there between them.

'I did…for about one minute. Then I realised that you would not do such a thing.'

'You did?' he asked.

'I did. Though you tried to make me believe the worst would happen to him.'

He nodded, having difficulty coming up with words when she gazed at him with respect.

'What will you do with him now?' she asked, as she led the way outside. Rob stood waiting for him there. When he did not reply as quickly as she'd like, she gave him the answer she wanted.

'You could send him back to my father. Negotiate with him to help settle this.' Rob turned to look at him. It was not something they had not discussed already.

'Your father will not do that, lady.'

'If I asked him, he would consider it.' She was lovely in her naiveté about her father, but then she seemed to need to believe the best of her father and the worst of him. 'If you returned Alan as a sign of good faith.'

'Do you really think he would even speak to the man who killed his son?' he asked.

Even if he was the lesser of the Mackintosh evils, there was no way that Euan Cameron would allow him to live. Even without Caelan in the high seat, there would be no peace if Brodie was the one to replace him and rule.

The truth drew down the wall between them. He saw it in her eyes as she realised it. As it always would stand between them. No matter the respect she might have for him about his treatment of her cousin. No matter the shared desire that he felt every time they spoke or were together. No matter…

'I should not have brought it up,' she whispered, backing away.

He reached out, heedless of those watching, and tilted her face up with his finger.

'Nay. I will always listen to your suggestions, Arabella. Just this one…' He shook his head and dropped his hand.

'I would see to his care this night, if you wiil permit it?'

Her soft words stunned him. Most of their conversations ended in anger or distrust. He just nodded this time and she went back inside. Brodie stood silent for a moment and then let out his breath.

'Have a care, Brodie,' Rob warned before walking off. He gave orders to one of the men to remain on guard there as he left. He did not mistake his friend's meaning.

'Have a care?' he said under his breath, to no one but himself. 'Twas too bloody late for that.

Chapter Fifteen

The worst thing Alan suffered for his first drunken experience was a bit of an ill stomach and a headache. Margaret, at Brodie's behest, sent over a noxious-smelling green potion that Alan stared at and refused to drink. For a time. Then when his symptoms became worse, he swallowed it down and complained loud and long about it. But it did help and by midday, he was asking for food.

For two days she did not see him...Brodie. Though her black was in the yard, she caught no sight of him in the camp. Was he avoiding her? She slept in either Margaret's or Bradana's tents, helped each of them see to tasks to keep the camp running, whether repairing garments, preparing food for meals or whatever needed to be accomplished.

She and Alan spoke many times and he brought word of many things from Drumlui and Achnacarry Castle. Alan said her father had left Mackintosh lands and, fearing Mackintosh aggression, was busy sending soldiers to protect their southern keep, Tor Castle. Worse, he was considering involving the king in this dispute. Although a prisoner, Alan's youth gained him softer treatment than a man would have received. He was permitted outside several times a day and Bradana saw to his care.

Arabella remained convinced that her father would help if he knew the truth and decided it was time to hear Brodie's side of this. If Alan could escape, if he had information to give her father, it might work out. So, she began to look for ways to help the boy escape. After all, he hadn't given his word as she had.

All he would need would be a short time undetected to make his way off the mountain and find a way to Achnacarry. Alan said they were about two days' straight ride to the northwest of Drumlui and almost to the shores of Loch Arkaig, so it would be about three or four days travel to Achnacarry by land. Shorter if they could use the loch and river.

Although she was in one of the caves visiting

Alan, she continued checking the others. She'd noticed that the supplies could be organised a bit differently and it would make it easier to keep track of them as they were used up. And, if they needed to abandon the camp, something everyone she spoke to feared was coming, it would be easier to find and take the most essential items. Planning to take her suggestions to Margaret now that things had calmed, Brodie's appearance surprised her.

And the fact that he looked as though he had not slept was more of a surprise. Dark circles smudged the skin beneath his eyes. His face was pale.

'Are you ill?' she asked, reaching up to touch his face. She stopped herself, but not before he saw the gesture. 'Have you a fever?'

'Nay, not ill, lady. Nothing to fear,' he said.

'If not ill, then what, Brodie?'

'Bradana said you were seeking me?' He neatly avoided answering her question.

'I was going to speak to Margaret about moving some of the supplies in the caves. It would be more efficient...'

'Efficient? For whom?'

'For the women who oversee them. For the people here who need to use them. For all of you if you need to abandon the camp, as some seem to think will be necessary soon.' He raised a brow at the last part.

'You've been asking your questions again, lady?' This time he did not sound so aggrieved at her curiosity.

'Aye. And I have been listening as your people talk. I have some experience with this,' she said, gesturing to the boxes and bundles around them. As chatelaine for her father's estates, she'd worked with their steward doing just this thing.

'Very well, Arabella. If Margaret agrees, I leave it in your capable hands and hers.' He stared at her now, as though seeing someone new. Then he began to leave.

She'd not said the most important part. In listening to his people, in watching him, even in being his prisoner, she'd begun to comprehend that there was so much more she needed to know and understand. About this feud. About Caelan's role in it and Brodie's. About her part and her future. Arabella lifted her head and straightened her shoulders, meeting his gaze directly.

'I think I am ready to hear your truth.'

There it was. Boldly and clearly put. Not demanded or angry. Now what would he say? He let out a soft sigh, a sound of utter exhaustion that she was not certain he realised, and then nodded.

'Join me for the evening meal and we can speak about this. And remember to speak to Margaret about your ideas.'

She smiled and nodded and watched him leave, aware of the effort it took for each step. Something was very wrong with Brodie and if he was not well, she suspected a lack of sleep.

The rest of the afternoon hours passed slowly and she spent most of it with Margaret, making suggestions and discussing her ideas. By the time the evening meal was ready, Arabella questioned the wisdom in the coming talks with Brodie. It made no sense unless she was willing to listen and believe his words.

The shocking truth she faced first was that she did believe him and trust him. That realisation came to her as she stood outside the cave he'd chosen, with one of Bradana's friends helping her carry the pot of stew, the loaves of bread and wheels of cheese. She stopped so quickly the other woman nearly dropped everything on the path.

How could she trust him? He had killed her brother and kidnapped her. And yet, deep inside, she knew he would stand by his word and his honour. He'd adopted these people, these exiles, as his own and fought to keep them safe. Against all odds and against all reason, he put them first and was determined to find a way to give them back their homes and their families.

'Did ye stumble there, lady?' Nara asked from behind her.

'Oh, aye, Nara. I beg your pardon for my clumsiness.' She tried to cover up the hesitation and moved on. The guard called out to Brodie and motioned her inside.

It took a few minutes to set out the pot and bowls on the small table and Nara helped her. Arabella could not help to steal a glance across the chamber to where Brodie stood reading some letter. He nodded in greeting but continued to read as they set out supper. After a quiet thanks to Nara, she waited for him to finish.

And then they were alone.

He put the letter aside and waited for her to sit. Bringing a jug of water with him, he sat and poured some in their cups. Arabella lifted the lid and scooped some of the thick stew into each bowl. He watched as she broke the bread and cheese into smaller pieces between them. Then, they shared the food, eating in a silence that should have been tense and filled with anticipation. Once they'd finished, she collected the leftover food and bowls and made them ready to return to Nara.

She watched as he stood and retrieved the small jug of whisky from his trunk and poured some into each of their cups. Remembering the results of this on Alan, she promised herself she would partake of little. When he did not begin to speak, she asked him about his condition.

'You look more exhausted than you did when we travelled here. I know you did not get much sleep and yet you never looked like this.' He smiled and held up his cup in salute to her.

'You do know how to compliment a man, my lady.'

'I did not mean… I meant… Why are you not sleeping, Brodie?' After the words had escaped her mouth she realised how prying and intimate they sounded. She should apologise.

'I am plagued by dreams.'

'Bad dreams?' He nodded. 'I had bad dreams for many years as a child after my mother passed. Aunt Gillie used to help me sleep by rubbing my forehead and whispering a silly song to me to chase them away.'

'Did it work?' He sipped from his cup, his

eyes darkening as he stared at her. She nearly forgot the question.

'Aye, most times.'

'I will have to remember that.' He paused and then changed their topic to the one she'd waited for. 'Arabella, how much do you know about how the feud began?'

'Broken promises. A lover's betrayal. Land. Gold. The usual ways a feud begins,' she said. 'The Cameron claim of lands near Drumlui was contested by the Mackintoshes. The fighting began and the battles continued over the last four or five generations.'

'And enough bloodshed and lost lives to destroy families. It was my father's and uncle's dream to bring it to an end.'

'And mine,' she added.

'Unfortunately, not Caelan's.'

'But he endorsed the truce. As chief, he accepted the terms already in place.'

'Aye, he did all those things in front of the clans, Arabella. Yet, all the while, he was negotiating his own arrangements with other clans in the Chattan Confederation and across the Highlands.'

The Mackintosh chief held the high chair of the Chattan Confederation, a group of clans, some bound by blood, others by oath, that extended its claim and control over a good part of the Highlands. The Confederation's involvement was the only reason, in her estimation, that the Camerons had not triumphed in this feud.

'How do you know this, Brodie?' she asked. She wanted to believe his explanation, but he would never succeed on just his word. At least not as an exiled outlaw.

He stared at her for a minute as though considering what and how much to say. So, when he stood and walked to his trunk, it surprised her. She watched as he moved the heavy case and lifted that chained one into view. Placing it before her, he removed the lock and opened it.

A pile of letters and documents, signed and marked with various wax wafers and seals, filled the box. He got the letter he'd been reading when she arrived and placed it on top. He gestured for her to examine them and walked away to stand in the shadows as she did. It took some time, but she read each of them and was disturbed more by the next and the next until she reached the bottom.

These documents outlined a thorough and deadly plot against her clan. This was no plan for a long and abiding peace, this was the complete annihilation of the Camerons. Every Cameron would be wiped out and their claims and titles buried with them. Caelan had even promised gold from her dowry as bribes and rewards for doing his bidding. Some of these plans went back for years and some were more recent, much more recent.

'But he claimed to want peace.'

'Caelan was, apparently, made to watch his parents being murdered by your father. It broke him in some way and he's planned this for years. Step by step, conspiracy by conspiracy.'

'My father?'

Arabella wanted to deny it, but she'd heard bits of this when the Camerons claimed their glorious victories of the past. She had not known about Caelan, though. She had only a moment's warning before her stomach convulsed in disgust and at the horror of it all. She made it over to the basin just in time. When it was over, he touched her shoulder and offered her a cup of water and a cloth.

Climbing to her feet, she faced him.

'How long have you known?' she asked.

'Not long. Since meeting you those months ago,' he said with a shrug. 'Because of you.' When her legs trembled, he caught her and eased her to sit on the pallet.

'Why me?' He handed her a cushion and she placed it behind her back. 'What did I do?' How could she have played a part in this?

'You made me question my assumptions, lady.' He sat next to her then and took her hand in his. 'When I found a completely different person hiding behind that facade you wore, it made me realise that something was not right about Caelan. I began to explore and question. But I did not have enough time...'

'And that's what you've been doing since? Finding proof?' She nodded at the box, still sitting on the table.

'Aye. The last pieces were only in our hands days ago.'

He had saved her. By kidnapping her, he had bought himself time, but he had saved her from Caelan. He stroked the back of her hand then and she met his eyes.

'And now what? What will you do with that?'

'I had hoped to meet with Caelan and convince him to do the right thing. To let him walk away. But...'

'He will never go. He has worked too hard on this. Oh, God in Heaven! Do you think he had anything to do with your uncle's death?'

A silent nod of his head sent chills down her

spine. Caelan had killed his uncle because Lachlan stood for peace. So who then?

'And…Malcolm?' she asked, daring not to hope.

'My dagger, Arabella. His blood on my hands. There were witnesses.'

'You could take this to my father. He would help. He already contemplates involving the king.'

'With this evidence, with these statements, your father could simply destroy the Mackintoshes. Wipe them off the earth even as Caelan planned to do with you.'

'My father would nev…' He watched her with intense eyes as she realised the truth—if given the chance and this evidence, her father would be as brutal as Caelan planned to be.

Silence surrounded them. Arabella tried to think of a way out of this. To preserve the peace. To keep them all alive.

His snore startled her when it came. Glancing at him, she saw his eyes had closed. Exhaustion etched dark lines around his eyes and a deep furrow in between them. Not wishing to disturb him, she sat there, her hand in his, thinking about all that she'd read.

And all he'd done. For her. And though he

could have tried, he had not tried to force her to believe. He'd done what he did best—he protected and helped and led. All the while, putting himself in danger and directly between his cousin's dangerous plan and her.

He was the first man to see her for herself. To see beneath the facade to the heart of who she was. He respected her even while holding her here, giving her a chance to use her mind and her efforts. Never valuing the appearance over the substance.

She looked down at their joined hands and realised that she had, at some point, fallen in love with Brodie Mackintosh.

Her heart pounded, confirming it.

She loved Brodie Mackintosh.

He stirred next to her, but she could not speak right now. She whispered his name and urged him to lay his head on her lap instead. Trying to sort out the feelings she only now acknowledged, she began to trace the patterns on his forehead and over the bridge of her nose as her aunt had done many, many times.

To ease her bad dreams. To ease the frequent megrims that throbbed in her head. To ease the pain in her heart over the loss of her mother and, then more recently, her brother.

And, though she could not understand how this man would have or could have taken her brother's life, apparently her heart had decided to accept him, anyway. She doubted any good could come from her feelings and she would not tell him. There were no assurances that he felt the same or that either or both of them would survive the coming battle.

Certainly, there would be battles to finish this. Of that, she had no doubt.

Arabella was sitting there in the quiet, thinking about all she'd learned, still holding his hand, when Rob entered and found her so. He opened his mouth to speak and she waved him off. Brodie had not slept for too long to wake him now. The shock clear on his face, Rob nodded and left, but not without giving her several quizzical looks.

Comfortable and warmed by his nearness, she drifted off to sleep as she was. Some time later, he released her hand and rolled to his side. She slid her fingers into his hair and caressed his head gently.

When he settled again, she stopped moving her fingers and just let her hand rest on his head. Content with her feelings about him, she fell deeper into sleep's grasp.

His restlessness woke her quickly. He struggled in his sleep, trying to move, but unable. Then he began calling out to people he saw in those dreams.

'The boy!' he said, gruffly. 'The boy.' She was going to try to wake him when he groaned, in pain.

'Malcolm! The dagger. The blood. Not Malcolm.'

God in Heaven, he was reliving that night! He thrashed around then, struggling against something or someone. The words were unintelligible, but the pain and grief and guilt were clear.

'Not Malcolm,' he moaned out. 'Pray God, not him. Not Bella's brother.'

Her own tears flowed freely at the sound of the name only her brother used for her and at the thought of what had happened between them that night. He quieted for a moment and then lifted his hand and pointed to something.

'The boy! The boy saw it.'

The boy. The only boy she could think of was…Alan! Had Alan been there? Had he followed her brother as was his habit and witnessed it all? Brodie calmed then, back into a more rest-ful sleep while she pondered the meaning of his words.

These dreams had begun just when Alan had stumbled into the camp and tried to help her es-cape. Brodie had reacted strangely to her cousin and she'd caught him staring at the lad several times since. As though his mind struggled to recognise him.

Had Alan's appearance spurred these dreams? Was his mind trying to remember the events he swore he could not? She did not believe Brodie would harm the boy, but if he had witnessed Bro-die kill her brother, others who would stand in his defence might take action.

If they knew. If he remembered. For if Caelan was discredited, there would be no other witness against Brodie but for Alan. If he remembered.

She must get Alan away from here. And she must send word to her father to prepare for at-tack.

Once Brodie slept deeply, she eased her way out from under his head and made her way across the cave. Glancing back, she was struck again by the love she felt for him. An impossible, irratio-nal love that would not, could not end well. But, as she walked back to Bradana's tent, Arabella knew she would treasure the time they'd had before their world here was destroyed.

Chapter Sixteen

Brodie woke with a start.

He lay on the pallet in the cave. The sun shone through the entrance, telling him it was long past dawn. The bowls and food from supper were gone from the table, though his strongbox was there. Open.

Arabella was gone.

They'd spoken at length. She'd read the proof he'd gathered over the last several months. And then…

He'd fallen asleep.

Pushing his hair out of his face, he stood and walked outside. The camp was awake and people carried out their tasks. Since no guard stood there, he knew Arabella had gone back to Bradana's. Before seeking Rob, he went back inside and secured the valuable papers in the box and placed it back under his trunk.

As he turned to leave, he noticed the cushion there, against the wall.

He'd fallen asleep next to her. Then he remembered feeling her gentle touch outlining his brow and forehead. Had she tended to him while he slept? Singing silly words to chase away his bad dreams? He smiled, thinking of the sound of her voice and the touch of her hand. Brodie left the cave and sought out Rob, who—from the expression on his face—was not happy to see him.

'You're awake, are you?' Rob said, walking through the camp and not stopping for him. He grabbed his shoulder and brought him to a halt.

'Is there a problem?' Rob stared at him and glanced around before speaking.

'Aye, there's a problem.' Brodie raised a brow at him. 'Her name is Arabella Cameron.'

'What has she done?' he asked, looking for the lady and not seeing her.

'Not "what has she done," Brodie. 'Tis more about what you have done.'

'Have a care, Rob,' he warned.

'Brodie, 'tis too late for that. I see how you look at her. I saw the two of you last night.'

'Last night?'

'You were sleeping on her lap. Holding hands.'

'Something changed between us, Rob. I cannot explain it. Almost as though…'

'Nay. It cannot be so. You know it, Brodie. You know it.' Rob paced back and forth before him, agitated by what he'd seen and what it meant.

Brodie knew the truth of the matter and there was no way to change it. So he saw no reason to argue over it. He reached out and grabbed Rob's arm.

'The plan is still the same. Nothing has changed.'

Rob glared at him, clearly disbelieving the words he uttered.

'You will walk away from her? You will leave her to marry the next tanist?'

If they succeeded, Brodie expected Grigor to take the chieftain's seat. One of the elders, he was the obvious choice, a blood relative to the last chief, and would be acceptable to all those with a stake in this. Then a new tanist would be chosen from among those men eligible from the other clans in the Confederation. No matter, it would not be him. The Camerons would never agree to terms if he took that position.

'She understands her duty, Rob. As do I.'

Rob stared at him, arms across his chest, considering his words. He shook his head and kicked at the dirt.

'Have you decided who should be our emissary?'

'Aye, my mother's brother, The MacPherson. He will listen to me and consider what we've discovered.'

'Will he support you in this?' Rob asked.

'I think so. He has no love for Caelan. And no reason to stand for him.'

'When do you plan to contact him?' Rob nodded as Brodie caught sight of the woman under discussion as she walked through the camp.

Brodie turned and watched her make her way along the path that would lead to Margaret's tent. The two were seeing to the suggestions about the supplies in the caves.

Rob whistled low, under his breath. ''Tis worse than I thought. If you keep gawping at her like that, everyone here will know the truth. Tell yourself she is not yours and move on with things, Brodie.'

'I have sent him word already,' he said, answering Rob's previous question. 'He is sending someone to discuss it.'

'So we wait?'

'Aye. We wait.' Brodie could feel some change in things. He did not get this premonition often, but he'd learned not to ignore it. 'Do the women and children know what to do if there's trouble? Do they remember the plan?' he asked.

'Trouble?' Rob signalled the men on duty with a shrill whistle and heard the answers declaring no danger. 'What are you expecting?'

'If the boy found us, so can others. Add to the guards down below. Review the escape route with Margaret and the others. We are getting too close to succeeding now and I do not want to risk failure.'

Rob nodded and would have walked away to carry out his orders if he had not stopped him.

'What would you suggest I do with the lady?'

'She is a liability, Brodie. She is nothing less than a distraction to you and nothing more than a hostage.' Rob raised his hand to him before he could object. 'Hear me out. We took her to give ourselves more time and...'

'And to protect her,' he added.

'But if something happens to her here, The Cameron will stand aside no longer. Then we will have both of them breathing down our necks. For our plan to work, The Cameron must agree to the terms with the new Mackintosh chieftain. Losing both a son and daughter will make that impossible.'

'So you are saying…?'

'Send her home. Now that we know The Cameron is back at Achnacarry, send her there. Then her safekeeping is his responsibility.' It made sense and yet he wanted her with him. He wanted…her.

'I will think about it, Rob. Your advice makes sense.'

'And the boy?' Rob asked. 'What will you do with him?'

Alan knew their location and could report it to anyone he could tell. The boy…

Flames again. Shadows.

Men laughing. Drinking.

Blood.

The boy…

'Brodie,' Rob called. 'What just happened? You seemed to lose yourself for a moment. And it's happened before. Several times in the last few days.'

Brodie shook himself free of the vision and turned to Rob. 'He has to stay until we move from here. Then we can release him to find his way home. Something I'll discuss with The MacPherson's man—a place for our women and children until this is done.'

He waved Rob off and went about his duties.

To battle the growing restlessness within him, he trained with some of the men. But mostly, he tried not to search for her around every corner.

He had fallen and fallen hard in spite of his words to Rob. The one woman who he had claimed could never be of interest to him was the one to capture his heart. The one whom he must turn over to another as part of this devil's bargain.

The one whom he knew was a perfect match for him.

Brodie decided that it would be an easier parting if he did not spend more time with her, so towards the end of the afternoon, he took the black and rode out of the camp, needing some time apart. The full moon's light was enough to make the paths visible and he did not push the horse as he would have in daylight.

He would have to give the horse back to her. He smiled at the way she was more upset that he'd stolen her horse than that he'd kidnapped her. Well, at least the black would see her safely home. Brodie knew he would have to follow Rob's advice. He knew that she was becoming too much a part of their lives there and it could not continue.

She was an heiress, the Lady Arabella Cameron, and she would marry to bring an end to their clans' feud.

If he carried out his plan, he would remain an outlaw, a man without a clan, without a name.

Resolved now to bring this to a close and to return her unharmed to her father, Brodie made his way back to their encampment, checking along the way for signs that they'd been discovered. His men were in place where they should be. Riding up along the mountainside, he found the entrance and gave the signal. Several guards acknowledged him as he made his way and saw to the horse's care before heading for his chamber.

Rubbing the back of his neck, he hoped that he had worked out enough of the tension in his body to get some sleep this night. As long as he did not think about her, did not long to touch and taste her… Damn, it promised to be another very long night. The sight of Dougal standing near the entrance to his cave said only one thing—the lady waited within. His flesh surged to life and images of her flooded his mind.

Pushing them away, for all of it was impossible, he nodded to the erstwhile bard and entered. 'Lady?'

She turned as he spoke and stared at him. Half in the shadows, he could see her shape outlined by the light given off by the brazier. Her lovely features appeared ghostly as she watched him move towards her. There was an air of skittishness about her that told him she was nervous.

'Sir,' she said softly. He smiled then at her attempt at formality but kept his distance. His control where she was concerned was not the strongest this night.

'Arabella, what brings you here at this hour?' he asked.

'I heard you are sending me home. Is that true?'

Bloody hell! How had she learned that? Rob with his loose tongue sharing it with one or another and word got passed around the camp. And now she knew.

'Aye. In a few days, you will be on your way home to your father.'

'And Alan? I heard you are keeping him prisoner?' She pressed on, never afraid to ask one more question.

'He knows where we are, Arabella. Surely you can understand the need to keep him here.'

'If he swore he would not reveal it? He can say he never found me, found us.' *Us?* His heart tore a little at the sound of it.

'And a bit of whisky or some of the punishments your father likes to mete out and he will not only tell, he will bring them here. I need time to move everyone to a safe place.'

He watched as she thought about his words. Her eyes darkened as a hint of something passed across them and she looked away. Guilt? Pain? Regret? Then taking a breath and letting it out, she faced him. Stark desire shone from her gaze now as she took a step towards him.

'Arabella...' He shook his head and stepped back a pace, but she continued forward.

'If you are sending me away and I will not see you again, then I have a question for you,' she whispered.

'Always questions!' he said, laughing. She'd reached him and stood so close that if she lifted her face up, he would feel her breath against his.

'I know you said you would not take what was not yours, Brodie...'

'Arabella,' he pleaded. 'Do not do this.' He knew what her next words would be and he would not be able to refuse her if she said them aloud. 'Go back to Bradana's. Now.'

But somehow his hands were on her shoulders, holding her to him. And she did lift her face to his. His honourable promise not to harm her melted away as she said the words. His eyes drifted closed as she spoke.

'If I give it to you freely, will you have…me?'

He'd been so arrogant, believing he could control the desire that burned through him for her. Her innocence should have forced him to walk away and yet, instead, it pulled him to her. He stared into her eyes as he leaned down and touched his mouth to hers, the barest of touches, to see if he could resist.

And he could not.

She opened to him and he dipped his tongue into her mouth, tasting her relentlessly until she touched him back with hers. He withdrew and allowed her to explore, to find her way, to taste him.

Until the sound of someone outside pierced the sensual haze around them and he released her. He walked to the entrance of the chamber and looked at her.

'This is your last chance to leave. If you do not go now, well, I will not be able to let you go later.'

She shivered, her body trembled and he recognised the arousal that was pulsing through her at his words.

'I am staying, Brodie,' she whispered.

He stepped outside and dismissed Dougal and

the other guards from their duties. He wanted no witnesses to what was to come. Tugging the rolled canvas loose, he let it fall over the opening, shielding them from prying eyes. Then he walked back to where she stood, staring with a wide gaze at him.

'So now what?' he asked, fighting the very strong need to take her completely. He knew she was a virgin and he did not want to frighten her with his ardour in the first minutes.

'I was hoping you might know.'

'Oh, lass, I do.' His mind raced with the things he wanted to do to her, with her, on top of her and beneath her. And in her, especially in her. He ached for her even as his body readied itself for her.

'Show me what to do.'

How he retained a semblance of control, he would never know, but he did. Though his blood raced as his heart pounded in his chest, he dropped his hands to his side, swearing he would not touch her...yet.

'Undress me, Arabella.'

It was more a plea than an order and he knew he was in deep trouble when she smiled and the edge of her tongue slipped out to lick her lips.

He'd watched her take to tasks with a curiosity and interest and he was now that task.

Her hands slid along his chest as she pushed the leather jack off his shoulders and let it fall to the floor. Then she untied his shirt, pulling the bottom edge of it free from his breeches. The friction of the fabric over his arousal made him clench his jaws. For now, the plaid wrapped and draped around his waist hid it from her sight.

'Did I hurt you?'

'Oh, nay, lass. You are doing fine,' he said.

Arabella ran her hands under the shirt, over his shoulders and down his arms until the garment fell. Her hands lingered, touching his skin and exploring the lines of his muscles, sliding back up on to his shoulders and then down on to his chest. He hissed at the sheer pleasure of her caresses. When she grazed his nipples, dragging her fingertips across them and through the hair on his chest, he silently promised retribution in kind.

She gazed up at him and then down at her next target. She was being wonderfully bold, just as he would have expected. Reaching for the end of his belt, she tugged until it came out of the buckle, allowing the length of plaid to follow his other garments to the floor. Her breathing grew ragged then and she paused as she reached for the ties on his breeches.

'Courage now, lass.'

When she hesitated, he drew her into his arms, pulling her up against his heated skin and filling her mouth with his tongue. She wrapped her arms around his neck and he lifted her against him, sliding his hand under her bottom and pressing his hard flesh against her. Her legs eased around his hips as much as her gown allowed and he knew she could feel him. Feel his arousal.

'You are wearing too many clothes,' he whispered, as he moved his mouth from hers. She slid her legs down his and stood before him. 'Let me take them for you.' She nodded and watched him through passion-glazed eyes.

He moved behind her and loosened the tie on her braid. Dragging his fingers through its length, he shook the hair free of its restraint and watched as it curled around her. Then, he wrapped it around his hand and lifted it, exposing the curve of her neck to him. He kissed her there, trailing kisses and caressing her skin with his tongue as he untied her laces and opened her, inch by inch, to his attentions.

When her gown was loosened all the way to her hips, he pushed it off and let it slide down over her belly and hips and legs to join his garments there. Then he kept his mouth on her neck, nipping along the edge of her ear until she trembled. She clutched behind her at his legs, trying to steady herself against him.

'Hold on to me, lass,' he whispered. Her body arched, opening to him and beckoning his touch. So he did.

Chapter Seventeen

Brodie moved his hands, sliding one around her waist to hold her close and the other to cup her breast, first one then the other. He teased her nipples with his thumb, rubbing against them until they hardened. She was gasping with each caress now. This was more than she had expected. This was nothing like she had expected.

His mouth was hot against her neck and she leaned her head back. He kissed and licked and then took the sensitive skin between his teeth and nipped at it. Shivers of ice and fire drove through her blood to a place deep inside of her. His arm trapped her between the teasing torment of his hand and the hard ridge of flesh pressed against her back.

Her body reacted on its own, pushing and arching against his every touch. Then she felt his hand slide over the material of her shift, gathering its length up and exposing her legs to the coolness of the cave. Only his arm wrapped around her held her up when his hand brushed the curls between her legs. The moan escaped before she knew it.

'Do you like that, lass?' he whispered against her ear. A moan was all the sound she could make and he laughed at it.

Biting her ear gently, he slid a finger between her legs and drew it up. Her legs shook at such pleasure and such a shocking touch as this was. But that place ached for more and her hips arched against his hand, asking for it.

'Open your legs for me, love.'

Her legs opened and he dipped his finger into the wetness there, finding the very spot that needed to be touched. He slid along the wetness, drawing it forward to a sensitive place that made her scream out. He reached up and turned her face to his, caressing her tongue, and he rubbed that place deep in the folds of her flesh.

Something ached there and every movement of his fingers as he used more of them to slide inside her and caress her woman's flesh made her tighten inside. Some connection made her feel every touch in her breasts and in her core.

She could only pant, her lungs sucking in short, shallow breaths with each slide of his fingers.

And then whatever tied her tighter and tighter snapped and she cried out against his relentless mouth as her body fell apart at his touch. She arched against his hand but he did not stop, pressing deeper and spreading her with his fingers. He whispered against her mouth, urging her for more and more and more until she was spent and collapsed against him. When he eased his hand from between her legs, another wave shuddered through her and another until she lost her breath.

Brodie eased them down on to the pile of clothing, holding her against his legs until he knelt and she sat on him. Before she knew what he did, he'd tossed the length of plaid across the floor there and laid her down. Small waves of pleasure echoed through her flesh, between her legs and deep within and she smiled at the sensation.

'You liked that?' he asked. She laughed then, finding that she could breathe.

'But we did not…join,' she said, realising that she'd been lost in whatever he'd caused her body to feel and he was still erect and clothed.

'There is time for that, Arabella,' he said, as he tugged her shift off and tossed it aside.

Wearing only her stockings, she felt wicked. And when he turned her over on to her back and lay next to her, she lost the ability to think at all. He could touch her anywhere now and he did. He moved to kneel over her and he kissed the length of her body, sucking on the tips of her breasts. Then he used his mouth to lick and taste every inch of her skin, down her belly and on to her thighs. Her legs fell open to him and she lifted her head to see what he was doing.

That was a mistake.

His gaze was so full of hunger and desire as he kissed along the inside of her thighs that she gasped and fell back. The first touch of his tongue on the flesh there shocked her, but her body liked it. Her hips rose and pressed against his mouth.

'What are you doing?' she asked, grasping at the plaid beneath her and panting as his tongue and mouth suckled the sensitive area.

'Tasting you, lass,' he said, his words vibrating against her flesh.

When his tongue delved deep where his fingers had been, her mind fled. When his fingers joined in and tormented her over and over, she lost herself to the pleasure he gave. Her body shook and bowed to his every touch, following his fingers and tongue and begging for more. Arabella spread her legs at his urging and he slid his hands beneath her, pulling her closer and tasting every bit of her there.

That exquisite tightness curled deep within her and her muscles began to shake as he pushed her relentlessly towards more and more pleasure. When he lifted his mouth and climbed up to kneel between her legs, she whimpered at the loss of him. He soothed her, tormented her, urged her on with his hand buried deep in the cleft of her flesh.

Then she felt him there and lifted her head as he pressed the hard ridge of his flesh into her. He met her gaze and watched her as he entered her, inch by inch, slowly stretching and burning and piercing her. Then, with one thrust he was as deep as he could be, and her body let go. He leaned down over her and kissed her mouth, possessing her there even as he joined with her.

Filled with him, his tongue in her mouth, his flesh in hers, Arabella ached with need. When she shifted her hips and took him in deeper, she heard his groan and laughed. He leaned back and gaze into her eyes.

'Ready, lass?' he asked in the last moment before he began moving. His hips lifted and plunged, sending his flesh deeper and deeper, touching another place she'd never known existed within her and pushing her to more pleasure. When she lifted her hips to meet his thrusts, he laughed against her mouth, so she did it again and again.

His flesh hardened within her and he withdrew until she cried out at the emptiness. Then he filled her with unrelenting strokes until her body fell over the edge of reason and into madness. She shattered around him, unable to stop the waves of pleasure from breaking through her. At the last moment of awareness, she felt his flesh harden as he spilled his seed within her.

How long they lay, their flesh joined, naked and sweating, skin to skin, she knew not. She cared not. Her body hummed with a new awareness, every inch of her had been pleasured and touched, even places she'd never known before. But he had known how to reach them and touch them and taste them. And he had. After some time, he eased out of her and he moved to her side, drawing her close to him. Tucking her head against his chest, he held her as all the sensations seeped from her body, leaving her unable to move but feeling more alive than ever before.

'Are you well?' he asked in a quiet voice.

She'd heard the women gossip about a maiden's first time. They all spoke of the pain, but none had shared the truth about the pleasure. Probably to keep young maidens from seeking it.

'I am...well,' she said, rolling away and stretching her body against his. He laughed as he gathered her in his arms and held her close again.

'I am glad.' He kissed her gently then, rubbing his cheek against hers and entwining their fingers. He lifted her hand up and kissed that, too.

Arabella lay there in wonderment of all that had happened between them. It did not take long for the passion to leach away and for guilt to enter her thoughts.

'Regretting it now, Arabella?' Brodie asked. When she met his gaze, he smiled. 'Your expression changed just then. I could see it there.'

'Regrets? Aye. You and this, nay,' she answered, turning to face him. He entwined their fingers together then, rubbing his thumb across the back of her hand. 'But many regrets.'

She watched as his eyes darkened and wanted to banish the sadness that entered there. She did not wish to think about all the repercussions and consequences of this night and her actions. She wanted to savour this night because she knew it would all change at dawn and then over the coming days.

But not now.

Arabella lifted her hand and traced a line down his chest. The curls tickled the tips of her fingers as she swirled through them. If he understood her aim, he did not say, but his breathing changed as she moved inch by inch lower. His trews lay opened and loose and as she touched his belly with the back of her hand, that male part of him began to rise.

'It's a randy fellow,' he said with a soft chuckle.

That turned to a gasp as she slid her hand around the randy fellow and closed her fingers. He hardened within her grasp as she watched. Then his hips arched and the flesh surged in her hand, growing larger and harder within seconds. Brodie reached down and moved her hand away.

'Did I hurt you?' she asked.

'Nay, Arabella. But I will hurt you if you let it have its way.'

'Oh.' She blinked at him, surprised at his arousal so quickly. She'd never spoken to her aunt about *this*, so it was new to her. So did this mean...?

'Do you want to do this again? To me. With me?'

The torrid kiss he gave her, taking her mouth and possessing and claiming it, should have been answer enough. The way his hardness rubbed against her belly as he pulled her closer was a clue. Then he took her hand and placed it back down there, guiding her fingers around his length and keeping his hand over hers. He rocked his hips, sliding into her grasp each time and her body remembered the feel of him deep within her.

'Aye, I want to do this again,' he whispered against her mouth. 'To you. With you. I have dreamt of many ways to have you, Arabella.'

His next kiss stole her breath. But his next words stole her ability to do anything but allow him his way.

'I have wanted you—' his hand released hers and slipped between her legs '—for months now, lass. Since the day you heard my insult and ignored it. Since you smiled at me, truly smiled at me.'

She could not help but wince as he touched that intimate place. He removed his hand, cursing under his breath much as his friend did and pulled away from her to stand. His breeches were still on, but they sagged down below his hips, giving her the most revealing look at that part of him that had joined with her, a part that showed the evidence of their joining. After tugging them up, he moved quickly around the chamber, gathering up items and bringing them to her. A basin of water, a cloth, some soap.

'You need to be tended to, Arabella,' he said as he placed them next to her on the plaid. Its dark colours and pattern hid what she knew must be there—her blood and his seed.

'I can see to myself.'

He nodded and walked over to the pallet, adding blankets and readying it. It took a few minutes to cleanse herself and when she handed the basin of bloodied water back to him, he walked outside and emptied it, remaining out there for several minutes.

Unfortunately, in those few minutes, all the sadness of having but this one night with him struck her. They would both carry out their duties—her to her clan and him to his in spite of their exile of him.

And they would never be together again.

Arabella turned away and gathered her clothing from the scattered place on the floor where he'd tossed it and wrapped his plaid around herself.

Her tears flowed.

His arms wrapped around her before she knew he'd returned and she let his strength surround her. How long they sat like that, she did not know, but he never let go of her. When her tears were spent, she raised her head.

'Would you like me to take you to Bradana's, then?' he asked, wiping the tears from her cheeks with his thumbs as he cradled her face in his hands. He stood and drew her up, her clothing held between them in a crumpled bundle.

What she wanted was to stay at his side and never be parted from him. She wanted to lie in his arms every night for the rest of her life. And she wanted always to have him gaze upon her as he had just a little while past—as though she were the only woman he would ever love. But… none of that could or would ever be, so she shook her head and took what she could.

'I would stay, if you will have me?'

'They will know,' he warned, nodding his head towards the outside of the cave. 'They know.'

This collection of people he'd gathered were a family and, like most, gossip travelled quickly. The women knew what would happen as soon as she'd left Bradana and Margaret behind to seek his cave. Dougal and the other guards would chatter quietly like old women at the well about being sent away. Other than the children who lived here and, hopefully, her cousin, everyone would be very aware that she'd lain with him this night.

And though she'd like to stay with him all night for purely selfish and intimate reasons, she also had to give Alan time enough to sneak away without being seen. So the longer the guards were away from this area around the caves the better.

'Ah, there's regret come once more into your eyes, Arabella.' He took her shift and began to hold it out for her, clearly expecting her to leave now.

'As I said, not regret over what we did, but over what we will never do,' she answered as she took the garments from him and tossed them aside. 'And since they already know what has happened here, there is no need to pretend it did not.'

Feeling a boldness brought on by knowing what pain awaited her on the morrow, she dropped his plaid and stood before him, naked but for her stockings, offering herself to him once more. He did not try to persuade her to leave this time. He closed the space between them with one step and gathered her up in his arms. Carrying her to the pallet, he laid her under the blankets there and slid next to her.

So quiet was he that she thought he meant them to sleep, curled up next to one another, so she closed her eyes and allowed his body's heat to warm her. As she drifted off, she remembered something he'd said to her and smiled.

'In what ways do you wish to have me, Brodie?' she asked.

The reaction was immediate and very noticeable as his flesh rose, long and hard, against her buttocks and spine. He thrust once against her and then groaned.

'Your questions will be the death of me yet, lass.'

She rolled on to on her belly and leaned up on her elbows. He did look angry as he sometimes did when she battered him with a long line of her questions. Instead, his deep-brown gaze shimmered as he watched her.

'We have but one night, Brodie. I would not want to leave with the regret that we did not do something we wanted to do. Especially since there can never be a repeat of this time together.'

'Headstrong. Stubborn. Intelligent. Questioning. I cannot imagine that you sprang from Euan Cameron's loins,' he said. Then he shook his head. 'Nay, I cannot say that's true. I think you are exactly the same as him. Though I suspect the questioning part came from your mother.'

She laughed then, for she remembered times when her father had cursed at her for some infraction or another with just those words. 'I tried his patience. I suspect that is not done yet.'

He took her hand in his and entwined their fingers—he seemed to like to do that. Then he kissed her hand. 'Aye, lass, I suspect you will try him in the coming weeks.'

They lay in silence just like that, touching, barely, but closer than she'd ever been to a man. It hurt to know that, come morning and over the next days, their lives would separate. And he would probably not forgive her for helping her cousin. He might understand her actions but forgiveness was another matter.

'So, you have avoided my question.' She glanced down at his cock when she continued. 'What ways do you wish to have me?'

Arabella could not help but smile as his body reacted to her purposeful tease. And it did, filling and standing out from the rest of his body. His eyes turned fierce then and her own body flushed with heat. Her breasts swelled and the nipples tightened.

'I will tell you, Arabella, just how I would like to have you,' he said, leaning closer to her.

Then he whispered scandalous things to her, about how he would join with her, where he would touch her, how their bodies would pleasure each other. His words were so vibrant and enticing that her body readied itself for him, shocking her as that place within her woman's flesh moistened and ached and throbbed. She wanted him. She wanted him to do all of these things to her. She wanted to touch him.

Finally she reached out and wrapped her fingers around his firm flesh as he had shown her before. His face grew intense and dark and he hissed as she slid her hand downwards to the base and then the rest of him she found there.

What began as her curiosity and desire to learn his body, turned into something different as Brodie reciprocated, touching her as she did him. Whether her mouth or her breasts or legs or the place between her legs, he drove her to madness even as she drove him. But, there was still one question in her mind before she relinquished herself to pleasure. Something she did not understand.

'How could I ride you?' she asked, breathless from the way she shivered and trembled as he pushed her towards that moment of dissolution she knew awaited her.

'Lass,' he whispered, shaking his head. 'You are too sore.'

She might be, but right now her flesh ached for him to fill her. Ached for them to join. Ached to find release when he did within her. 'Show me.'

If her voice quivered or if she sounded too demanding, she cared not. If her behaviour was not what was expected of a lady, of a Cameron, it bothered her not. The only thing that would bother her was if she'd shocked Brodie. When he reached for her waist and guided her up and over him, she knew he was not shocked.

'If this hurts, you must tell me, Arabella.' She worried her lip and nodded. He told her to kneel over his hips and she did so, the position very similar to sitting on a horse. His flesh rubbed between her legs when she lowered herself to him.

He pulled her down to him and they lay breasts to chest and hips to hips. As he kissed her, her hair fell around them like a curtain meant to keep the world away. Leaning over him, kissing him and feeling his hands kneading her legs and bottom, she rubbed her sensitive flesh against the ridge of his, sliding along it.

'Now, ride me, lass,' he said. Arabella sat

back and slid down the length of him. 'At your own pace.'

She closed her eyes and took him in, inch by inch, gasp by gasp, never dreaming that something like this would be so...decadent and pleasurable. When she looked down at him, his gaze was filled with concern as she moved on him. Then that expression changed and he held her hips, his fingers digging into her flesh as though to both hold her still and move her faster.

Soon, he drove deeper and deeper within her and her body prepared for that release she knew he would bring to her. He touched her everywhere, able to reach because she sat above him, and when he found that small spot near where he entered her, he stroked it, faster and faster, harder and harder until her body let go.

Then, he sat up, wrapping his arms around her as he turned them over. He was already deep but now he thrust even deeper, joining them and stroking the folds of her flesh until she cried out. He lifted almost out of her and then plunged to fill her completely and find his own release.

Only the sounds of their breathing filled the cave. At first, she could not even tell whose was whose. Shallow panting turned into deeper, laboured breaths and then slow, regular inhalations. Her body had lost its spine and she lay under him barely able to move. Brodie eased off her, but kept hold of her with his arm across her stomach.

Time passed as they lay together, touched and touching, exhausted and satisfied. Somehow she knew she would never find this kind of trust and sense of wild abandon with any other man. And when morning's grey light entered through the edges of the canvas flap, Arabella knew it was over.

When the whispers began outside, she knew they'd discovered Alan missing. When more footsteps paced along the path leading to the cave, she knew they wanted to call for Brodie, but dared not. But instead of waking him, she slid closer to him and smiled when he wrapped himself around her and slept even deeper.

Another hour would not matter—if Alan had escaped the camp's guards, no one would find him now. So she selfishly held on to him until the last possible moment.

Chapter Eighteen

'Brodie.'

He heard her whisper his name, but did not wish to open his eyes and bring this night to a close. Even the light he could see through his lids did not push him to accept the reality that day was here already. And that they were done.

'Brodie,' Arabella whispered once more. 'You must wake now.'

'Och, lass,' he whispered as he slid his arms around her and pulled her on top of him. 'I do not think I can pleasure you again. A man must have some rest,' he teased, knowing well that his body would ready itself if she gave a word or sign to him.

Then he noticed that it was not her bare skin that touched his. The fabric of a gown came between them. He shook off sleep's grasp and opened his eyes. True enough, Arabella was dressed and watched him with guarded eyes of her own.

'What is it?' he asked as he eased from underneath her and sat. Pushing his hair from his face and running his fingers through it, he saw that it was full day outside though only tiny shards of light pierced the cave's darkness around the flap he'd pulled over the entrance.

'Your men have been waiting outside,' she explained, setting her own hair to rights in a quickly made braid. 'I know you have not slept well these last nights, so I did not want to wake you.' There was something else that she was not saying.

'And?' he asked.

There was something different about her. He could not figure out what it was, but she seemed ill at ease now. Did she finally regret their actions? Had she realised what a mistake it had been?

'And I did not wish the night to end yet,' she admitted.

Her kissed her bruised lips gently and caressed her face with his hand. There was not a place on her that he had not tended to during this night of theirs but he felt as if he wanted to begin again. However...

They each had a duty to see to and they knew it.

'Nor I,' he replied as he climbed to his feet and found his breeches and shirt.

Tugging them on, he knew the magic they'd found was fading. Arabella moved around the chamber, folding blankets and putting things back in place. Soon, other than the bowls she held in her hands, there was not a trace of the incredible night they'd shared left here.

'Brodie?' Rob called from outside. Their movements must have been noticed. 'Are you awake yet?'

He laughed then, but noticed Arabella did not. Her face seemed set in stone. Had she just realised that she would have to confront others this soon? Was she embarrassed that they would know, they all knew, what had happened between them?

'Aye, Rob,' he said, walking to the entrance and rolling up the flap and tying it out of the way.

She looked away as though to allow her eyes to grow accustomed to the bright light. Rob and Duncan entered and walked towards him, their expressions grim. Something bad had happened.

'He's gone,' Rob said, staring at Arabella who would not look back.

'Who?' Brodie asked, glancing between the three. Then he knew the answer before anyone spoke a name. 'Alan.' Arabella turned away. His gut rolled knowing, just knowing. 'When?'

'Some time last night. He was there when Margaret brought him food. Then this morning, gone.'

He'd ordered the guards away last night. All of them. So that none would hear what he knew would happen. What she knew would happen. 'You know what to do. Go.'

Rob and Duncan did not question him and left swiftly to begin the search of the area. Still she did not meet his gaze, standing half turned away near the pallet where they'd…

'I told you I would release him soon. I told you that last night. You did not believe me?' he asked.

He could not sort this through. He'd not harmed either of them or mistreated them. God forgive him, he'd even fallen in love with her. And she had betrayed him. On purpose. So, she'd spent the night with him knowing the boy was escaping.

'And that's why you came to me last night. You knew I would try to protect your privacy and keep the guards away from the caves while we were together.'

'I am sorry, Brodie,' she whispered. He walked to her and took her by the shoulders, pulling her to face him.

'You knew.' He searched her pale face for something, some sign, that the night they'd spent together was not simply subterfuge for the escape. 'You gave yourself to me to keep my attentions here. In this place, on you.' When she did not deny it, he released her and she stumbled a few steps away.

'That was not the only reason for last night and you know it,' she said, straightening her shoulders and meeting his eyes. 'What I told you was—is—true. I wanted to be with you. I wanted to have the choice and not be given to some man I will never care for. I wanted…you.'

'So you arranged the escape, covered it by giving yourself to me and are now trying to tell me I should believe you?' She nodded. 'Tell me why I should believe you, Arabella. Tell me.'

'Because I love you, Brodie Mackintosh. Against all reason and sanity, I love you. In spite of knowing what you have done, I love you.' She spat the words out at him. 'And to keep you from having another innocent's blood on your hands, I helped him escape. Because I know your heart and soul could not bear another mean-ingless death.'

Though the heart and soul she mentioned wanted to rejoice in her declaration, it did not make sense. He'd killed her brother. For that and so much more, she could not love him. As the innocent one here, she must be mistaking the euphoria of their lovemaking with the deeper emotion.

'I do not understand. What innocent will die because of me?' He shook his head and frowned at her. 'Alan was safe.'

'Mayhap he was safe from you, but those who support you will rise against him when they know the truth.'

'Arabella, my people are not a danger to Alan. Nor you.'

She took in a deep breath and let it out before answering him.

'Alan was there that night.'

Her words struck him like the blow of a cudgel.

That night.

The boy. Malcolm. Blood. Dead.

Images and sounds filled his mind from that night that had changed everything in his life. The fire roared before him as he and Malcolm talked about…her. Smoke swirled around them and somehow in his head too. His eyes would not focus. He turned away from the flames and gazed at the trees around them, trying to clear his vision and he saw…

A boy. A boy hid there in the trees, watching them. Too young to join in their drinking, yet too old to be with the bairns. A boy.

Alan. Alan had been there.

'He saw it all.' He looked at her. 'He saw it happen.'

Arabella nodded at him, tears in her eyes. Tears for her brother. 'If Caelan is discredited, there would be no witness to stand against you. Except him.'

'Your father would never accept me,' he said. 'No matter if Caelan is the accuser or not, Malcolm's blood is on my hands. I killed him.' He'd held out his hands as though the blood was still visible. 'Why did he not admit it then?'

'Your accusers were Mackintoshes. Why would a Cameron boy come forward and blame you when their words were stronger and had already been taken for the truth?'

'I have accepted the blame and the guilt for what happened, Arabella.' Her eyes dimmed at those words. Even without mentioning her brother's name, he caused her pain.

'But your clan would not have trouble accepting you back if Caelan is not there to proclaim your guilt. These people you've gathered here are protecting you even as you protect them. If the only thing standing in the way of you being accepted back is that boy, after all your struggles to give them back their families and homes, do you not think someone would take care of it?'

Brodie could think of several of the men who would not hesitate to kill the boy. After all, he was a Cameron. A Cameron who stood in the way of his re-acceptance.

'What did he tell you?' he asked quietly. He still could not see anything but the beginning or the end of that night. Her face went grey in an instant, all the colour draining out. 'Christ! I did not mean for you to…' But he had wanted to know. The night swirled in scenes of fire and smoke and blood in his memory and he would have asked the boy if he'd known.

'He told me nothing. When I realised your dreams were actually memories, I told him never to speak to anyone about what he witnessed. That it could mean his life if anyone knew he'd been there and seen it.' He'd fallen asleep the other night on her lap. She'd never said a word about what she'd heard. 'And he will not say a word. And he will not reveal our location to anyone, even my father, Brodie. I swear he will not.'

Brodie knew differently. They'd plied the boy with spirits—others would not be so kind. The boy would break. The boy would speak and he would reveal anything or everything he knew.

'I wish you could have trusted me on this, Arabella. Now, everyone here is in danger.'

And that was the crux of the matter. She proclaimed love but had no trust in him. He'd done nothing to her that should cause her not trust him, he'd been honest with her. They both understood responsibility and duty and honour. Yet she did not trust him.

Somehow this tore him more deeply than being exiled. That she would give up her body to him, proclaim love for him and not believe he was worthy of her trust.

'Brodie,' Rob called from outside.

He left without another word. If he spoke to her again, he knew he would let his anger and pain guide him and he could destroy her. Yet, in spite of her betrayal, he did not want to do that.

The news was not good. Traces of Alan's path were found, so they knew he had headed north,

to the loch and most likely to the Camerons'
northern holding at Achnacarry. But, they had
also found other signs that strangers had been
coming close to the camp.

It would take them two days to pack and move
everyone here. One day if they only moved essential supplies. Within three hours of learning
about Alan's escape, he gave the orders to begin.

And within those same three hours, his camp
became a divided one.

He returned to the cave to discover her gone.
Which did not surprise him at all. Brodie knew
she would not face him now. As he walked
through the camp, overseeing the preparations
that would see the women, children and some of
the men head north to his uncle's lands, his re-
ception was a mixed one.

Some of the older men, especially those who
had fought the Camerons or had close kin taken
prisoners by them, nodded at him as though
pleased. It had not made sense until he remembered that old Tormod's sister had been taken…
and returned home some months later bearing
the very obvious sign of the price she'd paid for
being a female captive. They had expected that
Brodie would inflict the same on Arabella, since

she was his prisoner and a Cameron. So their night together was simply taking what was due him.

A few of the older women looked on him with disgust, as though they thought the same thing. They shook their heads and tsked at him as he passed them.

The worst were those who'd grown close to Arabella during her stay here. The ones she'd worked with and helped. The men who she had cared for when injured. Magnus, Margaret and Bradana were the worst of all. For it was not disgust, but for the first time, disappointment that filled their gazes.

And, as he walked the camp, helping with packing supplies and loading the few carts and wagons they had, he never once saw her. Somehow he'd expected her to be defiant and proclaim her righteousness. Or to be in the middle of things, helping Margaret. Instead, she'd disappeared. Since Rob and the other guards did not raise an alarm, he knew she was here somewhere.

His first true inkling that anything was amiss was the bowl of porridge that was to be their noon meal. Dark, blackened clumps of some inedible substance sat in his bowl instead of the creamy, smooth porridge he expected. When he took a mouthful of ale to wash it down, he found that it was mostly water.

He blamed it on the conditions in the camp. For in their rushing to pack and prepare, food sometimes overcooked or burned, and ale and water skins were confused.

Then there was the evening meal. Everyone served themselves from the large pot of stew, but when Brodie dipped the ladle in all he found was the dried-out, burned-on layer at the bottom. When he looked around to see if others had none, they'd all walked away. He sought out Margaret, knowing that she would be quite frank with him if she was angry with him.

'What is the meaning of this?' he asked, holding out the bowl of the burned stew scraps for her to see.

'You must have been late in getting to the stew pot,' she retorted without looking.

'What did she say?' he asked, not intending to dawdle around, pretending not to know who was the person at the centre of this small rebellion of sorts.

'She? Do you mean the lady?' Margaret said, facing him with her hands on her hips. 'Do you mean the lady whose virginity you took?' she whispered furiously. 'And without a care today of her condition?' Margaret glared at him and crossed her arms over her ample chest. 'That lady said nothing. She has not mentioned your name or what transpired between you.'

He'd not thought about her since he'd left the cave this morn. He was not a man to mistreat a woman who'd shared his bed and yet he'd not given any consideration to her comfort or discomfort on the day after he'd taken her body in so many ways he had lost count of it all. She had not stopped him from doing whatever he wanted to do, in spite of being a virgin.

'Oh, aye, now you think about it,' she said, shaking her head. 'A bit late.'

But now he knew it was all part of her plan to help Alan.

'You do not know what she did.'

Margaret was in his face, tapping her finger into his chest to make her point. 'I know what she did. We all know. And we all know what you did.' She stepped back and glanced down at his groin. 'You were thinking with the wee laddie and she got the best of you.' She laughed out. 'Just like a man.'

'There is more to it than that. More you do not know or understand, Margaret,' he said.

'I understand more than you think, Brodie. You have spent the last years not allowing a woman to get close, always ready to see to your duty to the clan. And this one, weel, you did not allow yourself to want her, either, believing that your cousin would win out. Now, I can see that she loves you and you love her. I can see that she had to make a choice she did not want to make but she made it.'

'Margaret...' he began to say. She put her hand up between them, forestalling him from speaking.

'You have not told her, have you? You are more fool than I thought you to be,' she said, shaking that same finger at him.

''Tis an impossible situation for us, Margaret. You know that. I know it and so does the lady.'

'You let your duty stand between you so you do not have to take the step you should. And that's even more reason to make sure she knows how you feel. Love does not come our way often and it is not something you give up, Brodie. Say the words. Let her leave and go to her duty knowing the truth in your heart, in spite of your stupid actions and pride.'

He shook his head and looked up at the sky in frustration. Until Margaret took his arm and tugged on it to gain his attention.

'The words, Brodie. If I could have one moment to say them again to Conall, I would pay whatever price was asked.' She looked away then and he knew tears were gathering. He'd so rarely seen this strong woman brought to tears that he was surprised. 'Give her that much. So that in the dark days to come, she will have your words to hold close in her heart. So that she knows her gift to you was honoured.'

And the dark days were coming. For good or bad, he would step out of exile and present his evidence. There would be no grey, shadowed result—it would be black or white, good or bad, life or death. He nodded then.

'I will think about your counsel, Margaret,' he said. She cursed under her breath, but he thought she might have cursed the wee laddie as well as the rest of him, too. He turned to walk away and realised he'd not asked about Arabella. 'How does she fare?'

'Well,' she said. 'She fares well, which is more than you deserve to know.'

He walked off then with Margaret still speaking her mind. But he did hear the last thing she said before she stopped.

'Do not wait, Brodie. There is little time.'

Brodie thought about her words, glad that Arabella was well after their passionate night. But later, as he finished his tasks for the day and sought refuge and sleep, he wondered just how much time there was for him and his quest.

The next day brought his answer…

No more.

Chapter Nineteen

As the sun rose, Arabella forced herself awake.

She'd sought the refuge of the smaller cave where they'd held Alan after Brodie discovered the truth, partly because of self-pity and partly because of embarrassment. But mostly because she was exhausted—heart, body and soul—and simply wanted to be alone.

After gathering together some blankets, she had added them to the pallet and then collapsed on them. There was not a place on her body that did not feel the strenuous use that had happened throughout the night before. Muscles deep in her legs ached. Her back protested. But those private places, untouched until hours ago, ached in a different way. The skin on the inside of her thighs bore the marks of his beard's stubble. Her lips and breasts yet felt swollen.

But, even with all the physical pain and soreness, it could not match that in her heart.

She had not trusted him even to tell him the truth. In spite of knowing how dearly he held true to his word and his promises to her, she did not trust him to see to Alan's safety. And she knew the exact moment he'd comprehended her ruse. She'd read it in his eyes and in his stance.

He probably did not even realise how he'd turned as though preparing for a blow, but she'd seen it. What past betrayals had prepared him for hers? Rob and Duncan saw it and it made them even angrier at her than they had been. When Brodie left, Rob had escorted her to this cave and left her without a word, but he'd practically glowed with the heat of his fury.

Some time later, hot water and soap had arrived, left at the opening to the cave by unseen hands without a word. Then Margaret had come with food. Arabella felt guilty since she knew the woman was always busy and she could have got it for herself, but Margaret had waved off her words of apology. She would not share the food she'd brought and instead simply watched Arabella's every move and step. Finally, she'd just asked the question that hung there in the space between them.

'Are you well, lady? Have you need of any remedy I can give you?' Margaret's gaze softened for a moment. 'Or have you questions you might want to ask, having no kinswoman here to speak to?'

'I am well enough, Margaret. My thanks for your concern.' Then as the woman was leaving, Arabella just could not help but ask her own question. 'Does everyone know?'

'Aye. Everyone kens.'

Arabella could feel the heat of a blush filling her cheeks then. What must they all think of her? She pressed her hands to her cheeks to cool them.

'Oh, about you and Brodie?' Margaret asked. When she met the woman's gaze, she saw the teasing there. 'I thought you meant…' Arabella shook her head.

'Aye, my lady, we know about your cousin, as well.'

Margaret turned to leave once more, but Arabella had another question.

'How does Brodie fare?'

'He will be fine, when he is done being stupid.'

She smiled for the first time that day. So she was not the only one he exasperated.

'I have known him all his life, him being Rob's

friend, and he is always willing to do for others. He puts his family first, even when he deserves that consideration,' she explained. 'And when he is being this stubborn, I want to smack him and tell him he is daft.'

Arabella could believe that Margaret was a woman who would do such a thing. Her father would never have stood for such behaviour from the women of the clan, or his daughter. But Brodie respected Margaret and her opinions and took the counsel of the women who'd escaped with him. He would make a good husband when he married.

The kind of husband she would like to have.

The pain of that realisation pierced her heart and she nearly gasped out loud. Luckily Margaret had turned to leave and did not seem to notice it.

The man who would be the perfect husband for her—if only he had not been the one to kill Malcolm. He'd been right in saying that her father would never accept a peace that included him. Her heart might have fallen to him, but her hand in marriage would not.

So, mayhap her actions which had pushed him away were for the best? He would never trust her again. She sighed and sat back down on the pallet once more.

With Margaret gone, Arabella had managed to sleep for several hours. She had woken to the sound of orders being called out and people passing by the cave carrying out those orders. Part of her had wanted to offer her help. The part that won knew she would be more of a distraction than a help so she had remained within, getting the rest she did not get the night before.

So, as the sun rose on this morn, she decided she must face the day and any repercussions to her actions—both those with Brodie and in helping Alan to get away. Pushing back the cocoon of blankets she'd fashioned, she stood up and shook out her gown. As she stood, her body protested once more, so she stretched tall to ease the tightness in her back and legs.

Although they would be busy with the preparations to move the camp that she could hear being ordered outside, there would be a cooking pot in the centre of the camp. She gathered her hair up into a braid, grabbed a length of plaid to use as a shawl in the cool air of morning and walked outside. Nodding to the guard who would now dog her every step, Arabella headed to the centre of the camp.

The reactions of those who met her gaze were varied. As Margaret had said, they all knew what had happened between her and Brodie. A mixture of curiosity, sympathy and knowing filled the eyes of those who looked at her. But some greeted her as she walked by, so that had not changed.

In the next moment, the somewhat organised chaos of the busy camp turned into mayhem.

Mounted warriors and more on foot flooded in from all sides. Their shouts blended with the screaming of men, women and children who fled their swinging swords. She pressed herself into a copse of trees and tried to find the safest way out. And then she saw one man on a horse pursuing Fia from behind.

Running out from her shadowed hiding place, she scrambled around the fighting and got to her first. Pulling the crying girl close, she ran to the nearest shelter and pushed her inside. Across the clearing, Arabella saw more children and women clustered in fear and not moving. Skirting the horses and the men, she ran to them. She heard Brodie's voice calling out orders to his men and then saw him leading a group of his men against the invaders.

For a part of a moment their gazes connected across the camp. Her heart pounded in her chest at the way he stared.

'Get to safety!' he yelled, and the spell broke between them.

She grabbed the hands of two of the boys and called for the women to come. Ducking and running, stopping when they got too close to the warriors now engaged in battle, Arabella managed to get this small group to one of the caves. As she ran back to find Margaret, she heard her name being called and stopped to look.

A man bore down on her with his sword in hand. Just before he began to swing his sword down at her, he pulled up hard on the reins and brought his horse to a halt in front of her. Shielding her eyes from the spraying dirt sent into the air by the horse's hooves, she stumbled and fell.

Someone grabbed her arm and pulled her to stand. Arabella then found herself face down over the saddle of a man's legs. When she tried to push off, a strong hand on her back held her in place.

'Have no fear, Lady Arabella. I will get you to safety. Be still!'

Through the confusion and screaming, the fighting and people running around below her, she could not tell the direction they travelled, but soon they were away from all of that and on the road leading down the mountain.

'I cannot stop until we are safely away, lady,' the rider warned her.

She heard the sound of a small group of riders massing along and around them and then nothing.

'What do you mean she's gone?' Brodie asked as he ran towards the place where they were gathering the wounded. 'I saw her taking the women to the caves.'

'Aye, she did. Then she came back this way. Was she struck down?' Rob asked.

A terrible fear pierced deep into him then. Had she been killed in this attack? They ran along the path, checking every injured person and not finding her. He called out for help when they found someone needing attention. Margaret and the other women were already helping.

'Arabella!' he called out as they made their way around.

Then he stopped and looked one more time across the clearing where he'd seen her.

'The man took her.' Brodie whirled around and found Bradana's daughter there.

'What man?' he asked, crouching down to speak to her. Rob came to his side and waited.

'The man on the horse. He grabbed her up and

rode off there with the others,' Fia said, pointing towards the path out of the camp. The girl winced as both he and Rob let loose several curses.

'Go to your mother, Fia,' he said, pushing the girl to where he could see Bradana working.

'Ye will bring her back, Brodie? She looked scared. She didna want to go,' the little girl said. He wanted to give his word, but he could not. Not right now.

'Go to your mam now.' She ran off as he said, but her sad eyes pleaded with him to follow Arabella. Then he turned to his friend. 'Gather the men,' he ordered. He knew the horses were safe so they could follow them.

'Nay.'

Brodie turned to look at Rob. 'Nay?'

'Chasing them down the mountain is likely to end up with the lady's death. We know the paths and trails, they do not. It will be a simple thing to ride off the cliffs near the turns. Is that what you want?' When he did not answer quickly, Rob pushed it. 'Well, do you?'

'You know I do not.'

'Stop for a minute and think about this. They were Mackintoshes from Caelan. They will return to Drumlui Keep. That's where they're taking her. Caelan wants her back.'

True. Caelan would take her back, if for nothing else than to prove he could best Brodie. But did he still plan to go through with his plot? To marry her and destroy the Camerons? If he wed her, and the betrothal yet stood as legal unless her father broke it, then he would control a fortune and be able to pay out the promised bribes.

'And we know how to get into the keep.'

'Aye, we do. But we cannot defeat all of them with the men we have. We've lost at least three just now and more are injured.'

'Then our best weapon is our planning and stealth. That has kept us alive all these months. Do not play into his hand now.'

Brodie tried to bring his thoughts to clarity. Rob made sense. He nodded. 'Our original plan but with a few changes. We need to get the others moving north, just as we planned. Then, once we have a better idea of how many can fight, we will know what we can do.'

They spent the rest of the day gathering up survivors, treating the injured and organising those who would leave in the morning. Just before they sought their night's rest, Brodie called them together—men and women—to discuss their next step.

* * *

The next morning, after escorting those going to his uncle's lands down to the road that would take them north, he waited until they were well away and then gathered those remaining and told them his true plan.

'We do not have enough men to fight our way in or out of Drumlui Keep,' he announced. 'We have the proof we need but not enough of us to see it through.'

Rob cast him a dark look and Brodie shrugged.

'We could…' Rob began.

'Nay. I will not be the one who orders you to your deaths. You have fought well at my side, for my quest.'

'We didna fight for ye, Brodie. We fought for our families and our homes,' Duncan said. 'Well, we fought for ye also.' A few laughs and chuckles echoed around them.

'And now it is time to seek new homes with my uncle. Pledge your service and loyalty to him.'

'What will ye do?' Hamish asked. 'Ye rescued the lady once. Will ye leave her to her fate now with that bloody bastard?'

Rob had been watching him closely and now

stepped forward, arms crossed over his chest. 'So what is your plan then, Brodie?'

Brodie had thought about this all night. Without enough men, he could never be successful in his challenge. Their conflict had already torn apart the Mackintoshes and split loyalties.

'In order to put Grigor in the chieftain's chair, we need to remove Caelan and destroy his right to hold that seat in the eyes of both our allies and our enemies.

'The documents and evidence that've been gathered there—' he stopped and pointed to the locked strongbox that sat next to him on the ground '—are part of it. The other part is getting the Camerons to agree to back this.'

The shouting he knew would erupt did, so he waited while they all called out their objections, some rational and calm and others seething mad. He said nothing, but only acknowledged their contributions, until everyone, even Margaret and the other women, had spoken their piece.

The lass had given him the only possible answer to this quandary when she'd said she would convince her father about Caelan. If Euan Cameron had not truly wanted peace, he would have broken the betrothal contract and attacked the Mackintoshes when his son was killed. That

Lachlan had been able to work out a new truce and treaty spoke of The Cameron's commitment to ending this feud, ending the relentless deaths and destruction.

Brodie planned to take advantage of knowing that when he approached Arabella's father. If he lived long enough to actually speak to the man.

'My plan is to go to Achnacarry and speak to Euan.' At their shouts, he paused. ''Tis up to you whether or not you follow me.' More shouts and objections. 'I think the man wants peace. I think he wants his daughter back. I think he will help us.'

'Before or after he guts you and hangs your innards from his wall?' Rob said. Brodie walked to his friend and placed his hand on Rob's shoulder.

'That is where you will come and play your part. I will make my attempt and you and any who stand with us will wait outside Achnacarry with the proof that we have paid for with our blood and tears. If The Cameron agrees, we will attack Drumlui together to rescue Arabella and defeat Caelan.'

'And if he does not?' Jamie asked. 'If you are dead?'

'Then you must decide if your fight is over or not. Take the proof to my uncle. If nothing else, it will buy you all a place with him. It will be up to you to make that choice.'

Silence descended over them as they considered his words and their very limited choices. They had been at his back through every day and week since the moment of his exile. Rob had left with him, trailing him by only hours and finding him in their favourite hunting place. The rest came and, as word spread about his gathering flock, more and more had appeared. Everyone had done their part and given a full measure of effort and loyalty.

Never once had they refused his orders. But would they accept his plan now? And could it work?

'Seeing as how you saved my arse more than once, I will have your back in this, Brodie.' Magnus stepped forward, offering his hand. Though barely healed, he had refused to go north with the others.

'I canna let him have all the fun,' Duncan said. 'And Bradana and my lass would tan my hide if I did not help get the lady back safely.' Brodie reached out and accepted his hand.

One by one, they all accepted his words and his insane plan. All but Rob, who watched as all the others came forward. Rob's faith in him and his friendship was all that had kept him alive during this ordeal. If he did not support him now...

'You think that Grigor is the man to lead us, then?' Rob asked, facing him. 'And not you?'

'Grigor would have my full backing, Rob. You know he will be able to pick up the damaged pieces and put them back together. The elders will unite behind him once Caelan is exposed.'

'Why not you? You should be tanist.' Murmurs and whispers of agreement made their way through the group.

'You know well why it cannot ever be. With the blood of The Cameron's heir on my hands, it would never be accepted.'

'But they've been murdering thieves for generations. Euan himself put many Mackintoshes to the sword,' Hamish called out.

'Killing a man in the middle of a truce is a different matter,' he said. That was what made his crime worse than many that had come before.

'But if Caelan is discredited, no one will believe his friend's words, either. Mayhap they are even lying?' Duncan suggested.

He clenched his jaws together. This was exactly what Arabella had tried to tell him.

'There was another witness there that night.'

Rob walked up to him. 'Why did you not tell me this?'

'I just discovered it.'

'Not the lady? Surely she would not have been there?' he asked as the noise of the others began to lessen.

'One who believed himself too old to be stuck in the nursery with the bairns that night.' Rob's eyes widened as he comprehended who the witness was.

'Before or after his escape?'

'The reason for it,' Brodie admitted. 'In fear of something like this.' Brodie called out to them now. 'We have talked over this matter many times. Grigor is our best hope. He stands high in the respect of many of our allies. Will you support him? Will you be at my back now?'

A short time later, they made their way to the north-east, towards Loch Arkaig. If the weather held and the fates smiled, they would arrive at Achnacarry before Arabella reached Drumlui. He only prayed that he would be alive to say the words to her that he should have said that night.

Chapter Twenty

They passed the clearing where Brodie had brought her to share the incredible views of Mackintosh lands and she struggled to keep up the charade of being grateful to be rescued. All she wanted to do was return to the mountains and find out if he was still alive. If any of them were.

The past three days had passed slowly for her, her heart and thoughts filled with fear while she had to smile and act as the gracious lady these warriors expected her to be. She'd slowed them down with every possible excuse, including one real reason. Her courses had come upon her that first night and had truly made her ill.

She used it to gain almost a day of rest, for men could not bear to hear about the pains and other unpleasant parts that women faced each month. She required more rest and more stops along the way to see to her private needs. These men were young enough that they did not know the truth of it and polite enough not to ask too closely.

At first she thought that Brodie would follow them, but then she realised that he would see to everyone's safety and needs before his own. From the glance they'd exchanged in the camp during the attack, she knew that it was not finished between them. So, she had no doubt that he would come for her. None at all.

Until she rode into Drumlui and stood before Caelan.

That was when his men gave their report and her heart broke with every word they spoke. Worse, she could not show it or Caelan would know she knew about his plan.

Instead, she did what would be expected of the gracious, ladylike Arabella—she wept incessantly.

And then fainted.

Caelan saw what he wanted to see—his rescued betrothed, overwrought and overwhelmed and exhausted from being held prisoner by his dastardly cousin. Her skills at acting the part were out of practice for she had become used to behaving as the woman she truly was while she lived with Brodie. He had given her the freedom to use her mind and her skills and was not threatened by her.

Her betrothed called the servants to see to her needs and sent the healer to her chambers. When she asked for her father and her aunt, knowing well they were not here, Caelan promised to send for them immediately. If she had not known the truth, she could have believed him when he said how distraught he'd been at this separation and how he had sent so many search parties out to find her. And, she acted her part, fuelled by Brodie's bitter truth.

She'd been at Drumlui for two days and he'd summoned her to the hall to speak to her. This could not be good. The servants would tell her nothing. At least she'd eaten well and had soaked in the longest, hottest bath in her life. And she discovered a gold-and-jewelled circlet waiting for her as she was dressed—a gift to celebrate her safe return.

Garbed in a shift, gown and stockings that were her own and with her new circlet in her hair now arranged in an artful braid instead of the plain, serviceable ones she'd become accustomed to these last weeks, Arabella Cameron, the only daughter and heir to The Cameron, entered the hall and prepared for the fight of her life.

But first, she placed *that* smile, the one that drove Brodie to madness and the one that pacified Caelan, on her face. It would be more shield than any targe carried into battle.

'My lady,' Caelan said as she stood before him. 'I am gladdened that you have left your chamber to be here with us for the noon meal. Too much time has passed since you graced us with your presence and I thank the Almighty for your safe return.'

He sat in the chieftain's chair as he had before, but now she noticed so much about him. How his smile was more a smirk. How he stared at her breasts. How others kept their distance from him. How his words were as much a falsehood as hers were.

She dipped low into a curtsy, allowing a good amount of time to go by as she waited there. Then she rose and smiled at him and he clapped in approval. He rushed down the steps from the dais to help her up to the table.

'My lord,' she whispered as he waited for her to sit. 'I am honoured by such treatment.' Once seated, she reached out and touched his hand for good measure. 'And your gift was so thoughtful. What a lovely surprise to find waiting for me!'

The servants began bringing forth trays of

food and filling the trencher she would share with him. She made some appropriate comment as each new good was placed there. Arabella glanced down the table and realised that she knew no one. One of the older men, a clan elder, nodded to her and he looked familiar but she had paid little attention during her time here. Was that the Grigor she'd heard mentioned? When they'd eaten, she took a breath and asked her first question.

'My lord…' she began.

'Pray you, you must still call me Caelan.' She smiled at him, looking from under her lashes.

'Very well, Caelan. I thought my father and my aunt would have been here by now. Have you any word on when they will arrive?'

It was about a three-day journey to Achna-carry from Drumlui and about the same in the other direction to Tor Castle, their southern hold-ing. But a strong horse and a good rider could make it in less. If they had a reason to.

'I sent a man out as soon as we received word that you were safe. I would think a week more at most.'

'And then we will marry?' she asked, adding a breathless, little sigh to the end of the question.

'Impatient, are you?' he asked, leaning in and

kissing her cheek. She kept her smile in place and allowed it. 'I confess, I am anxious, as well, but the elders here have convinced me that your father should be present at such a momentous occasion. After all, he paid with the life of his only son for this truce and treaty.'

Not for all the gold in the kingdom could she keep her distress from showing. She glanced away and blinked, trying to gain control once more.

'That was thoughtless of me, Arabella. You have suffered, too, for this treaty.' She lifted her cup to her mouth and drank deeply from it before turning back to him.

'Aye, Caelan. Many have suffered. Too many. And so our marriage will put an end to that for generations to come,' she said.

He lifted his cup and took a mouthful, sparing a passing glance for her. The coldness in his gaze made her recoil for a second before she forced herself to accept the cup when he held it to her mouth. She needed to change the topic or she would unmask herself.

'I hope my aunt brings the rest of my clothing and jewellery with her. I have been too long in the garb of peasants and villeins in that encampment.'

'Tell me of that, if it does not upset you too much. I would not have you retiring to your chamber because you are overwrought again but I am curious about my cousin.' He nodded at her. 'Did he deny his crime to you?'

'Nay,' she said, honestly. 'He accepts his guilt in Malcolm's death. Even revelled in it.'

'The damned traitor!' Caelan exclaimed, and then he looked at her. 'Forgive my outburst, Arabella. I cannot imagine the indignities you suffered at his hands while his prisoner.' His eyes flashed then, something dark and dangerous, before he spoke again. 'Did he keep you bound? Gagged?'

'Aye, for the first weeks. Then he forced me to labour with the meanest of them, carrying out whatever tasks he ordered.' She shuddered then and held out her hands. 'I am embarrassed even to show them to you,' she said, mournfully.

The skin on her hands was not the same smooth, unworked skin as it had been. The weeks of working there, side by side with the other women, had left her skin calloused and her nails broken. Their condition bore out her tale. A lady's hands were not meant to show evidence of physical labour.

'He will pay, doubt it not, Arabella,' he said.

He lifted her hand to his lips for a kiss, but barely grazed it.

'I know you will see to him,' she said, nodding in approval. He basked in the praise and confidence of her words. She wanted to vomit on his boots.

If she was going to be ready when Brodie came, and she had no one doubt he would come for her, she needed to be able to move around the keep and yard and even the village. So, she asked for a boon.

'I cannot tell you how good it feels to be here with you, my lo…Caelan.' She nodded at the light coming through the high windows in the walls of the great hall. 'For many days and nights, he imprisoned me in a cave. I could not tell when it was day or night. It is good to see the sun again.' She glanced at the others at table and then smiled at Caelan.

'Now that I am free, I would like to walk to regain my strength. With your permission, of course.'

'Lady—' he began to answer, but she interrupted him.

'Arabella,' she offered.

'Arabella, I do not think it safe for you to go outside. My men told me that there were many who escaped during your rescue. I would not risk your safety, if they chose to attack.'

'May I walk in the hall, then? Or up on the battlements? Surely no place could be safer than here or there?'

'I think you should regain your strength by resting these next days. In preparation for our wedding. In preparation for our wedding night,' he added, whispering so only she heard those words.

Whether or not he knew she played a role, she could not tell. But, fighting or arguing with him would not bring the results she needed, so she bowed her head to him and accepted his orders.

'Very well, Caelan,' she acquiesced to him. 'I will always appreciate your guidance and your strength.'

He stood and motioned to two of the many guards who stood around the perimeter of the large chamber. They waited at the bottom of the steps. He took her hand and escorted her down to them.

'Fear not, my love,' he said as he leaned in and kissed her cheek. 'I will bring him to justice, for you and all that he has inflicted on you.'

She dipped down as low as she could then, to get away from him mostly, but also to make a public showing of her humility and acceptance of their match. The longer he did not suspect her, the better. With a smile when she rose, Arabella left the chamber, with one guard before her and one after her.

A week. Brodie would come for her before the week was out, to save her once more.

He had watched her every move and listened carefully and closely to every word she spoke. Her servants had reported to him directly. And yet, since she'd returned, there had not been an untoward word or action.

She reacted to him as she had before her kidnapping. She accepted his affections, though a bit stiffly. Still, for someone, a lady, who'd been subjected to such rough treatment, it was understandable. So now, with her return and their marriage, his plans were in place and on schedule.

He'd not sent word to her father at all. The documents had been witnessed and signed and she was, for all legal and religious intents, his already. All it would take would be the reciting of vows and a consummation to claim her and her dowry. Whether her father was present mattered not to him, nor to the priest who would speak the words.

As she walked away now, he could still feel the shiver that had passed through her when he'd mentioned their wedding night and he smiled at that thought. He'd been concerned about whether or not she came to him untouched and would discover the truth soon enough. One of his men reported that she was unwell on the journey home—'had bled for days' in the man's mumbled words—so at least she carried no bastard to his bed.

For now, he would keep a close watch on her and make the arrangements. After a few more days of rest, she would be ready for him. He would make use of her while he needed her alive but he did wonder if Brodie had done so, too. Prisoners, especially women, were often beaten and ravaged during their imprisonment. She said he'd forced her to work for him—had he also forced her to service him? Service his men?

It mattered not. He was not marrying her for her reputation or her looks or her genteel manners. He did it only for the gold he needed to bribe the right people to help him annihilate her entire clan. When this was over, he would find the appropriate wife for a man as powerful as he would be.

A few more days and it would all be well in hand.

* * *

Two days after her abduction, Brodie stood some yards away from the gates of Achnacarry Keep with his hands on his head. He wore no armour and he carried no weapons. He'd left his men a mile or so back in the woods that crept to the edge of Loch Arkaig, far enough away that they would not be seen. If things went badly, they would have enough time to escape.

He knew the guards atop the gate had seen him. Now, they were probably summoning their laird for orders about what to do. He hoped that an arrow in his head or heart would not be the first action taken. When the gate lifted and a troop of warriors headed for him, he thought himself lucky.

Alive was his priority. Alive to save his clan and to save her. *Alive*, he chanted in his thoughts. A short time later, battered, beaten and bloodied, he was not certain that alive he would remain.

The first five did not wait or explain, they fell on him with punches and kicks. They did not stop until he lay on the ground unable to move or speak. Satisfied with their work, they dragged him in through the gates.

He could not see out of one eye, between the blood and the swelling, it was hopeless. His ribs were broken and he wanted to scream with every breath he took. The last bit of control he had was lost when they tossed him face-first on the cold stone floor before The Cameron and tied his hands behind his back and his feet together.

'I will get the rope,' someone said. 'Draw and quarter him, my lord!'

Rob was right in his guess of how he would meet his end. He would be hanged and then his guts pulled out while he watched. Death would be kind at that point.

'Wait!' He recognised Euan's voice and heard the crunch of boots on the floor coming closer. 'I would look on the man who killed my son.' Hands grabbed him roughly and turned him, crushing his arms beneath him. At least one hand was broken.

Then someone knelt on his stomach, crushing the breath from him. The point of a dagger was stuck in his neck and dragged down, cutting through his clothing and exposing his skin. He felt the sting of the blade as it marked him.

'Talk,' he forced out. Barely able to drag in breath, he said it again. 'Talk.'

'Talk? You think to talk to me? You think I would talk to you now? I have waited for months to avenge the murder of my son.' The dagger went deeper and Brodie could feel blood seeping from the wound. 'I think I will not give you such a quick ending. A gut wound will have you suffering for days.' The blade pierced the skin on his belly. 'Days when you will beg for death and it will not be given.'

Those around cheered their laird and Brodie could feel himself slipping away. He must stop this now.

'Arabella…' He panted. Now he spiralled down into some dark place.

Cold water shocked him, causing him to spasm and gasp for breath. Every movement and cough that tore through him caused agony anew. He prayed for the strength to survive. For if he did not, neither would…

'Arabella,' he said louder.

'Do not speak of my daughter, you damned murderer!' Euan yelled. A fist pounded into his face. 'I will not have the man who took the life of my son speak her name.'

'He did not kill Malcolm.'

Brodie hung on to consciousness by a thin thread and thought he'd imagined the voice and the words. They were followed by such an uproar, it would have wakened the dead. It took some time for the laird to regain control over his men and his hall. Brodie tried to lift his head, tried to see who'd spoken but he could not.

'What did you say, boy?' Euan demanded.

Boy.

Boy?

Alan.

'I said Brodie did not kill Malcolm. The other one did.'

Could it be that simple? Could a child's word give him absolution for a crime he'd accepted on his own soul? Did the boy speak the truth?

'Clear this chamber!' Euan called out. Over many vocal protests, they left as he ordered until it was quiet. 'Come here, Alan,' he said. A pause while the boy must have come to his uncle's side.

'Now tell me truly. Were you there that night?'

'Aye.' The boy's voice was barely a whisper.

'You followed Malcolm, then? As you were told not to do while we were there?' Courage, boy, he thought.

'Aye, Uncle,' Alan admitted. 'I just wanted to see what they would do.'

'And what did they do?' Euan asked. 'Come now, you've admitted your disobedience. Tell me the rest of it. It will not change your punishment.'

If Brodie could have moved at all, he would reach up and throttle the older man. Why would any boy speak a word after such a threat? 'Boy,' he forced out. 'What did you see?'

'The other one stayed awake when Malcolm and Brodie and the others slept. They fell asleep all over the ground.' Alan paused. 'I can drink more than they did, Uncle!'

'Then what happened, Alan? When Malcolm slept on the ground.'

'He...'

'Lord Caelan?'

'Aye, Lord Caelan stabbed Malcolm. I thought he would wake and save himself, but he did not.' He could hear the distress in the boy's voice. He was crying. 'Then Lord Caelan threw Malcolm on Brodie and left him there.' He cried openly now as he explained how his beloved cousin had died.

'See to him,' Euan said.

Thinking he meant the boy, Brodie was surprised when the ropes that bound him were cut and he was freed. As the feeling rushed back into his arms and legs, he was dragged to his feet and held there.

'Why did you not tell me this sooner?' Euan asked Alan. 'If you knew the truth of it?'

'I was not supposed to be there. I knew you'd be angry. And then Lord Caelan said he'd seen

Brodie stab Malcolm. I did not dare to call him a liar.'

'Wise boy there,' Brodie said, coughing and spitting out blood. 'Caelan would have found a way to kill him, too.'

'Did you know this?' Euan asked him. He walked over to Brodie and stared at him. 'Why did you never dispute your cousin's word?'

'I still do not remember the night,' he answered. 'Only Alan can tell us the tale.'

'Does anyone else know that you were there?'

'Arabella,' they both said.

'She knows?' her father asked.

Brodie shook his head. 'She knows he was there. She does not know what he witnessed.'

'Arabella made me swear not to tell anyone that I'd been there. She said it could mean my death if anyone knew.'

Once more silence reigned there as both of them digested the information given by the boy. His own addled brain would not accept it. He'd lived with the guilt for so long, he'd believed it as fact. Now, he knew it was not. His knees buckled and he would have pitched forward but for the hands that yet held him.

'Sorcha, summon the healer,' Euan called out.

'Nora, see him to a chamber.' Brodie reached out to grab Euan's arm as he passed.

'My men wait for me to the west. By the lakeside. Summon them.'

Those were the last words he would speak for some time.

Chapter Twenty-One

When Brodie came to awareness, several people were hovering over him. Rob he knew, the other man and woman he did not. From the poking and prodding of his injuries under Rob's watchful gaze, one of the strangers was the clan's healer and the other a servant of some kind.

'Ah, so you are awake,' the man said. 'Not too bad.'

Rob raised his brow at the pronouncement, clearly having a different assessment of his friend's condition. 'A few broken ribs. Gashes and bruises. Your left hand is broken, too. And your nose, he thinks.'

'And you have lost a considerable amount of blood,' the healer offered. 'But you should survive.'

He'd suffered those and more in his years of

fighting, but possibly not all at the same time. 'When can I ride?'

The healer and Rob exchanged a glance and then both laughed aloud. The servant woman shook her head in disgust.

Brodie pushed up, intending to find Euan and settle this, but he did not get very far. His body betrayed him, sending him reeling backwards. This would not do. He must get out of this bed. He must get to her and tell her the truth he'd just discovered.

'Lord Euan will be here to speak to you,' Rob explained. 'You might want to rest now so we can leave sooner.'

'Did you bring the box?' he asked Rob. A nod was his only response. 'Bring it here.'

Rob left and Brodie gave himself over to the healer's ministrations.

When Euan arrived, his injuries had been cleaned and dressed. By the time Euan had read all the documents collected in the box, Brodie was able to get out of bed and stand. Sipping some noxious brew that was supposed to speed his healing, he waited for The Cameron's reaction.

'I had no idea.'

'You were not supposed to know. He played each one of us against all the rest,' Brodie said. 'And you would not know even as he was destroying you bit by bit.'

'Why?' Euan asked. 'Oh, this feud is like many others. It's become almost sport between us, when it does not get out of hand. But this,' he said, holding out the parchment he was reading, 'this is personal.'

'You killed his parents in front of him. Certainly it is personal for him,' Brodie said. He hated what his cousin was doing but he could understand the need for revenge.

'It was a brutal time. One that brought us, both of our clans, to the brink of madness. But, I did not kill his mother.' Something darkened in the old man's gaze, his face grey for a moment. 'She ran into the middle of the fight and was struck down. I have regretted their deaths since that day.'

'There is something more?' Brodie asked.

'His mother died the same way my Fiona died,' Euan said, looking away for a moment. 'At the same festival. It had been Fiona's idea.'

It was the last time the clans had tried to end the feud. A festival that had brought many to its promised haven and it had turned into a massacre when squabbles between factions of both clans had escalated into violence. Fighting had broken out.

'Was Arabella there?' he asked, wondering if she was Caelan's focus for more than one reason. Had she played some part in that, too?

'Aye, she was there. Not much more than a bairn. But old enough to disobey me and sneak out of our tent. Fiona went searching for her and ran into the fighting as it began. We found her curled around Arabella, saving her life with her own.'

A hardness entered the man's voice then. And Brodie realised that…

'You blame Arabella for her death.' Many things fell into place then. The man's brutal treatment of his children, especially Arabella. His pursuit of a peace. 'Does she know?'

'I couldna bear to look upon her afterwards, for she has the look and eyes of her mother. I think I grew to resent her.'

'Does she know?' he asked again.

'I never spoke about it with her,' he admitted, sitting on the bed. 'I do not think she kens the real reason. She learned to stay out of my way. She did as she was told.'

All the things a child does to protect herself

when others do not. If he had the strength then, Brodie would have beaten the man as he had often raised his hands to his children. Even making a fist was not possible now, so it would have to wait. But it would come to the old man.

Arabella had become a different person in dealing with her father, to protect herself and her brother. She hid her curiosity and strength within, never letting Euan see it. But Brodie had seen it. Brodie saw the true Arabella hiding inside the hurt woman. Once Caelan was handled, he would make certain no one hurt her again.

'Does Caelan know it was an accident? That you regretted his mother's death and your involvement?'

'Nay. Whenever we spoke, he never seemed to recognise me. So I thought he'd forgotten me.'

'Forgotten? Nay. Just buried the hatred deep so no one could see.' As Arabella had buried herself.

'As I said, brutal times.' Euan met Brodie's gaze then. ''Twas about the same time that Arabella's aunt had been kidnapped by one of your clansmen—the one called Grigor.'

'Her aunt?' Brodie had never heard this.

'Aye. There were some stories about the two having meetings in secret that were discovered. But the truth is that Grigor kidnapped and ruined her and we had to attack to get her back.'

He looked over at Rob who was as surprised as he was. They both knew that the woman had been meeting Grigor while at Drumlui Keep. More than once, she'd been seen with him long after her charge had retired for the night. And Grigor's gaze followed the woman whenever she was in the same room. Brodie suspected that none of them knew the truth of the matter.

'But, killing in the heat of battle is different from planning to assassinate someone in cold blood and then doing it under the sign of a truce. And blaming someone else for it. He must pay for that,' Euan said, his tone saying that he would not allow any other outcome.

Brodie held no sympathy for his cousin or his actions and when the time came, he could step aside and allow Euan his vengeance. But, he also desired to strike the blow that would end his cousin's destructive plans.

It took several hours to lay out their plan. Brodie hoped that Arabella was using her wits to stay alive and well until they could get there. And he prayed that she understood that he would always come for her, no matter what.

Once, in the middle of their discussions, he wondered to himself if Arabella was asking Caelan as many questions as she asked him. He chuckled aloud, bringing strange glances from the others. She would hold her own with his cousin, he had no doubt. But, whether they faced the twelve plagues of Egypt or every demon from hell, he would see her safely out of Drumlui.

Finally, the planning was done and Brodie's body pushed for rest. The others left, but Euan remained behind. Brodie could tell exactly what the man wanted to know from the way he could not find the words to begin.

'You held her prisoner,' he said. Brodie nodded. 'For nigh on four weeks.' Another nod. 'Did you take her virginity?'

Brodie did not want to insult the man about his daughter so he was choosing his words carefully when Euan blurted out, 'Knowing the girl, she offered it to you.'

He laughed then and it hurt. Clutching his side, he tried to breathe slowly to make the waves of pain subside.

'That is what I thought.' Arabella's father shook his head. 'She trusted you if she went to your bed.' Euan squinted at him then, as though seeing him for the first time. 'I did not think you would suit, but you just might.'

'I have pledged my loyalty to Grigor, Lord Euan. He is the one to lead the Mackintoshes and oversee the treaty and the peace. And he will choose another to be tanist from the other clans in the Confederation.'

'I do not think your men are doing this to put Grigor in the chieftain's chair,' Euan said with a shrug.

Think what he might, it would not be Euan making that decision. The man did want peace, Brodie knew that much, but he had agreed to this extraordinary arrangement to save his daughter. And, for the additional concessions that Brodie would broker for him when the time came.

'Get some rest,' Euan advised him. 'We ride at morning's light.'

At dawn, as Brodie climbed stiffly onto the black for the ride to Drumlui, he suspected that this was only the beginning of the road through hell.

Arabella tried to hide her true feelings, but each hour that passed made it more and more difficult. The two women he'd assigned to her looked on her with suspicion and loathing. She would never again complain about Ailean's sour disposition after spending the past few days with these two.

At first she thought she could sway them from staunch support and absolute obedience, but she failed at that. So, she stopped talking to them. Whenever another servant arrived, whether with food from the kitchen or clean linens for her bed, she tried to engage them in conversation.

All her attempts to discover his plans failed. All her attempts to gain some freedom of movement failed. Then she had a visitor that the two servants could not order away. Grigor Mackintosh knocked at her door and asked to speak to her. While the two women were chattering about what to do, Arabella opened the door and bade him enter.

'Lady Arabella, I thought to look in on you,' he said politely as he sat next to her. 'You look as though you are recovering from your ordeal.'

'Go and fetch some wine and some food for my guest,' she said to Bethoc, the young woman. When she looked as though she would refuse, Arabella smiled at her. 'Remember who will be your lady in just a few days, Bethoc. It might be better to be in my good graces since I will over-see this household.'

'Begin as you mean to go, my lady,' Grigor added, making the young woman pale as she considered this new twist to her situation. Deciding that fetching refreshments was safer than directly disobeying her, Bethoc nearly ran from the room. Once she was gone, Arabella smiled at the other one. But Grigor surprised her by speaking first.

'I would speak with the lady privately.'

He nodded to the door and stood, taking only a step towards it before Una fled, too. Arabella had no doubt that she would go directly to Caelan, so they had little time.

'Is Brodie alive? And the others?' he asked.

She knew that Brodie and his men trusted Grigor, she knew he'd helped get Magnus out of the keep for them, but she could not understand why he would think he could trust her?

'Come now, your aunt said you could be trusted.'

Her mouth fell open then. Of all of the things she thought he would say, that was not one of them. Her aunt? She would speak about that later.

'They were when I was taken from the en-campment. Some, though…' She shrugged.

'What do you think he will do?'

'He was sending the women and children north to his uncle. The men? I do not know.' Then she did. 'He will come for me.' Lifting her head and smiling, she repeated it. 'He will come for me.'

That expression in his eyes when he saw her across the clearing in the camp. It was love looking back at her. He did love her. He would come for her again.

'You must be ready. He will be here soon. But I have no idea how many will be with him.' The sound of approaching footsteps down the corridor made her hurry with the rest. 'He had the proof he needs. Tell those who would fight against him, he is the rightful chieftain.'

Grigor raised a brow at her words. Although Brodie spoke of supporting Grigor's claim, she thought it should be Grigor supporting Brodie and said so. 'They will need someone who has always put the clan's interests first. He is the stronger warrior with the skills to bring this clan back together. He is honourable and worthy and—'

Grigor held his hands up in mock horror to stop her.

'Aye, my lady. I have always believed it, but

the lad did not. Maybe with us both demanding it, he will see reason?'

When the door flung open, Caelan found them sitting quietly, with Grigor offering his kind words about the ordeal she had suffered. The servants at his back stared in, expecting to find something else.

'And so, I do hope you will not hold that criminal's actions against the rest of us? That rogue will be stopped,' he said, standing to leave. 'Ah, Caelan, come to visit your lady, have you?' He patted Caelan's on the shoulder and nodded. 'Young love, 'tis a glorious thing to witness.'

'Caelan,' Arabella said. 'I did not expect you, but it is good to see you. May we speak?' Caelan was still looking at Grigor as he walked down the corridor when she touched his arm. 'Would you be free from your duties soon, so that we might walk together? I know you worry about my safety, but if you are with me, then all will be well.'

In trying to keep up his game, it was hard to refuse her.

So, Arabella found herself walking along the path around the keep with an irritated Caelan. Their walk was interrupted when the guards called out that riders approached. Caelan did not even wait to find out who rode to the gates.

Whoever it was could not be a good thing for him.

Within minutes, the gates were closed, guards lined the walls and she was dragged back to her chambers. Caelan dropped all pretence then, calling out for the priest as he pulled her up the stairs and shoved her inside a small chamber.

'Ready yourself, Lady Arabella. We marry as soon as the priest comes.'

'I will not consent. The priest will not hear those words from me.'

'Oh, aye, he will.' The smile he gave her then made her skin crawl. She wanted to back away but there was little room to do so in that chamber. He had a plan and would use whatever force he needed, she knew that now.

He pulled the door closed and Arabella heard him drop the bar to lock her in. She pulled on it and pushed against it but it would not give way. She cried out and called for help but no one came. Then, a short while later, he opened the door and strode back in, carrying a small bottle.

'This is a wondrous potion. A few drops and you will say whatever you are told to say,' he explained, pulling the cork free and tilting the bottle to show her.

Then he set the bottle on a shelf on the wall and grabbed for her. No matter how much she struggled, he soon had her subdued, pushed against the wall with his hand holding her throat tightly so she could not move her head.

'Only a couple of drops now, or you will fall unconscious,' he warned as he held the bottle over her mouth. She clenched her lips tight so he could not pour it in.

'Do not fight this,' he said, pressing his knee into her back and tightening his grasp on her throat until she gasped against the pain.

The bitter taste landed on her tongue and she tried to spit it out. He covered her mouth and pinched her nose until she struggled to pull in a breath, forcing her to swallow the potion. It burned its way down her throat into her stomach. Then, he released her and tossed her to the floor.

'The priest awaits us below. Come now,' he said.

Her stomach rolled and her head spun. She wanted to ignore his words, but her body did not follow her wishes. He took her hand and pulled her up to stand.

'What did you give me?' she asked as he

wrapped his arm around her waist and helped her walk. The chambers passed in a haze as did the people. Her mouth felt dry then.

'The same thing I gave Brodie. It makes you pliable and obedient. You will do as I say,' he whispered in her ear.

'I will…' She could not think very clearly. One thing did strike her. He had given this to Brodie. 'Brodie would not kill,' she forced out.

'Nay, he had too much and slept. So I did the rest. He remembered nothing and I still managed to have him blamed for it.' He laughed then and it washed over her, making her sick.

Everything blurred then in her mind and in her memory. She tried to pull away but he held her close, his breaths coming hard and fast against her neck. Then she could swear that Brodie suddenly appeared there in the hall before them.

And her father.

And more men climbing out of the walls. She laughed at that.

Brodie called out to her then. *Bella*, he yelled to her and she wanted to reach out for him or say his name. Then he began moving and did not stop until he stood in front of them. The others followed him, sliding and slipping forward it seemed to her, from one place to another.

Caelan pushed her in front of himself and she saw the fierce look on Brodie's face. On a face covered in bruises and cuts. But she knew it meant he loved her. Brodie could not say the words, but he showed them on his face. And in his eyes.

Words were shouted and men fought and she heard swords striking swords. She reached out for Brodie, to ease the pain he held within himself. And the guilt. But mostly she just wanted to love him.

The stones in the walls stopped pushing men out but the noise seemed to grow. Soon, the hall was filled with warriors of all sorts. Even in the confusion she recognised some of them for a moment or two though their names would not come to her.

The man, the voice behind her grew louder, screaming curses and promising retribution before he pushed her, flinging her from him. With nothing but air beneath her, Arabella flew off the high dais and then her own screams filled the space around her. First she first rose and then fell and fell and fell towards the stone floor below her.

Until Brodie's strong arms surrounded her.

'I have you, love,' Brodie whispered then. 'I have you.'

He would keep her safe. He would protect her. He would love her. So, she held on to him and fell the rest of the way into his embrace.

Chapter Twenty-Two

'Arabella?'

She threw her arms around her head and tried to shield herself from the horrible screaming.

'Arabella, love,' he said again.

'Shh,' she urged but then that noise shook inside her head, too.

'Drink this.' Someone lifted her head and touched a cup to her lips. 'Just a sip.'

Cold water. It tasted so good to her parched mouth that she wanted more. And she would have had more if the cup had not disappeared.

'You must try to open your eyes and wake now.'

It was Brodie's voice she heard and she wanted to see him, but the confusion and dizziness still assailed her terribly. She fell back into the stupor and knew nothing.

* * *

Until she did.

Surrounded by heat, she opened her eyes and found herself in a large bed, with Brodie curled around her. She lifted her head slowly and discovered the light-headedness was dissipating. If she moved a little bit at a time, she could turn her head.

He lay there, his bandaged hand and arm draped over her hip. She wore garments as did he, which she discovered when she pushed herself around to face him.

He looked terrible! She'd thought the potion Caelan had forced into her had caused her to see such a distorted version of his face, but now she could see it clearly. His one eye was swollen shut and his nose was puffed up and bruised badly. Though some had been dressed, she could count more than five gashes on his face and neck.

Then, searching back through those strange visions, she realised what had happened.

'Caelan?' she asked, already knowing he must be dead.

'Your father saw to his end.' She shivered, knowing it was better that she had not witnessed her father taking revenge for her brother's life.

'So you did go to my father for help.'

He opened the one eye that would and nodded. 'Aye.'

'And this was his help?' Her father was a hard man, but this was...

'This was when he believed I had killed Malcolm.'

'The potion. Caelan said he'd used too much on you and Malcolm.' She touched his face then. 'You did not kill my brother.' She'd been so wrong about him, as had everyone else. And yet he had kept faith with all of them. 'Can you forgive me for thinking the worst of you?'

He nodded and a smile brought the edges of his mouth up. 'Aye.'

'That quickly? You can forgive me?'

'You loved me even believing I killed him. If you could do that,' he whispered, 'how could I not forgive you?'

He leaned over to kiss her but the door burst open and people poured in. Still groggy, she shook her head as she watched both Camerons and Mackintoshes fill the chamber. If anyone thought it amiss that she lay there with him, no one, not even her father, objected.

The strangest thing was that her father helped her off the bed and hugged her fiercely, whispering endearments and promises in her ear. From the satisfied look on his face and the way he nodded and smiled at her, she knew Brodie had something to do with this, as well.

From what she could see and what she'd heard, he would need some time to remain abed and heal. But the daft man tried to stand up when Grigor arrived in the chamber.

She understood—a man stood when his chieftain entered a room and so Brodie tried once more to push his beaten body from the bed only to be pushed back by the elder.

'Rest now. You deserve it, Brodie.'

Grigor glanced around the chamber and nodded. To a one, the Mackintoshes dropped to their knees around the bed. Brodie began to object then, but Grigor silenced him with a gesture.

'While you have been here,' he said, 'the elders have finally been tending to clan business. We examined the documents and the rest of the evidence you gathered and settled the matter of inheritance. Well, most of the elders did. Some left in haste during the night.' Some of the men laughed and she did not doubt that a few of the elders had been urged along in their leaving.

'With Caelan's death, the seat was opened. The council has voted and appoints you, Brodie Mackintosh, as chieftain.'

Brodie began to object, to offer his loyalty to Grigor as he'd planned to do, when Grigor went down on his knee and bowed his head in obeisance, ignoring him. He struggled to rise from the bed when the chanting began.

'A Mackintosh! *Loch moigh!*'

Arabella knew it was the Mackintosh battle cry and it rose and echoed throughout Drumlui Keep. She leaned over and whispered to him.

'You kept your faith in them. Let them keep faith with you, Brodie.'

He fell back, taking her hand and entwining their fingers as he liked to do. When he pulled her closer to kiss her, she saw that his lips were split and bruised. So, she kissed him on the one place on his forehead that was not bruised.

It took several weeks to sort through the clan's business and set things to rights. Messengers came and went from Drumlui as Brodie made new alliances, strengthened others and severed a few rotten ones. Her father counselled him, as did Grigor, and Rob and some other trusted warriors. Caelan had caused such damage in trying to seek vengeance and it would take time to correct it all. But they would have that time.

Her father told her the rest of it when she left Brodie to rest. They grieved together for the loss of their Malcolm, now knowing the truth of how he'd died. And he spoke of her mother for the first time, explaining and apologising for the distance between them.

She also discovered that she had been betrothed to Brodie as part of the new contracts and agreements. Arabella smiled at that arrangement, wondering if he would ask her himself before they married.

A week later, she learned the answer when she arrived in the hall for their noon meal.

'My lady.'

She turned to find the women who'd lived in the camp there. Margaret, Bradana and the rest. She hugged them all, asking about the children and their husbands.

'Brodie sent word for us to return,' Margaret explained.

'He did not want to accept it,' she told them. They laughed over his stubbornness until he left the table and came to them.

'Welcome home, Margaret,' he said. 'Does Rob know you are here yet?'

'He does now,' Arabella said, watching as Rob

strode across the hall to his sister and grabbed her in a fierce embrace.

'Bradana, I wondered if Fia would like to serve as my maid,' Arabella asked. The girl was pleasant and it would give her a respected place in their household.

'Oh, my lady! She will be so pleased,' Bradana said.

'And I have asked young Alan to serve me,' Brodie said.

Already there were signs of a blending of their kith and kin. A good sign. Brodie moved to her side and then gestured for quiet.

'I know that we are betrothed, Arabella, but a wise woman once told me that I should say the right words to you and I have not had the chance,' he said. Margaret laughed the loudest and nodded at him, telling her and everyone just which wise woman had spoken her piece to him.

'You had every reason to hate me, but you did not. You had every reason to fear me, but you did not. Instead, you made me question myself and everything I believed.' Tears filled her eyes as he spoke of things she never thought to hear. 'You loved me in spite of what you believed. You loved me in spite of being enemies. You had faith in me when I did not.'

He paused then and looked to her. 'So, I will give you the only thing I can give you. Freedom. 'Tis your choice. You are not bound by any contract to me unless you wish it to be so.' He kissed her then, taking her breath and her wits. 'But I hope you will choose me.'

Before she could say anything, a woman called out, 'Ye daft man, she chose you a long time ago!'

He waited, watching her and giving her the freedom of her own mind, though it was, as had been said, a choice she'd made some time ago. That night when she'd gone to his cave to betray him and instead had given him her love.

'You are my choice, Brodie.'

'You heard her, Father,' Brodie called out to the priest she had not seen there earlier. 'A wedding it is.'

The hall erupted into cheering and Arabella found herself carried to the dais in Brodie's arms and placed before the new priest sent to serve God's people in Drumlui.

'I had faith you would say aye.' He winked at her as the priest began the ceremony and they exchanged vows there before her family and his.

The noon meal became their wedding feast and Arabella enjoyed it more as she watched Brodie finally accept his place there. It was hours before they were able to make their way to their bedchamber.

And, hours more before she could move or think or put words together.

He turned to watch her as she slept, still not able to believe she was his in every way that meant anything. Oh, the contracts covered the law and the Church, but she had chosen to say aye to him and the love he brought to her. Lifting her hair out of her face, he counted the seconds of each breath she took and smiled as she mumbled under her breath.

Apparently, 'twas a bad habit she'd picked up while his prisoner. As was her habit of questioning him every chance she could. He did not mind her earlier questions at all for they were about the ways he wanted to take her. She'd remembered that comment and brought it up all through the day, leaving him hard for all those hours between the wedding and their leave-taking. But she had paid for it once they reached their chambers.

Or had he paid the price?

It mattered not.

'What are you doing?' she asked in the husky

voice of sleep that made his body respond... again.

'Just waiting for you to wake,' he said, kissing the tip of her nose. He hesitated for a moment, thinking that she would tell him no since he'd wakened her several, well, four times this night already. Lucky for them that they had married in late autumn when the nights grew very long, giving them plenty of time to be abed.

'I wonder if I should tell you of my wicked dreams this time?' she asked, leaning up on her elbow and stretching out alongside him so their bodies touched.

'When did you begin having wicked dreams?' he asked, wrapping his arm around her and kissing her.

She might be the death of him if she continued to accept his every overture, but right now, as his body and heart and soul warmed next to her, he cared not.

'Well, there was this cave in my dream...' she began. As she whispered, she touched. As she touched, she loved him and healed him of the betrayals and hurts of the past.

And he loved her more than all the horses and cattle they'd bought with the gold from her dowry.

Epilogue

Six months later

'You are kin.'

'Not close enough for this,' Rob said. Crossing his arms over his chest, he was the image of defiance and refusal.

'Now you know how women feel,' Arabella said with a laugh. She remembered her brother's words saying he would be bought or sold just as she was being and laughed again at his disgruntled, insulted expression.

'Margaret thinks it a good match,' Brodie said with a shrug. Arabella liked that he relied on the women who'd helped him during his struggle and not just the elders and other men.

'Make certain to promise enough cattle this time,' she offered. It was a joke between them now. Whenever difficulties arose, horses and cattle were pledged.

'I do not think you are taking this seriously, lady,' Rob pointed out. 'And neither of you are taking my objections seriously, either.'

'Rob, it was your idea that I should be made chieftain, so you now must put up with the consequences.'

'I offered you my loyalty. I offered you my service and my sword, Brodie,' Rob said. 'But I do not remember saying you could sell me to another clan.'

Brodie glanced at her and then walked to where she stood looking out the window of their chamber. Though she felt large and cumbersome, he never failed to touch her or place his hand on her growing belly to wait for movement beneath it. And she did not mind at all. Wrapped in his arms, she leaned her head back against him as the battle raged on between Brodie and his best friend.

The matter at hand was a betrothal being discussed by one of the clans newly allied with the Camerons and Mackintoshes. Being unmarried and a blood relative of the chieftain, Rob was the perfect man to be named. However, he was too busy enjoying his life, flitting from woman to woman, bed to bed.

'I am not selling you,' Brodie said. 'I am asking you to go and meet the young woman. If you think you suit, then we will make an offer.'

"Tis not as though you will have to leave your home and move to hers. Your place here is secure,' Arabella added.

'Is it?' Rob asked. Arabella left Brodie's embrace and went to their friend. Touching his hand, she nodded.

'Of that, have no worries. You kept him alive for me. For all those dark months. Your place here and in our hearts is safe. Always.'

'Damn it to hell, Arabella!' Rob cursed. 'How am I supposed to refuse it now?' He turned and strode out, still cursing under his breath as he left. They waited a whole minute before they burst out laughing.

'Do you think it a good match, Brodie?' she asked. 'Is that what Margaret said?' She'd not spoken to the woman about this possible marriage, waiting for Brodie to broach the topic with his friend first.

'I did not ask her.' When she stared at him, he laughed. 'I only said that to confound him.'

'You torment him so,' she said. 'Tell me true, is this good for him?'

'I need someone I trust to make this alliance. I need kin. I need Rob.' He'd taken to his duties and responsibilities quickly and she marvelled at the wisdom he showed in branching out their clan's interests and connections.

'After all his moaning and cursing, you know he will do it.' She kissed him. 'For his clan and for you.'

Many miles to the north and west, at the very edges of the Scottish Highlands, a young woman received that same news—of a possible betrothal to a Mackintosh—and was so unhappy about it that she ran away the very next morning...leaving her parents to face that Mackintosh when he arrived some weeks later.

* * * * *

This is the first book in
Terri Brisbin's gripping new series
A HIGHLAND FEUDING.
Keep an eye out for more stories, coming soon!

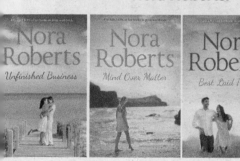
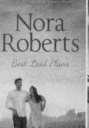
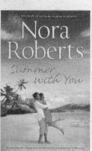

MILLS & BOON®

The Chatsfield Collection!

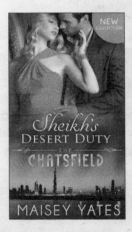

Style, spectacle, scandal…!

With the eight Chatsfield siblings happily married and settling down, it's time for a new generation of Chatsfields to shine, in this brand-new 8-book collection! The prospect of a merger with the Harrington family's boutique hotels will shape the future forever. But who will come out on top?

**Find out at
www.millsandboon.co.uk/TheChatsfield2**

CHATSFIELD_PROMO_BK

MILLS & BOON®

& HISTORICAL

AWAKEN THE ROMANCE OF THE PAST

A sneak peek at next month's titles...

In stores from 1st May 2015:

- **A Lady for Lord Randall** – Sarah Mallory
- **The Husband Season** – Mary Nichols
- **The Rake to Reveal Her** – Julia Justiss
- **A Dance with Danger** – Jeannie Lin
- **Lucy Lane and the Lieutenant** – Helen Dickson
- **A Fortune for the Outlaw's Daughter** – Lauri Robinson

Join our *EXCLUSIVE* eBook club

FROM JUST £1.99 A MONTH!

Never miss a book again with our hassle-free eBook subscription.

★ Pick how many titles you want from each series with our flexible subscription

★ Your titles are delivered to your device on the first of every month

★ Zero risk, zero obligation!

There really is nothing standing in the way of you and your favourite books!

Start your eBook subscription today at www.millsandboon.co.uk/subscribe